To Alex

SAVAGE IMPULSES

KINGS OF OLYMPUS U

MICHELLE HERCULES

KINGS OF OLYMPUS U

Editor: Hot Tree Editing
Proofreading: My Brother's Editor
Photography: Michelle Lancaster
Model: Chad Hurst

Paperback ISBN: 978-1-950991-90-7

PROLOGUE

HADES

ELEVEN YEARS AGO

Flattening my back against the wall, I stick my head out to check if the coast is clear. The scrawny puppy in my arms whimpers, but he's too malnourished to do anything else.

"It's okay, little buddy. We're almost there."

The staff finally leave the kitchen, carrying their trays to serve breakfast to my father. This is my chance. Ignoring the delicious smell of cinnamon rolls, I dash through the kitchen, heading to the service stairs; I can't risk using the main set. No one will be on the second floor right now. They won't start cleaning until my father is gone and I'm on my way to school.

Once I reach the hallway, I make a beeline for the stairs leading to the attic. The door is always locked, and the staff have been instructed to stay away from it. I don't know why my father doesn't want anyone snooping around—he never comes here, and there aren't any juicy secrets stored up there either. It works for me, though. Last year, I borrowed his key and made a copy. I needed a space for my project.

The hinges creak loudly when I push the door open. Once inside, it takes my eyes a while to get used to the darkness. I lock the door again and head up the old stairs. The boards groan as I put my weight on them. My nose itches thanks to the dust, but I try to hold the sneeze in. I lose the fight once I reach the landing. My succession of sneezes seems to frighten the puppy, who squirms in my arms, trying to break free for the first time since I picked him up.

The noise alerts the other dogs of my presence, and they bark excitedly from their crates. I don't like to keep them locked up, but there's no other option. The attic is filled with old furniture and objects, so letting them loose here when I'm not around would be dangerous. They could bump into something and get hurt.

"Hi, guys. I brought you a new friend."

I open the first crate, letting Bruno free. He was the first stray dog I saved from the mean streets of Olympus Bay. He's an old, mangy gray mutt who's missing an eye. Wagging his tail, he jumps to greet me. I drop down, crouching at first, so he can say hello to the little fella in my hand.

"That's right, say hello to Patricio."

The attic door opens with a bang, making me jump to my feet. Bruno and the other dogs bark as the heavy steps come up the stairs. I clutch Patricio tighter against my chest as my eyes widen. My father is standing there, glowering at me.

"What's the meaning of this?" he thunders.

"They had nowhere to go!"

Hercules and two other minions step from behind my father, who orders, "Take them all."

"No! Please, Dad. Don't take them away. I've been taking good care of them."

"Good care? This place reeks of shit and piss."

Hercules doesn't meet my pleading gaze as he pushes Bruno back into his crate. The other bullies are already busy moving the other dogs down the stairs. I'm too small to stop them. My heart is shattered.

I glance at my father again, not bothering to hide the tears in my eyes. He hates when I cry, but I can't hide my emotions right now. "What are you going to do with them?"

He sneers and then turns to Hercules. "Get rid of them. *Permanently.*"

"No!" I launch myself at Hercules, trying to make him drop Bruno's crate. But the man is a giant, stronger than anyone I've ever met.

"I'm sorry, kid," he says.

I'm yanked off him by the back of my shirt and tossed to the floor.

"Stop with this spectacle at once!" my father yells, and then he takes Patricio from me. "Give me that."

The dog whimpers.

"Please don't hurt him."

Before I can stop him, he twists the puppy's neck, breaking it with a loud crack.

Fury courses through my veins. I jump to my feet and then try to hit my father, but I only land one blow before his fist connects with the side of my face. The force sends me back to the floor. Blood fills my mouth, and the pain makes me dizzy.

"Don't you dare raise your hand at me again. Do you understand me?" he asks in a voice that's deadly calm. I know better than to talk back.

I nod, helpless, and then turn to Hercules, who's standing still as a statue. It's almost like he wants to tell me something, but then my father barks at him, and he disappears down the stairs.

"Get up," my father orders.

I do as he says, and I can't help but stare at him with my chin raised in defiance. The right side of my face throbs; it will probably turn purple. He narrows his eyes, maybe noticing my attitude, and then throws another punch at my jaw this time. I stagger back, managing to stay on my feet.

"You're a disgrace to the Godaire name. I should have drowned you when I had the chance."

He turns around and heads down the stairs. It's only when I no longer hear the sound of his footsteps that I sit down and hug my legs. My face is on fire, but I don't cry. I'm too angry for that.

A moment later, someone comes up.

"What are you doing sitting there?" Zeus, my older brother, asks.

"Leave me alone." I let my head hang between my shoulders.

He crouches in front of me and forces my chin up. There isn't any sympathy in his cold blue eyes. "Your dogs are dead."

I flinch, trying to look away, but he roughly holds my face in place.

"How does that make you feel, little brother?"

"Sad."

He digs his fingers in my skin, inflicting more pain. "Wrong answer. Try again."

"Fucking angry, okay?"

His lips twist into a cruel grin. "Good. It's high time we get rid of the old man."

I frown. "What do you mean, get rid of him?"

Zeus unfurls from his crouch, standing tall in front of me. "You're old enough to guess."

As much as I hate our father, I'd never considered that possibility. Now that I hear Zeus's insinuation, I reject it.

"I'm not going to help you commit patricide."

He raises an eyebrow. "I can't believe you know that word."

"I'm ten, not a moron."

He watches me through narrowed eyes. "I'm only going to

give you one chance, Hades. You're either with me or against me. I suggest you choose wisely."

"What about Poseidon?"

He chuckles. "What do you think, brat? Naturally, he's with me."

Zeus and Poseidon are much older than me; both were in their twenties when I was born. They've never made it any secret that they hate that our father acquired a third heir to split his empire. If I choose them, there's no guarantee that I'm not next to die.

But in the end, the decision is easy. Stick with the devil I know.

"Well, I'm not."

His eyes flash with rage. "Big mistake, little bro." He takes a step forward. "You say one word about this conversation to Dad, and you'll meet the same fate as your mutts."

I stay frozen, sprawled on the floor as I watch him leave. I barely feel the sting of my father's punches anymore. The agony swirling in my chest is greater. Mom died when I was a baby, and my father never cared about me. The strays I rescued were the closest thing to a family I had, and now they're gone.

I'm truly alone, and I'd better get used to it.

1

PERSEPHONE

An annoying sound blares through my ears, jolting me awake. Damn, I was having a nice dream. Glowering at the device, I pick it up to shut the blasted thing off only to curse in the next breath.

Fuck! I'm late.

I jump out of bed, tripping over my shoes and almost landing on my face. It's a miracle that I manage to keep off the floor this time. My mother always said I was born with two left feet, and sadly, she isn't wrong about that part.

I glance at my reflection in the mirror and decide I can skip a shower this morning. I'll be laboring away anyway, so who cares if my curly hair resembles a bird's nest? I fell asleep with my clothes on last night, burning the midnight oil to prepare for my test later today. My flower print oversized sweatshirt is a bit wrinkled, but it looks clean. I bring the fabric to my nose; it doesn't smell ripe, so I don't need to change either.

I have fifteen minutes to get to work, so I sprint down the hallway but skid to a halt when I hear Persi's loud snoring. *Son of a bitch*. He also overslept. Where the hell is my mother, who didn't wake him for school?

I push the door open and yell, "Perseus, get up!"

"Go away." He hides his head under the pillow.

I venture in and am immediately assaulted by the stench of dirty socks and old pizza. I pull the cover off him, making him curl into a ball.

"Come on, Persi. I don't have time to play the mother card with you. I can't be late for work."

"Who's asking you to play Mom?"

"Someone has to." I march to his window and yank the curtains open. "Besides, don't you want to get out of his hellhole one day?"

"Right now, all I want is to go back to sleep."

"Not an option. You need to get your ass to school. Don't force me to use the bucket of ice again."

"Ugh. Fine!" He sits up and tosses the pillow at me.

I dodge, and it ends up knocking his desk lamp to the floor.

"You'll probably need to ride your bike today. You've already missed the bus."

"Why can't you give me a ride?" He scratches his head but makes no move to get out of bed.

"I already told you. I'm late for work." I head for the door. "You'd better get moving, Persi."

"Yeah, yeah."

I would have given him a ride if only to make sure he got to school on time, but I can't push my luck. I've already received a warning from my boss about being late before, and I can't lose my job. I desperately need the money, but I also love what I do.

On my way to the kitchen, I stop by Mom's room. No surprise that I find it empty. She didn't spend the night—*again*.

I wish I had time for coffee, but that will take too long. I settle for a banana that's already turning brown. As I peel the gooey fruit, I see a pile of bills with "final notice" stamps on the envelopes. My stomach twists at the sight, or maybe it was the bite of overripe banana that's making me queasy. I force myself to finish it, because who knows when I'll have the chance to eat again.

Outside, I greet my car like I always do. "Good morning, Petunia. Are you ready for another wonderful day in Olympus Bay?"

"Stop talking to that piece of shit you call a car, young lady. People will think you're nuts," our neighbor Jack complains.

"But I *am* crazy." I smile from ear to ear like a deranged person.

The old man shakes his head and goes inside his house.

"Don't listen to him, Petunia," I coo. "You aren't a piece of shit."

I slide behind the steering wheel and pray I can get the engine started on the first try. Petunia can be a little temperamental. There's a little hiccup, but the rumble of the motor soon comes through.

"Thank God," I say, but as I put the car in first gear, I notice the nearly empty gas tank. *Crap*. I'll have to drive slower than molasses to make the little bit of gas last until I can put some money in it.

There's no chance in hell I'll arrive on time now.

I MAKE it to Le Chant Flowers just as Otto, a.k.a. the boss, is finishing loading the van. I'm sputtering excuses as I get out of the car, but he raises his hand and levels me with a glare.

"Save it, Persephone. I don't have time to hear your BS. Get in the van."

"You don't need me at the store?"

"No. A last-minute job came up. You're in charge of the flower arrangements for Mrs. Harrods's funeral."

My eyebrows rise, almost meeting my hairline. "I'm in charge?"

He gives me a droll look. "Don't sound so surprised. The only reason you still have this job despite your lack of punctuality is that you're a damn talented floral designer."

A blush spreads through my cheeks. Otto never hands out compliments. He's an old grump most of the time.

"Thank you."

"Thank me by getting in the van already," he grumbles.

"Where am I going?" I ask, but it's pointless. There's only one major funeral home business in Olympus Bay.

"Styx Funeral Services, where else?"

"What time is the service?"

"In a few hours. Mrs. Harrods's daughter will be there to share her *vision* for the flowers." Contempt drips from his tone, which means the client is a pain in the ass.

"Great!" I reply with extra cheer, which only makes him glare harder.

I jump into the van before Otto decides he can fire me after all.

I've never designed floral arrangements for a funeral before, but I can't imagine it will be different than any other event. As I drive, I start to daydream about what I could do, though it's a little pointless since I don't know what type of flowers I'll be working with.

The drive to Styx doesn't take long, and when I arrive, the parking lot at the front is almost empty. However, I drive to the back so I can unload all the flowers without getting in the way of their customers. Unfortunately, there's a truck already occupying the unloading spot, which means I either wait until they're done or I use the front door.

I look at the clock on the dashboard. If I wait, it means I'll have to rush through the job to finish on time.

"Screw it."

I put the van in Reverse and return to the front. There's no one around anyway. I do notice the new vehicle parked right at the front. It's a shiny black sports car that looks like the Batmobile. The windows are tinted, making it impossible to see inside. I make sure to park far away from it; with my luck, I'd end up putting a dent in it.

To get into the zone, I put on my headphones and select the playlist titled "Getting It Done." The first song that starts blasting is "Hello" from the *Ted Lasso* soundtrack. In an instant, I get lost in my world and start transferring the flowers to the cart. It's no surprise that I don't hear anyone's approach until my headphones are yanked from my ears.

I yell out and jump to the side, colliding with the semifull cart, which tumbles down with all the flowers in it.

"Shit! What the hell!" I glower at the tall blond dude responsible for my scare and mishap.

"My words exactly. What the hell?" He returns the glare.

"You're the one who almost gave me a heart attack."

"That wouldn't have happened if you weren't listening to music so loudly that even I could hear it."

"Well, no one forced you to listen to it."

He narrows his gaze, his cheeks hollowing in as he clenches his jaw, then he looks at the mess of flowers on the asphalt. "You must be here for Mrs. Harrods's funeral. The unloading dock is in the back of the building."

Why is he telling me that? I look over his shoulder toward the shiny car. There's a huge beast of a dog sitting next to it, watching us. I glance at the guy again and really pay attention to his face. The squared jaw, the chin dimple, and that trademark arrogant vibe all members of the Godaire family have.

Shit. Now that my brain isn't freaking out over getting scared to death, I can finally recognize who I pissed off.

Hades Godaire, the king of Olympus U and the owner of Styx Funeral Services.

I'm so fucked.

2

HADES

I know the moment flower girl realizes who she's speaking to. Her beautiful jade-green eyes turn rounder, and her plump lips make a perfect *O*. Even annoyed as hell, I've managed to notice every desirable trait she has.

"The unloading dock was occupied," she replies with her chin raised high. "And I'm on a tight schedule."

Most people are too afraid of me to be assertive. Her attitude, even though it's grating, is also a breath of fresh air. It doesn't mean I'll go easy on her.

"Do I look like I care? Clean up this mess and drive to the back."

Her cheeks are bright red, and her jaw clenching is one of the hardest I've caused. I wait for her reply, perversely hoping she'll defy me again. I was having a shitty morning, but it turns out sparring with this stranger is working to lift my bad mood.

"Fine," she grits out. "I'll use the dock."

I step back and watch her collect the flowers scattered on the ground for a moment. I won't deny that I'm enjoying the view despite the ugly sweatshirt she's wearing, but an incoming phone call cuts my fun short. With a single glance, I know my day is only going to get worse. It's Zeus's office calling, which means my big bro is hounding me. I reject the call and head to Styx's entrance.

With a whistle, I call Cerberus to me. He's the only bright side in my life at the moment.

I pat his head and smile. "Good boy."

Once inside, I give the place a cursory glance. If it weren't for the coffin display in one of the rooms, one would think they were inside a five-star hotel. This place was a dump when I inherited it. I never wanted to work in this field, but I'm fucking proud of what I've accomplished.

I usually don't come here at opening hours, preferring the solitude of working at night. I chuckle as I head to my office in the back. Zeus thought he was so clever when he gave me Styx after our asshole father died. It was meant as a joke, but when I turned eighteen and could actually do something with it, I made the business extremely profitable without resorting to illicit activities—unlike him. Now Styx is the McDonald's of funeral services. Death is the only certainty in life, and I've made sure Styx is the first name that comes to mind when people think about it.

That much can't be said about any of Zeus's companies or Poseidon's. Of course, that doesn't stop them from trying to fuck me over. Once a bully, always a bully.

I go about my business, trying to forget my asshole brothers. Besides running my empire, I have a damn report to finish for school. I'm determined to graduate from Olympus U with honors, just to prove to Zeus that I can do it all and be the fucking best at everything.

It doesn't take long for the world to disturb me, though. Ten minutes after I get settled, there's a knock on my door.

"What?" I bark.

"It's me, Hercules."

"Come in."

A mountain of a man, and a jack-of-all-trades, he's been on the Godaire payroll for as long as I can remember, which is surprising because he hated my father's guts just as much as he hates my brothers. Hence why I made sure to bring him with me when I moved out of Zeus's house. My bastard brother gained custody of me when he went through with his vile plan and killed Dad. I honestly thought I wouldn't last long under his care, but he never made an attempt against my life.

I suspect Hercules is in part responsible for me being alive today. He was one of the many things Zeus inherited when our father died. We never discussed his involvement with what happened on my darkest day. He was following orders, and I don't blame him; the survival rate for those who disobeyed Cronos was zero.

Hercules's eternal frown is even more pronounced today, which doesn't bode well.

"What now?"

"I just had to dispatch some of your brother's goons who wanted to inspect the new coffin delivery."

There isn't a single hair out of place, and his clothes look fine. That brings a grin to my lips.

"Is that so? How many did Zeus send this time?"

"Five." He shrugs.

Shaking my head, I chuckle. "Pathetic."

"He's not going to give up, you know? He wasn't happy when you put a stop to his little operation."

My entire body tenses as I narrow my eyes. "I don't give a fuck about what Zeus wants. I won't use my business to help him move drugs across the borders."

A bark followed by a loud crash outside puts me on a high alert in an instant. Hercules kept the door open when he came in, and Cerberus must have slipped out. I jump from my chair and go investigate. Hercules is closer to the door and gets to the corridor first.

"I'm so sorry. The dog spooked me," a female voice says.

It's flower girl again. I walk around Hercules, who was blocking my view, to find her sprawled on the floor and surrounded once again by her damn flowers.

Her face is white as a sheet, though, and there isn't a spark of defiance in her eyes. That leads me to two possible scenarios: she's either afraid of Hercules, or she overheard our conversation.

"Do I need to call your employer and complain about your ineptitude?" I ask.

She jumps to her feet. "No. Please don't call him. I'll clean this up in a minute. I promise."

"I'll help," Hercules grumbles, surprising the shit out of me.

"Th-Thanks."

My first impulse is to tell him she needs to clean the mess herself, but I refrain from acting on it. Instead, I watch them work together and then disappear back into the main part of the building. In fact, I couldn't keep my eyes away from flower girl. Something must be wrong with me.

My phone's ringtone snaps me out of my daze. This time it's Hecate calling.

"What's up? You're up early."

"All thanks to your stupid-ass friend."

The man in question yells a "Hello" in the background, earning a "Shut the fuck up" in response from her.

"What's Dionysus doing there?" I ask.

"How do I know? He's *your* friend."

"Let me talk to him."

A second later, his lazy voice comes to the phone. "Hades, where are you?"

"At work, dumbass. What do you think?"

"Why? You're like the richest motherfucker I know." He hiccups.

For fuck's sake. He's drunk, and it's not even nine in the morning yet.

"Did you just come from a party?"

"Someone has to enjoy college life to the fullest."

"Well, you're pissing off Hecate. You'd better leave before she rips your nutsack off."

"Fine. The raid on your fridge was a bust. You eat like shit."

I snort. "I eat healthy. I suppose that's shit according to your standards."

"Anyway, you're still coming tonight, right?"

"You bet your ass I am. With the way my day is going, I'll be jonesing to break some bones later."

"Excellent! Ouch!"

"What now?" I pinch the bridge of my nose.

"Your damn housemate threw a pineapple at me."

I try to keep my laugh bottled up. "Uh, I wonder where she got that."

"*That's* your concern? I almost got killed!"

"Then I suggest you go home."

"I can't."

"I'm afraid to ask." I rub my forehead. Talking to him is giving me a headache already.

His breathing becomes labored, as if he started to run. "She's got a knife!"

A groan escapes my lips. I must be a glutton for punishment, because all my friends are deranged fucks.

There's a loud bang in the background that sounds like a door shutting. "Okay. I think I'm safe now. I locked myself in one of your guest bedrooms."

"Whatever. Just don't make a mess like the last time."

Hercules is returning from helping flower girl, so I end the call with Dio to ask why he volunteered to help her.

One glance from me and he knows what's on my mind.

"I needed to find out what she heard," he says.

"And?"

"She heard about the drugs," he replies with a straight face.

I raise an eyebrow. "She confessed just like that?"

"No, she lied to me."

Not surprised he could tell. I've never been able to hide shit from him. He's a lie detector.

I narrow my eyes. "Hmm."

"What do you want me to do about it?"

"Do? Why would I care if she overheard us? I'm not the one breaking the law."

Hercules opens and shuts his mouth like a fish out of water, but whatever he wanted to say at first, he decides against it.

"So you don't want me to dig up intel on her?"

I wasn't planning on it, but now that he's presented the idea, I discover that I'm quite keen on it.

"On the contrary. I want to know everything about her."

He nods. "Consider it done."

I start toward my office when I notice Cerberus isn't in the corridor anymore.

"Have you seen Cerbie?"

Frowning, Hercules scratches the back of his head. "He wasn't up front."

"The back entrance… was it open?"

"I believe so."

Fuck.

3

PERSEPHONE

I never thought I'd pray for a floral arrangement gig to be over. The customer wasn't as bad as I thought she would be. The issue was Hades and then his assistant... bodyguard... whatever. He only offered to help in order to shower me with questions. Yes, I overheard their conversation, but so what? Everyone knows the Godaire family is powerful through shady means. It's not likely I'll go run off to the police. Wouldn't do me any good, and would probably get me killed. The Godaires own this city.

I glance at the time and realize I'm once again behind schedule. I have to be at school in twenty minutes or I'll miss the test. I can't afford to let my GPA drop or I might lose my scholarship. I do wish I had time to go home to shower and change, though. I was passable earlier, but now I feel like there's a green cloud wafting off me just like in *The Sims* when a character is in dire need of a shower.

I reach for my purse and try to find the sample of perfume I tossed in there. Instead, I prick my finger on God knows what.

"Ouch. Son of a bitch." I peel my eyes off the road for a

second to inspect the damage when, from the corner of my eye, I see a black blur cross in front of the van.

I press on the brake hard, making the tires screech and burn rubber. The whimper of an animal tells me I didn't stop the vehicle in time. With my heart stuck in my throat, I jump out of the van and run to the front.

"Fuck my life."

It's Hades's dog.

I drop to my knees, praying I didn't kill him. His eyes are open, but when I touch his head, he whimpers pitifully again. It looks like one of the tires caught his hind leg, and there's blood. I have to take him to a vet ASAP.

"I'm so sorry. I know this will hurt, buddy, but it's the only way."

I reach underneath his body and try to lift him as if he were a baby. Big mistake. The dog is built of solid muscle.

Come on, Persephone. You can do it.

Grinding my teeth, I somehow find the strength to lift the beast off the ground, walk around the passenger side, and open the door without causing another disaster.

I'm only a block away from Styx. I could go back and tell Hades about what happened.

I scratch that idea immediately. He already doesn't like me. He's going to kill me if he sees what I did to his poor dog, even if it was an accident.

The vet it is, then.

I press the pedal to the metal while frantically waiting for Google to tell me where the nearest vet is. If I'm not careful, I'll end up in a car wreck. Mercifully, the damn thing finally gives me an answer, and I'm relieved that there's one five minutes from here.

"Hang on, sweetie. We're almost there."

The dog doesn't make a sound, but at least he's awake. My

heart has shriveled to nothing. I hate to see innocent animals in pain.

I make it to the vet's office in four minutes. To my dismay, there isn't a single parking spot available in front.

"Screw it. This is an emergency."

I park the van right in front of the sliding doors, blocking a few cars in. I rush to the other side of the van just as a couple is walking out of the office.

"Hey, you can't park there," the woman complains.

"Lady, this is an emergency. I'll move the van in a minute."

She says something to the guy with her, but I tune her out. My arms strain with the weight of Hades's dog, but I suck it up and rush through the front door.

"I need help," I almost yell, or maybe I actually did.

The woman behind the reception counter glances up from her computer screen and widens her eyes. "What happened?"

I thought I had my nerves under control, but her question proves that I was barely holding on. Now the dam breaks, turning me into a stuttering mess.

"He came out of nowhere. I didn't mean to. I tried to brake," I attempt to explain through hiccups and tears.

"It's okay, honey. The vet will take care of him."

A man wearing a white coat comes out the door next to the reception area and takes the dog from me. I don't know if that was the vet or the assistant all thanks to my nonstop crying.

"I need you to fill out this form for me," the receptionist tells me.

"Okay." I take the clipboard from her and find a seat.

I'm conscious that people in the reception area are staring at me, but I don't give a flying fuck that I have witnesses to my meltdown. I stare at the questions on the form, and I have no idea what information to write except for my contact information. It occurs to me then that the bill for this visit will be hefty, and I'll probably have to sell a kidney to cover the costs.

I consider filling out fake information and then slipping out, but that wouldn't be right. I made the mistake, and now I must pay the price.

"Hey, van girl. Are you moving your vehicle or what?" the man from before asks.

"Shit." I jump from the seat and hurry to move the van before he decides to call the cops.

The universe seems to take pity on me, because someone just vacated a parking space. I'm still distraught when I return to the office, though. In a daze, I bring the discarded clipboard back to the reception desk and hand it over.

"I'm afraid I don't know much about the dog."

"It's okay, dear. We scanned his tag and contacted the owner. He'll be here shortly."

My stomach twists savagely and then drops to the ground. Shakes wreak havoc on my body, and I fear I might barf right over her pristine counter.

"You! What have you done to my dog?"

My blood freezes in my veins, rendering me paralyzed save for the tremors.

Hades is here.

How the hell did he get here so fast?

"Oh dear," the receptionist mumbles.

A rough hand clasps around my arm painfully and turns me around. "Answer me!"

"I-I'm sorry. He came out of nowhere."

His blue eyes spark with fury and so much hate that I'm glad he's holding me in a vicious grip; otherwise, I think I might crumble under that stare.

"You're a menace," he grits out, then pushes me aside to stride past the reception desk toward the door into the office.

"Wait, you can't go in there." The receptionist stands up.

He looks in her direction, his gaze hard and unyielding. "Try to stop me. I dare you."

She blanches and then falls back into her seat. As for me, I don't know what to do.

"You should probably go," she tells me.

I shake my head. "No. I have to stay and deal with the consequences."

"Consequences? Are you insane, girl? You ran over Hades Godaire's dog. You're lucky he didn't kill you on the spot."

"I know, but I can't leave without knowing if his dog is okay or not."

She stares at me without blinking, then shakes her head. "It's your funeral, then."

The irony of her statement almost makes me laugh. *Almost*. I haven't lost my mind completely yet.

4

HADES

I was prepared to destroy the person who hurt Cerberus, but my thirst for blood vanished when I saw who was responsible. Flower girl. I don't know why I held back with her when the anger was still pumping in my veins.

I burst through the vet's examining room, startling him. But the moment I see Cerbie on the table, he gets my undivided attention.

"What's the meaning of this?" the vet demands. "You aren't—"

"Save it, Doc. How is he?"

"His left hind leg seems to be broken. I'll know for sure after the X-ray."

"Is he going to be all right?" I pat his head, and my heart breaks when he whimpers.

"He's a healthy dog. I don't see any reason why he shouldn't make a full recovery."

"Do whatever it takes."

"He got lucky."

I whip around to face him, not hiding my displeasure.

"Excuse me? My dog was run over by a van, and you think he was lucky?"

The douche's eyes widen. "Yes. If that girl hadn't stopped in time, it could have been much worse."

My rage returns with a vengeance. Now that I'm not distracted by whatever spell she put on me, there's nothing putting a damper on my emotions.

"She didn't stop in time," I grit out. "If she had, Cerberus wouldn't be here. Why don't you concentrate on helping my dog instead of sharing your fucking opinions?"

He swallows so hard it's audible. He knows who I am and what I'm capable of.

"Of course, Mr. Godaire. I'll take Cerberus to get his X-ray right away. Why don't you wait outside?"

I veer for the single chair in the room and sit down. "I'll wait right here. You'd better get moving, Doc. The more my dog suffers, the more aggravated I'll be."

His face blanches, but at least he keeps his piehole shut. He wheels Cerbie out of the room, and the moment he's out of my sight, my chest becomes tighter. Cerberus has been with me since high school and helped me through a lot of shit. If something happens to him, flower girl will pay despite the strange hold she has on me.

I pull my cell phone out and type her name in the Google search bar—information that Hercules got out of her when he was giving the girl the third degree. Persephone Flores. The top link on the page is to her Instagram account. I click on it first, but it offers me nothing useful besides telling me she's into floral design and she isn't bad at it.

I move on and continue my search until I find something I can work with. She goes to Olympus U. A sophomore, major undecided. She must not be a social person or I would have seen her before. There's no chance I wouldn't have noticed her if she were in the same room as me.

The vet returns with Cerbie and confirms his leg is broken, but it was a clean break, and no surgery is needed. My anxiety releases its hold on my chest, but not by much. I won't have to kill Persephone today, but it doesn't mean she's off the hook.

Getting Cerbie in a cast takes another hour, and by the time I'm ready to take him home, I'm surprised to find Persephone is still there.

She springs to her feet and asks, "Is he okay?"

I try to hold on to my anger, but damn it, her bright eyes and tear-streaked face once again work in her favor.

"No. His leg is broken."

"I'm so sorry."

"Not as sorry as you'd be if something worse had happened to him."

She dips her chin and stares at the ground. "Trust me, nothing you could do to me would be worse than the guilt swirling in my chest. I couldn't live with myself if I had ki—" She shakes her head and looks up.

I know bullshit—I grew up surrounded by narcissist assholes, after all. Her confession is heartfelt, and I don't know how to react to it.

"If there's anything I can do—" she starts.

"Stay the hell away from me and my business." I walk around her and keep going without looking back despite the urge to glance at her again.

One more reason to avoid her like the plague. She's making me soft, and I can't have that.

PERSEPHONE

I wait until Hades is gone to walk out of the office. My phone rings the moment I step foot outside. It's my best friend, Helen, calling.

"Hey," I answer.

"Where the hell have you been, girl? You missed the test!"

Curse all the gods. "Shit. I completely forgot about that."

"How could you? You've been studying for days."

I pinch the bridge of my nose. "There's been an emergency, and I spaced out."

"What happened?"

"I ran over someone's dog."

"Oh no! Did you ki—"

"No! Thank God. I brought him to the vet. It was a broken leg, but I'm shaken, and the owner is crazy pissed."

"I'm sorry. Were they super awful to you?"

"I thought he was going to kill me at first."

"Well, you're talking to me, so I take it he didn't." She laughs, grating on my already fried nerves.

Wrong time to be cracking jokes, Helen.

"No. But it doesn't matter. I made an enemy for life."

"Oh, honey. You're so dramatic sometimes."

"I'm not kidding, Helen. Hades won't forget this."

There's a noticeable pause. "Wait a second. You maimed Hades Godaire's dog?"

"Yep. Now you can officially call me Disaster Queen."

"Jesus, you have the worst luck in the world. What were the chances you'd run over that psycho's dog? The Fates must really hate you."

"You can say that again. Now I have to beg Prof. Cashore to retake the test. I can't afford for my grades to drop."

"I'm sure he'll let you do it. You're his star pupil."

I grimace. The old perv does have a soft spot for me, and on more than one occasion, he's hinted that he'd give me straight As if I fucked him. *Why are men pigs?*

"That's what I'm afraid of. What will he ask in return?"

"You know, I bet if you dropped the Hades name, Prof. Perv would stop harassing you."

"How would saying I'm on Hades's shit list help me?"

She sighs, clearly exasperated. "You don't need to tell him that tiny detail. Let him believe Hades is your boyfriend or something."

"Helen, you're insane. I'm not having this conversation with you."

"Fine. Anyway, I wasn't calling only to ask where you were. I have an invitation for you."

"To what?"

"Remember when I told you about the underground fighting on campus?"

"Yeah."

"I got us passes. Well, technically, Paris did. But anyway, we're in."

I groan. "What makes you think I wanna go to that? Besides, you know I hate being the third wheel."

"You won't be. Hector will be there too."

"Goody. I'll be stuck with Mr. Grumpy Pants while you suck face with your boyfriend."

"Come on, Seph," she pleads. "After the shitty day you had, you need to have a fun night out. Besides, there will be tons of hotties there. You don't need to hang out with Hector."

She's not wrong, and I know more crap is coming my way before the day is over. I still have to deal with my mother—that is, if she decides to show up.

"Okay, you win. I'll make an appearance."

"Make an appearance, my ass. I'm picking you up."

I roll my eyes. "Whatever. I'll see you later."

Helen can be a pain sometimes, but she means well. We've

been best friends since elementary school, despite the fact that her parents make a lot of money, and I'm probably the poorest student at Olympus U. Not that she's ever made me feel less for it.

My phone rings again, but this time, it's my boss.

Shit. I never returned the van.

Man, how much trouble can I get in before the day is over?

5

PERSEPHONE

"What have you been up to, Seph? I haven't seen you in ages," Paris asks.

"Not much. I haven't had a chance to do anything besides study and work."

"Are you still working at the flower shop?"

"Yeah."

"You can't possibly be making any money there," Hector pipes up.

My cheeks warm. I don't mind talking about money—or my lack of it—with Helen. It's a different story discussing my financial issues with other people, especially with the Alexander brothers, who are a bit snobbish. They only tolerate me because of my friend.

"Jesus, Hector. Have you no filter?" Helen complains.

"What did I say that was bad? I was making an observation, that's all."

"It's fine," I reply. "No, the money isn't great. But I love working there."

"If you need more cash, our mother is always looking for waitstaff," Paris chimes in. "The tips are wicked good."

"How do you know?" Hector asks, annoyed. "I don't remember you ever working at any of the restaurants."

"I was told. Unlike you, brother, I make friends with everyone."

Okay, maybe Paris isn't that snobbish, but I know Hector is.

It's not the first time he and Helen have suggested waitressing, but I know I'd be a disaster with my lack of coordination. However, there's a high chance I won't have any other option but to give it a try. My job at the flower shop is hanging by a thread, and there's that pile of unpaid bills waiting at home.

I didn't dare open those envelopes, knowing it would obliterate my evening, and I do want to have some fun tonight. The bills will still be there tomorrow.

"I'll think about it," I say. "Have you guys been to one of those fights before?"

"Yes," Paris and Hector answer at the same time.

"What's it like?"

"Madness." Paris chuckles. "But a lot of fun."

"Do you know who's fighting tonight?" Helen asks.

"Ares for sure. He never misses it," Paris replies. "And Hector."

"What? You're fighting?" Helen asks, clearly surprised.

There's also an accusation in her tone, which I find strange. It's like she believes he should have told her about it, but they don't even get along. Why would he tell her anything?

"Yes," he answers curtly.

She crosses her arms and pouts. "You didn't tell me."

Man, I was right. She *is* pissed that she didn't know.

"Why would Hector tell you?" Paris turns to look at her, sporting a frown.

Yes, Helen. Why?

I watch my friend, immediately noticing her consternation. Something's up.

"Well… I don't know."

"I didn't tell anyone besides Paris because I didn't want to hear a sermon about how dangerous those fights are," Hector replies calmly.

"Are they, though? Dangerous, I mean," I butt in.

"Not if you know what you're doing," Hector answers.

Paris turns the radio on, putting the volume as high as it goes. But despite the deafening sound, I can't ignore the sudden tension in the car. I'm too curious to wait until I'm alone with Helen to ask, so I text her.

ME: What's the deal with you and Hector?

HELEN: There is no deal.

ME: I thought you didn't get along.

HELEN: We don't. You're a busybody tonight.

I give up trying to get her to talk to me. I'll have to wait until she's ready to tell me the truth. She's always been like that, keeping secrets until they become too much to bear. Then she won't shut up about them.

I try to get distracted by the music as I look out the window, but my mind goes to a place it shouldn't, and Hades takes center stage. I don't like how I can't make up my mind about how I should feel about him. He had every right to be furious with me after the accident, but he was a jerk before that, so I can only come to the conclusion that he's an asshole. Yet I'm tempted to go after him and ask for forgiveness again. It sucks that I'm on his shit list, but I shouldn't care so much about it. There's a slim chance we'll cross paths again.

It doesn't take long for us to arrive at the old warehouse on the outskirts of Olympus Bay. It sits next to the abandoned railroad tracks, which used to be a popular hangout for the high school kids. I've been here a couple of times with Helen. No one from high school comes here anymore, not since the underground fights began.

Hector takes off in front of us. Helen laces her arm with Paris's, and they follow him. I bring up the rear. As I walk in front of a group of guys, they wolf whistle and laugh. I cross my arms over my chest, trying to hide my boobs. I hate when assholes act like creeps.

I speed up until I'm walking next to Hector. He gives me a side-glance but doesn't say anything. I'd rather suffer his company than be subjected to more ogling. No one will dare mess with me if they believe I'm with him.

The noise is deafening inside the warehouse, and the fights haven't even started yet. The place is massive, and the installations look brand new. The ring in the center rivals what I've seen on TV. Every time Helen mentioned these fights, I pictured a dark and smelly basement, which is a stupid image since I've always known they happened here. I'd probably latched on to Brad Pitt's *Fight Club* when I thought about it. Helen says big money keeps the cops looking the other way. Who's paying them off, no one knows for sure, but I suspect the Godaires.

"I'm going to report to Atlas," Hector tells us and then disappears in the crowd.

"Who's Atlas?" I ask.

"One of the organizers," Paris replies. "Come on. Let's get something to drink and then find a good spot. I want to be up front when the fight starts."

"Do you know who Hector is fighting?" Helen asks.

He shakes his head. "No clue. He didn't say. I'm not sure he knows."

Paris carves a path for us toward the nearest bar, but it's already a zoo, so we hang back and let him order the drinks.

Now that I'm alone with Helen, my curiosity gets the better of me.

"You're really not going to tell me what's going on with you and Hector?"

She sighs. "I knew you wouldn't let it rest. There's nothing to tell."

"You sounded surprised that he didn't tell you he'd be fighting tonight."

"Yeah, only because he loves to show off and boast about his fighting skills." She shrugs.

Paris returns with our beers, so I have to bite my tongue for now.

Getting closer to the ring proves more difficult than going to the bar, but thanks to Paris's height and build, he manages to guide us to the front.

"How much longer do we have to wait until it starts?" Helen asks, fidgeting from side to side.

Patience is not a virtue she possesses, but tonight she seems edgier than ever.

"Not long now," Paris says.

Five minutes later, a dude sporting a blue mohawk and wearing a deep-purple silk robe over his dark jeans steps into the ring.

"Who's the Hugh Hefner wannabe?" Helen asks.

"That's Atlas."

He brings the mic to his mouth. "Good evening, ladies and gentlemen. Are you ready to see some awesome ass kicking tonight?"

The crowd goes wild, shouting and whistling. Atlas waits until the noise dies down a little to continue his speech, and it goes on for another minute before he announces the first fighters of the night. It's Hector and a guy named Patroclus.

"Hell," Paris curses under his breath.

"What is it?" Helen turns to him.

"Patroclus is a beast."

Indeed, the guy Hector is facing is built like a mountain. His arms are so thick they translate as trees to me. However, Hector doesn't seem one bit intimidated by his opponent's size. He watches him with a calculating gleam, and when the fight starts, it doesn't take long to realize size isn't everything. Patroclus knows how to fight, but Hector is better. The match lasts less than ten minutes before Hector delivers a knockout punch that sends Patroclus to the floor.

The crowd screams as if the world is about to end, making me wince. I turn to Helen in time to see her exhale as if a great weight was lifted off her shoulders. Paris is jumping up and down, screaming like a maniac.

When the cacophony dies down a bit, I say, "I don't know about you guys, but I think that was enough violence for me."

Paris's eyebrows arch. "You want to leave *now*?"

"I wouldn't mind going either," Helen chimes in.

"But we can't. We haven't seen Ares fight yet, and that's something you really don't want to miss."

I open my mouth to reply, but Helen beats me to the punch and agrees to stay. Since they gave me a ride, I have to suck it up until they're ready to go.

"I need to use the restroom," I say.

Helen nods. "Oh, I'll come too."

Paris twists his face into a scowl. "Uh, I don't want to leave and lose our spot."

"Jesus, Paris. We can manage to find the restroom on our own," I retort.

My comment doesn't smooth the crinkles on his forehead, though. If anything, it only makes them more obvious.

"It's fine, babe. We'll be back in a minute." Helen kisses his cheek, then grabs my hand and steers me away from the ring.

"Is it me, or is Paris getting more and more possessive?" I ask.

"He's not possessive. He's protective. That's different."

"If you say so."

No surprise, we find a huge line outside the girls' restroom. I'm glad I don't have to go badly; I just wanted a break from the rowdy crowd. Tonight, I don't mind the wait. Hopefully, we'll miss most of Ares's fight.

6

HADES

I told Dionysus that I was looking forward to breaking some bones, but now that I'm here, I'm not as keen to fight. Oh well. Too late to back down now that the names have been drawn and I'm facing Ares, my nephew who's a month older than me and never lets me forget that fact. He's a veritable pain in the ass, but considering who his father is, it's a miracle he isn't worse. As it is, I get along with him fine, but if I withdraw, he'll never let me forget it.

He appears before me, jumping from side to side like the Energizer Bunny on speed.

"What's with the frown, Uncle Hades? Are you afraid to face me?" He smirks.

"Sure."

"I heard about Cerberus. Is he going to be okay?"

I wish he hadn't brought it up. One of the reasons I came tonight is to stop the worry from consuming me whole.

"Yeah. Long recovery, though."

"I'm surprised I didn't read anything in the papers about a murder."

I give him a droll look. "What are you talking about now?"

"You didn't kill the motherfucker who ran over your dog. Or maybe you did and got rid of the body." He raises an eyebrow.

My lips curl into a grin. "Do you really think if I *had* killed anyone, I'd tell you?"

He widens his eyes innocently. "I wouldn't blabber. I'm not Hermes."

I shake my head. Ares's younger brother deals in secrets. The pest has an undeniable talent for digging up dirt on people, a skill I've used many times in the past. But I wouldn't go as far as calling him a friend. His loyalty is to whoever pays him more.

"You live with him, which means he knows everything you do."

Ares grimaces. "Not everything."

His attention diverts to Atlas, who just entered the locker room, followed by Hector Alexander and a dazed Patroclus. The giant has a bloody cloth over his nose and the slumped shoulders of someone who just lost.

"Damn. I can't believe that noob broke Patroclus's nose." Ares shakes his head.

"Size isn't everything," I say as I stare at Hector.

He comes from a traditional Olympus Bay family, and all my life, I've never seen or heard any stories about him or his younger brother, Paris. They like to keep to themselves, rarely cause trouble, so I'm surprised he signed up to fight tonight.

"Your fight is next," Atlas tells us.

"Excellent." Ares claps his hands. "Does the crowd know I'm fighting my dear uncle?"

"Not yet. I figured it's best to let them remain in the dark for as long as I can. This is too good of a pairing. I have to milk it. I'll announce you first, Ares."

He twists his face into a scowl. "Why me first and not Hades?"

"Because I rarely come, and you practically live here," I answer, knowing exactly why he's bothered.

“Exactly. Besides, Hades is Hades.” Atlas shrugs.

“What’s that supposed to mean?” Ares bristles.

“It means I’m the motherfucking king of Olympus U, *nephew*.” I give him a toothy grin.

He flips me off and goes to sulk in a corner.

“Oh, you’re in for a match now.” Atlas laughs.

“And you think I wasn’t before?” I quirk an eyebrow.

After another minute or so, we head to the ring. I wait in the corridor, hidden from the crowd until Atlas and Ares finish their performances. I wish this was a real underground fight without all the theatrics. I just came for the sport. I could do without the circus.

I put my game face on when my name blares through the speakers, avoiding making eye contact as I run toward the ring. I worked hard for my reputation on campus, and no matter what’s happening in my life, that’s something I can’t risk getting ruined. Winning against Ares is also crucial, but I’m not worried about that. He’s never been able to beat me in a fight.

PERSEPHONE

The restroom visit didn’t take as long as I’d hoped, so I steered Helen to the bar to get new drinks. For once, she isn’t in a hurry to return to Paris’s side. They’ve been together since freshman year of high school, and up until now, I thought they were destined for the altar. But now I’m not so sure if that’s in the cards for them.

“So, what happened with Prof. Cashore?” she asks. “Is he going to let you retake the test?”

“I sent him an email, and he asked me to come see him in person.”

Helen's lips become a thin, flat line. "Jerk. I'm telling you, use Hades as the excuse."

I take a sip of my beer. "I'll think about it."

As if we summoned the man just by speaking his name, Atlas announces Hades to the crowd.

Helen's eyes go round. "Holy shit! Hades is fighting tonight. We can't miss that." She grabs my hand before I can protest and drags me back to where Paris is, shoving people out of her way like she's on a mission.

"Helen, slow down. You'll get us killed."

I send an apologetic glance to a dude she just elbowed. His annoyance turns into a leery grin that sends shivers down my back. *God, why can't women be nice to guys without triggering their creep mode?* Mercifully, we're making quick progress, and soon the crowd swallows us.

When we reach the front, the fight has already started. Hades and Ares are circling each other, but the first punch has yet to be thrown.

Paris turns to us as soon as Helen steps next to him. "Where have you been?"

"There was a huge line for the restroom, and then we figured we should get new drinks."

"Where's mine?"

"Err…." Helen's face turns beet red.

"Sorry, we forgot," I say.

The audience cheers, drawing our attention back to the ring. Ares is wiping off blood from the corner of his mouth. I guess Hades just hit him, but the guy doesn't seem bothered that his uncle got him first. There's a deranged glint in his eyes that makes me believe he enjoyed getting punched.

I quickly return my eyes to Hades, and I can't look away. If he was impressive wearing his sharp work clothes, I can't find the words to describe him when he's shirtless and his tats are on full display. A funny feeling unfurls in the pit of my stomach, and my heart seems to beat faster. I move closer to the ring, as if I'm caught in Hades's gravitational pull.

Ares throws a punch, which Hades dodges easily. For all the muscles he has, he's nimble, fast as a cobra. His brows are furrowed, and his eyes are locked on his opponent. They circle for a few more seconds before Ares starts taunting him. Hades remains unfazed until he steps forward, and then all I see is a blur of movements. Ares is forced to retreat to a corner as Hades pounds on him. The violence should turn me off, but instead, it ignites something in my blood. I couldn't look away even if I tried.

Instead of finishing Ares off, Hades steps back, grinning. I guess he doesn't want the fight to end too soon. Ares eyes him with murder in his gaze and then launches on the offensive. Hades seems to anticipate all his moves, though. But then his eyes flick toward the crowd and land on me. I didn't realize how close I had gotten to the ring until now. I can see the surprise in Hades's eyes.

But that's gone in a flash when Ares, taking advantage of Hades's momentary distraction, lands a punch square on his jaw. His head is thrown back, and then, to my dismay, he falls. I gasp, covering my mouth with my hands.

The crowd goes silent for a moment. I think everyone is stunned like me. But it only lasts a few seconds before the warehouse is brought down in a deafening roar. Hades is still sprawled on the floor, and my chest is now tight with worry.

Ares is declared the winner, but instead of basking in his victory, he goes to check on Hades. I can't see what's happening now because other people jump in the ring and surround him.

Helen tugs on my sleeve. "We need to go. The crowd is getting out of control."

No sooner does she say that than we're pushed forward. If we don't leave now, we'll get crushed.

"Come on. Let's get out of here," Paris shouts to be overheard over the noise.

Helen grabs my hand and drags me away from the ring. I look over my shoulder, trying to see if Hades has gotten back to his feet, but it's impossible to see anything now.

It's crazy how worried I am about him. He's made no secret how much he loathes me, yet I can't stop my heart from constricting painfully because of him.

HADES

My ears are ringing as I stare at the warehouse ceiling, and my head feels like it's going to split in two. It's been years since I've been sucker punched like this, and I forgot what it was like. The noise around me is muffled, but I can imagine the crowd is going crazy. I let my guard down, and Ares took full advantage of that. All because of Persephone Flores.

Fuck me.

I was surprised to see her in the crowd, but more so when I couldn't take my eyes off her. I'd probably still be staring if Ares hadn't knocked me out.

His stupid face appears above me. His mouth is moving, but I can't hear a word he's saying. He glances at Atlas and seems worried about me.

"I'm okay," I say even though it's a bald-faced lie. I feel like roadkill.

I sit up, and the entire world begins to spin. *Shit*. I didn't realize his right hook was so damn powerful. I touch my jaw to make sure it isn't broken.

He crouches in front of me. "Are you okay, man?"

"I'll live."

"Good. If I killed you, my old man would make my life more

hellish than he already does. You know he wants the honor to off you."

"I'm well aware of Zeus's intentions for me."

Ares offers me his hand and helps me to my feet.

I scoff. "I can't believe you aren't basking in the glory of my defeat."

He shakes his head. "As much as I like to win, I take no joy in doing so when your head clearly wasn't in the fight."

That's the problem. I was one hundred percent in the zone until I saw Persephone. Then it was like my brain went haywire and I forgot where I was. I can't let this stand. First, she hurt Cerberus, and now she made me lose the fight. I have to deal with her one way or another.

The question is what do I do about her?

7

PERSEPHONE

I slept like shit last night, worrying about Hades. I kept checking his social media accounts for any updates, which was foolish because he clearly doesn't waste his time posting anything. I don't know enough about his circle of friends to stalk their accounts, and Ares didn't update his either.

I'm bleary eyed when I step into the kitchen in desperate need of coffee, but the surprise of seeing my mother there jolts me awake. She's sitting still at the table, staring into space, and doesn't acknowledge my presence. The cigarette between her fingers is half burned, and the ash tip is about to fall on her plate. Not that she'd care.

"You're finally home. Where have you been?" I ask.

Her glazed eyes meet mine. "I've ruined everything, child. Everything."

Shit. For her to admit that, she must have screwed up royally.

I pull up the chair next to hers and sit down. "What happened?"

Her expression crumbles, and then she starts to cry. She drops the cigarette, still lit, and then covers her face with her hands.

"I tried to stop, Seph. I really did, but I'm not strong enough."

My stomach sinks. I should have presumed why she'd been MIA for so long. I guess I was sticking my head in the sand. I was hoping she had a new boyfriend. It was a better scenario than to acknowledge she was using drugs again.

"You *are* strong enough, Mom. You need to get clean. If not for me, then do it for Persi."

She looks at me and grabs my hands. "That's not the worst of it, Seph. I was desperate for cash, so I borrowed it."

A huge lump forms in my throat. Only a shark would lend money to a junkie. "From whom?"

She drops my hands and looks away. "I only know him by his first name. Deimos. He said if I don't pay by the end of next week...." She whimpers.

I grab her by the shoulders and turn her back around. "What will he do?"

"He's going to hurt you and Persi." The waterworks start again, but this time, I take no pity on her.

"Let me get this straight. You borrowed money from a criminal to pay for your nasty habit, and now my life and Persi's are in danger?"

"I didn't mean for this to happen. I thought I'd get the money."

I jump to my feet. "How did you think you'd get the money? You haven't been able to hold a job that pays the bills in years."

"Maybe you could borrow money from your friend Helen."

"How much do you owe?"

"Twenty-five thousand dollars."

"What? Are you telling me you blew twenty-five grand on drugs?" My voice rises to a pitch. I'm surprised Persi hasn't woken yet.

"No. Of course not. My debt was smaller than that. To pay it off, I agreed to do some work for him."

I glare at her through slitted eyes. "What kind of work?"

"Please don't get mad at me."

"Oh, Mother, it's already too late for that."

"I agreed to move some merchandise for him across the border."

I curl my hands into fists, trying to fight the sudden anger that's spreading through my veins like wildfire. "You agreed to be his mule?"

"What choice did I have?"

"How about not borrow money from a fucking shark!"

She winces, and her eyes well with tears again. "I'm sorry."

"You still haven't explained how you ended up owing him that much money."

"Things didn't go well on my last trip. The cops were suspicious, so I had to abandon the merchandise or risk getting caught."

I throw my hands in the air. "You're unbelievable."

"Did you want me to go to prison?"

"Yes, that would have been a better outcome. How the hell are we going to come up with all that money?"

"He—"

"I can't ask Helen for cash!"

"Because of stupid pride? Would you rather see your brother get hurt?"

I take a step in her direction, jabbing my finger at her. "Don't you fucking dare try to guilt-trip me! This is *your* doing."

"But you can help me."

"I don't think I can this time. And it isn't about pride. Helen doesn't have that kind of money."

"There's another way we can pay."

The hairs on the back of my neck stand on end. I'm afraid of what's going to come out of her mouth next.

"How?" I grit out.

"Deimos's employer owns a private club. He said if you're a virgin, you could fetch a good price at an auction. And I know you haven't been with any boy. You always thought you were above them all."

I feel the blood drain from my face. I can't believe she just suggested that I whore myself to pay for her debt.

"You want me to auction my virginity? Is that it?"

"It wouldn't be that bad. Trust me. People make a big deal about the first time, but it's not that important."

I press my closed fist against my forehead. "Stop talking before I do something I'll regret."

"Think about it, Seph."

"There's nothing to think about, Mother. Nothing."

I'm glad I came to the kitchen already dressed for school. I grab my purse from the counter and walk out of the house. It's not until I put a good distance between me and that odious woman that I allow the tears to fall.

I don't know how I manage to arrive on campus without getting into a car accident. It doesn't matter, though. I may be in one piece, but I'm a wreck inside.

My phone pings with the reminder I set yesterday. I have an appointment with Prof. Cashore. But I can't see him like this. I need to put myself back together before I go plead my case.

I pray that the man behaves today. I don't think I can deal with another scum of the earth in such a short period of time.

HADES

I keep my shades on as I stride across the quad. Unfortunately, Ares didn't give me a black eye I could cover up with sunglasses. No, the motherfucker got me square on my jaw, and the bruise there isn't concealable. Not that it matters anyway; by now, everyone knows about my disgraceful loss.

I have every intention of going straight to my next class until

I see Persephone dash around the corner. Grinding my teeth, I follow her. I wasn't planning to deal with her today, but it seems the Fates want to shove her down my throat no matter what. I've been at this school for nearly four years, and not once has she ever crossed my path. Now, I can't go a day without bumping into her, and every single time, her presence makes my life hell.

She seemed to be in a hurry before, but now she's just standing in the middle of the hallway with her chin dipped low.

"Everywhere I go, there you are. If I didn't know any better, I'd say you're stalking me," I say.

She turns around and stares at me with wide eyes. Then I see the moisture in them. She was either crying or about to. A sliver of remorse pierces my chest, but I fight the feeling from taking root.

"What do you want?" She hastily wipes her tears away.

"I want to know why you're hell-bent on pissing me off. I told you to stay away from me."

Her spine turns rigid in an instant, and I see the fight gather in her eyes. "I go to this school. As far as I know, you don't own the campus."

"Don't be so sure of that. What were you doing at the fight last night?"

"I went with my friends. I had no idea you would be there, but honestly, I'm glad I was. It was good to see someone knock you off your pedestal."

I step closer to her, invading her personal space. I'm at least a head taller, so she needs to crane her neck to hold my stare. My proximity doesn't intimidate her, though. She's acting different than she did at Styx and later at the vet. Does she think I'm no longer a threat because I lost one damn fight?

"You're toying with danger, sweetheart. I'd be very careful if I were you."

"I'm not afraid of you, Hades. You can't keep bullying me because of a mistake I had no intention of making."

"Oh, can't I? I wouldn't be so sure of that."

Her nostrils flare, and I know then, without a shadow of a doubt, that her new attitude has nothing to do with me. Something happened to her that was worse than pissing me off, something that made her think I'm the lesser threat.

I reach for her arm, holding it tight. "Why were you crying?"

Her defiant eyebrows arch, almost meeting her hairline. She doesn't answer for a couple of beats, and those seconds up close to her make me want to do more than torment her. She's getting under my skin and she's not even trying.

Finally, her gaze hardens. "That's none of your business. Now let go of me before I scream."

I laugh. "Go on. Scream, then. I dare you."

There's enough anger in her eyes to warn me that she's contemplating it. It wouldn't be pleasant, but it would be interesting if she did.

"Seph!" someone shouts in the distance, making her turn.

A blonde girl is waving at her from the middle of the park that separates two of the buildings. She's standing next to Paris Alexander. I decide then that I don't need that extra complication.

I drop Persephone's arm and step back. "Go on. Join your little friends, but this conversation isn't over."

I can read a million retorts in her stormy eyes, but she doesn't voice any of them. Pity.

I watch her walk away, and for the first time, I give myself permission to check her out. She's slim but curvy where it matters. And those jeans fit her like a glove. She not only has a gorgeous face. She's got the whole package.

Hermes wolf whistles, stepping next to me. "You too, huh?"

"Me too what?"

"You've also fallen under the spell of Persephone Flores."

I glower at him. "I haven't fallen under anyone's spell."

"Sure, sure. Rumor has it she's a virgin, you know."

A strange sense of protectiveness takes hold of me. His comment—true or not—rubs me the wrong way. I'm annoyed that people are discussing her sex life.

"And why would I care if she is?" I turn around with the intention of walking away, but the pest follows me.

"That's not the only thing I may or may not know about her."

Keeping my stride, I look at him. "What are you getting at, Hermes? You know I don't have the patience for your games."

"I'm just saying I might have information about Persephone that would perhaps interest you. I mean, the Hades I know wouldn't simply allow the person who hurt his dog to go unpunished, would he?"

I stop suddenly and turn to him. "All right. Fine. What do you know?"

He smiles slyly, knowing he got me. "Not so fast. How much is the intel I possess worth to you?"

Here we go. Hermes knows I'll pay whatever price he sets, but he loves the negotiation process more than the exchange.

"A lot."

8

PERSEPHONE

"Was Hades giving you a hard time, Seph?" Helen asks, searching my face for answers.

"Not really," I lie.

He was being a bully, but considering the astronomical problem I have, dealing with him felt good.

"You have to be careful with the Godaires. There isn't one in the family who's not tainted in some way," Paris pipes up.

"You don't have to say it twice. Trust me. I want nothing to do with them."

"So, how was the meeting with Prof. Perv?" Helen changes the subject, but unfortunately, it isn't a topic I want to discuss.

"As expected."

Her face falls. "Oh no. What did he say?"

"The usual insinuations. He won't let me retake the test, though."

"Wait. But you have a valid excuse," Paris interjects. "You were in an accident."

"He doesn't care."

Not as long as I don't do what he wants. If he would only say it out loud, I could record it and report him to the administration. But the bastard is smart. He chooses his words carefully. Usually, I can take his innuendos, but today, I just couldn't deal. I broke down afterward, and Hades was there to witness it. Damn that guy.

"Helen, do you think I could have a word with you in private?" I ask.

She furrows her eyebrows and then glances at Paris.

I can't imagine what their loaded look means, but I don't care what they suspect. The prospect of doing what my mother suggested brings bile to my mouth, so I'll break all my rules, forget my pride, and ask my best friend for her help. I just don't know yet how much I'm willing to tell her.

We head over to a tree nearby, but when it comes time to tell her about what my mother did, I can't bring myself to say the words. The story is too sordid. Helen would try to help me, but she can't do it without involving her parents. And her father is a lawyer. He'd go to the cops.

"What is it, Seph? You're as white as a ghost."

I shake my head. "It's…. I'm just upset about Prof. Cashore."

She cocks her head and watches me closely. "Is this about Hades? What did he say to you?"

"He wasn't happy that I was at the fight last night."

Her eyes widen. "I knew he was giving you a hard time. Who does he think he is?"

"The king of the world, apparently."

"He's not even the king of Olympus Bay. That title belongs to his asshole brother Zeus. My parents hate him."

Helen doesn't get aggravated often, but it's impossible to miss the signs when she does. Her face turns bright red.

"Did something happen?" I ask.

She sighs. "Yeah. Zeus raised the rent on all his properties on the boardwalk. The association is threatening to sue. My parents have been busy, working on their case for weeks. And you know what he did?"

"No."

"He sent one of his goons to threaten them, a jerkface who only goes by the name of Deimos."

My blood seems to grow cold. *Oh my God.* I can't believe I didn't suspect who Deimos's employer might have been. Rumors abound that the Godaires' fortune comes from illicit activities, including drug trafficking.

"Seph? Are you okay?" Helen touches my arm.

I blink fast, trying to erase the freaked-out expression I know I'm sporting now.

"Yes, I'm fine. I gotta run. I'll talk to you later, okay?"

I take off toward the nearest building, even though that's not where my next class is. I only turn around and go in the right direction when I'm sure Helen and Paris are gone. Checking the time, I know I'll have to sprint again or I'll be late.

My phone rings, but I choose to ignore it. I'll check once I'm inside the classroom. But it keeps ringing nonstop, so I fish it out of my bag to see who's calling. It's Perseus. *Shit.* It's not like him to insist on reaching me unless it's an emergency.

I skid to a halt and breathlessly answer, "Persi, where's the fire?"

"Se-Seph? I need your help."

My heart skips a beat. He sounds terrified, and immediately I know something is wrong.

"What happened? Where are you?"

"I'm near the old fairgrounds."

"That's nowhere near school."

"I was taken by some thugs who wanted to deliver a message to Mom."

A sharp ache in my chest robs me of the ability to breathe. Fucking Deimos is already putting pressure on her.

"Are you hurt?"

"Yeah. Can you please get me, Seph? Please?"

"I'm on my way. Don't move, okay? And keep your phone on you."

PETUNIA, bless her, performed better than she has in ages. I drove as fast as I could, and she didn't complain. It's crazy to think of a car as a person, but no one can convince me that my pleas and pep talks don't help.

The sky decided this situation wasn't shitty enough, however, and it brought forth an angry storm to make everything ten times gloomier. I'm drenched in a second once I get out of the car, and naturally, I never have an umbrella on me.

The old fairgrounds are supposed to be off-limits, but the chain keeping the gate closed is old and rusty, and there's enough slack that I can slip through the opening. Once upon a time, this was a place of laughter and happiness, but the company running it went out of business when Zeus revitalized the boardwalk. Now the place, along with the carnival rides has been left forgotten, a junkyard of lost dreams.

I call Perseus again to get his exact location. If he was out in the open, I hope he took cover. He answers on the first ring.

"Where are you?" I ask.

"I'm in the carousel."

I still remember where every ride is here. Our father used to bring Persi and me when we were little. I try not to think about those memories. Dwelling on the past doesn't help.

I run, ignoring the puddles on the way. Mud splashes all over my jeans, and my wet sneakers and socks feel gross against my skin. But my discomfort takes a back seat when I finally spot Persi leaning against a plastic horse, hunched over and cradling his arm.

"Persi!"

"Seph, thank God you're here."

I crouch in front of him, holding his face between my hands. His lower lip is busted, and there's a scratch on his forehead.

"Who did this to you?"

"I don't know. They didn't say their names, only that this was a message for Mom." His hazel eyes are wide with fear. "What kind of trouble is she in now?"

There's no point trying to hide the truth when he already took the brunt of it.

"She owes money to someone very powerful and dangerous."

His Adam's apple bobs up and down before he asks, "Who?"

"Zeus."

His tanned face turns ashen. "Drugs?"

I nod, fighting to keep my shit together. Mom has been a user since before my father died; she just hid it better from us when he was still alive.

"How much does she owe him?"

"We can talk about this later. I need to get you to the ER."

I help him get back on his feet, but he won't move forward. "Is it a lot?"

"Yeah, but don't worry about it. We'll figure something out."

He doesn't reply to my lie. This is not our first rodeo, and he's no longer a kid. He knows a sacrifice will have to be made by us.

He just doesn't know it will be by me.

9

PERSEPHONE

There's no point in delaying what needs to be done. Perseus's arm in a cast is a cruel reminder that if I don't step up and protect him, no one else will.

Mom is a hot mess when we get home. Her makeup is smeared, and her eyes are red. I also catch a whiff of alcohol emanating from her, which makes me even more certain of the decision I made. It doesn't matter how hard it is, or how I agonized over it on the way here. I can't keep ignoring that having her around is doing us more harm than good.

She makes a big fuss over Perseus, and he lets her because he's doped up on painkillers. I take him to his room, and only when he's sound asleep do I return to the kitchen to have the most important conversation of my life.

"Are you happy?" I ask her.

Her expression falls. "Of course I'm not happy. I didn't mean—"

"Save it." I raise my hand. "I don't want to hear any more excuses from you."

"I didn't think they'd do anything to you so soon. The deadline isn't until next week." She hunches her shoulders, defeated. "We don't have a choice, Seph. You must act—"

"Shut up! Just fucking shut up!"

Her eyes widen. "How dare you speak to me like that? I'm still your mother."

"No, you aren't. Not anymore. You're dead to me."

The words hurt more than I thought possible, but they needed to be said. I have to protect Perseus from her.

Pressing a hand to her chest, she gasps. "You don't mean that."

"I want you to pack your shit and leave."

"You're kicking me out? You can't do that."

"I can, and I will. The rent is under my name, and I pay for it."

She stands up. "How can you be so cruel? I gave you life! You wouldn't be here if I didn't want you to be."

Despite the barrier I erected around myself, I wince. It's not the first time she's thrown those hurtful words at us.

"And I think Perseus and I have paid dearly for your *gift*. But it's over. This is the last time you'll fuck up our lives."

"Kicking me out won't change anything. Deimos will still come after you."

"You let me worry about that scum. I'm going to take a shower. When I'm done, I want you gone."

"But… where will I go?"

"I don't care." I stride to my room, fighting to keep my face from showing how much this is destroying me.

I never thought there would be a day when I wished Mom had died instead of Dad. It's not right to feel this way, but I can't help it, not when she put Persi's life in danger, I'm being forced to debase myself to God knows who, and she doesn't show an ounce of true remorse. A good mother would never sacrifice her children like that.

I slam my door shut, locking it for good measure. I don't

care that she might raid the house and take every valuable thing she can carry. I just want her gone, and I don't want to look at her face for one more second.

My eyes prickle with the tears that are quickly forming, but I refuse to shed them. Opening that torrent will only weaken me. I have to be strong right now, for myself and for Perseus. So I do what I said I would. I take a shower and spend an eternity there. I don't care that I'm wasting water or energy. When I finally step out, I'm pruney.

I get dressed as if I were a robot. I don't even know what clothes I choose. When I leave my room, I look in her bedroom. Judging by the mess and the empty drawers, she did as I told her. I check on Perseus, finding him snoring.

Before I head out to seal my doom, I make him a sandwich and write him a note. I don't want him to worry in case he wakes up before I return.

As I'm about to step out of the house, I glance at my reflection in the hallway mirror. I look like shit. Without makeup, there's no hiding the dark circles and the lack of vigor. This won't do. If I'm going to become a whore, I need to make sure I'm the hottest thing that ever went to see Deimos.

I return to my bedroom, and half an hour later, I look like someone who's worth way more than twenty-five grand. I'm not a heroine from a generic rom-com who doesn't know she's a hot piece of ass. I never flaunt it because I hate when I'm objectified.

My hair is styled properly so my curls aren't all over the place, I'm wearing makeup, and my dress hugs my body, accentuating all my assets.

After Deimos's thugs broke Persi's arm, they left behind his calling card, which has the address for an upscale club in the nicest area of Olympus Bay. When I park in front of the club, I can't help noticing how Petunia is out of place here.

The bouncer at the door eyes me up and down, and then a disgusting grin unfurls on his lips.

"This is a club for gentlemen only, sweetheart."

"I was invited." I hand him Deimos's card.

"I see." He returns the card and opens the door for me.

Inside, the smell of cigars and whiskey reaches my nose. It's dark and cold, and despite my long-sleeve dress, I shiver. I have no idea what Deimos looks like, but I don't have to wander far into the place before another beefy security guard finds me and escorts me to the rear of the club. I keep my gaze glued to his back because I don't want to lock gazes with one of the creeps here. I might lose my bravado, and my courage is already hanging on by a thread.

The bouncer knocks on a door, and when a rough voice tells him to come in, he opens the door for me. But before I'm allowed in, he says, "Hand over your purse."

"What? Why?"

"Don't argue. Just do it," the man inside says.

I've come this far; protesting their rules won't do me any good. I give the bouncer my purse and then walk in.

I expected Deimos to be a disgusting middle-aged man, not a dude who could have graced the cover of *GQ* ten years ago. He has a chin and Roman nose that would photograph well. His dark hair is cut in a classic style and kept in place by a good amount of product. But for all his good looks, my skin crawls when his shrewd gaze takes me in. I have to fight the urge to squirm under his appraising eyes.

"I see you got my message," he says.

"I did, and it was unnecessary. We weren't late."

He narrows his eyes. "I'm the one who decides what's necessary or not. Don't ever forget that."

"We don't have the money."

He chuckles. "I know. You're here to offer yourself as payment."

My stomach twists into knots, making me sick.

"Yes." I force the word out.

"You're attractive, no denying that. But are you untouched?"

I grimace. "Untouched? What century are you from?"

His eyes darken with annoyance. "Do not test me, girl. There's no pussy in the world that can earn a free pass to antagonize me."

"Even if it's untouched?" I raise an eyebrow. "I suspect that there aren't a lot of virgins offering themselves to be auctioned these days."

He snorts. "You'd be surprised." He looks me over again, then sighs. "Well, if you're lying, the debt won't be settled, and we'll come for your brother again, but this time, we won't stop at breaking his arm. So you'd better not be trying to fuck me over."

I swallow the huge lump in my throat. I'm telling the truth. I've always wanted my first time to be with someone I cared about, and I never met any guy who made me feel that way. And now here I am. But what if whoever wins the auction isn't satisfied and decides to fuck up my life even more?

"I'm not lying. So when will this auction take place?"

He grins like a wolf. "Aren't you eager?"

"To be rid of you? Absolutely."

"Tomorrow. We'll send a car for you at four."

My stomach tightens even more. *So soon.*

"I can get here on my own." It's a miracle I can keep my voice steady.

"You're not coming here."

My eyebrows arch. "Where, then?"

"That's for me to know and for you to never find out."

Alarm bells ring in my ears. This is probably the biggest red flag I've ever seen. There's nothing stopping this asshole from kidnapping me and selling me as a sex slave. But there isn't much I can do. Going to the police won't work. I have no proof

—no wonder the bouncer took my purse and phone so I couldn't attempt to record this conversation.

There's only one path, but that doesn't mean I can't leave a letter behind for Helen or Perseus if something goes wrong and I disappear.

I think about the person responsible for putting me in this awful situation and wish she was dead again.

10

HADES

I'm not surprised to see my brother's right hand manning the entrance to Zeus's depraved party. I've known about these events since I learned about the birds and the bees, but I've only been to one. I was fourteen, and Zeus and Poseidon thought it appropriate to bring me so I could become a man. Their idea of what that entailed is too sordid to even think about.

I vowed to never return here, but when Hermes told me what Zeus had planned for tonight, I couldn't stay away. I'm hoping Hermes is wrong for once or that the idiotic girl changed her mind. But only a desperate person would entertain the idea of doing what Persephone agreed to.

When Hermes first approached me with his gossip, nothing had been set in stone yet, but the pieces were in motion. Later, he confirmed it, and then he got me an invitation to attend. What he couldn't unearth—and that's a first for him—is why Persephone had been handpicked like that.

I'll find out tonight.

If I were a better person, I'd try to put a stop to it. But

considering the type of control she already has over me, it's best if I let things play out.

The mask I have to wear is an annoyance but a requirement to attend Zeus's parties. It's supposed to give the illusion of anonymity, which is bullshit since the masks don't hide everything, and everyone knows everyone in this town.

I take a glass of champagne from a waiter who crosses my path as I'm heading to the center of the party. This is one of Zeus's many properties in Olympus Bay. He rarely uses this mansion, but thanks to its secluded location, it's where he's always held his infamous parties. The place isn't to my taste, but I can't ignore its appeal. It screams wealth. The grand foyer has a domed ceiling where frescoes depict the lives of deities. The deep-red Sicilian Diaspro floor mirrors the warm tone of the wood paneling and the extravagant oil paintings hanging from them.

There's a sea of men wearing their finest tuxedos, mingling and talking, and at first, one would think this is just another black-tie event. But beyond the entry foyer and through the tall double doors is where the devil plays.

I spot Hermes, who wouldn't miss this party for anything in the world, talking with Aphrodite, one of the few women present. Next to her stands her younger brother, Eros, who's watching the crowd as if he were bored.

I stride in their direction, and halfway there, I catch Hermes's stare. He smiles, and then both Aphrodite and Eros turn to me.

"Are you ready for the show?" Hermes asks.

"Don't sound so eager," I reply, annoyed, though I don't know why.

"I've never seen you at these parties, Hades. I didn't think it was your thing," Aphrodite points out.

"It isn't."

"Why are you here, then?" Eros asks, not as friendly as his sister.

I smile tightly, choosing not to dignify him with an answer.

The gong sounds, announcing the main event is about to start. The double doors open, and in an orderly fashion, the guests flood into the room. I make sure to lose Hermes and his friends; I don't want to be standing close to anyone I know when Persephone steps onto the stage.

A small orchestra provides the background music, making everything seem so civilized. Never mind that in a few minutes, a girl will auction off her virginity. I can't wrap my mind around the motive that would prompt her to do that.

Damn it. Why do I care?

I spot Poseidon in a corner close to the stage, looking regal. There's no sign of Triton, which surprises me. I thought Poseidon was already molding my nephew to be a narcissistic prick like him. He and Zeus believe women walk the earth to satisfy their every whim.

Dealing with either of my brothers is the last thing I want tonight, so I head in the opposite direction until I find an alcove that will keep me concealed and, at the same time, give me an unobstructed view of the stage.

Not a minute later, Zeus makes his grand entrance with a beautiful young woman attached to his side. His mask is the most ostentatious in the room, with swirls in gold and red that are almost vulgar. I guess money can't buy style. He doesn't join Poseidon; instead, he stops right in front of the stage, positioning himself in the middle of the small circle the crowd formed for him.

The emcee finally appears on the stage and welcomes the guests, then thanks Zeus, the host, before singling out one guest in particular, Salas Ciriano. Tension immediately wraps around me. I've never met him in person, but I've heard of him. He's evil incarnate and makes Zeus's cruelty seem like child's play in comparison. I doubt he's here only to score a virgin. There's a more nefarious reason for his presence.

My musings are interrupted when the emcee announces Persephone. I turn my attention to the stage, and then it's like the world goes off-kilter. My surroundings seem to disappear, and I get tunnel vision. All I can see is her.

"Isn't she lovely?" the emcee asks the crowd. "Let's start the bid at twenty-five thousand."

And so begins the succession of raised hands. I can barely keep track, but I do notice one person in particular keeps outbidding the others—Salas. Grinding my teeth, I force my eyes off Persephone to glance at him, and then I flick my gaze toward Zeus. He's looking too pleased with himself, which means this auction is a means to something much more sinister.

Regardless of that detail, I can't let Salas—or any other man, for that matter—win the auction. There's a primordial feeling in my chest telling me no one can have her because she's mine.

"One million," the jackass says.

The crowd grows silent, and no new bid comes forth. As stunning as Persephone is, that's a high price to pay for a fuck.

Not to me, though. He's not having her.

I raise my hand. "Five million."

Instead of silence, my offer is followed by a rush of sound. People gasp and murmur. I purposefully avoid looking at Persephone. I keep my gaze on Zeus, who is now openly glaring at me. His blue eyes flash with fury. The murderous look is so intense, not even his ridiculous mask can hide it.

"That's five times the amount of the last bid," the emcee says, unable to hide the nervousness in his tone. "Do I hear six?"

"This is absurd!" Salas blurts out. "I did not come here to be humiliated in this manner."

He glowers at me first, then at Zeus before striding out of the room, shoving to the side whoever is in his path. Whatever deal Zeus was hoping to make with the man, it's now in tatters. I can't help the smile that tugs at the corners of my mouth.

"If there aren't any more offers, the lovely Persephone Flores is now sold to Hades Godaire."

I finally allow myself to glance at her. She's looking at me like a deer caught in headlights. The emcee leads her off the stage, and I mean to follow him, but I'm intercepted by Zeus.

"You fucking asshole. Do you have any idea what you've done?"

He's trying to be intimidating, but that stupid mask is making it impossible for me to take him seriously.

"Yes, I just bought a virgin, and you're five million dollars richer."

His nostrils flare. "You cost me far more than five million dollars, prick."

"If I upset whatever deal you had with that scum because he lost a virgin at an auction, it reflects on your poor negotiation skills."

Zeus takes a step forward, invading my space. "You humiliated the man by outbidding him, and now he thinks I had a hand in it because you're my brother."

"How is that my problem?"

His lips curl into a sadistic smile. "Oh, little brother, it *is* your problem now. I went through a lot of trouble to procure Persephone Flores, but you had to take her. I know you too well to realize you wouldn't have done it if she didn't mean something to you."

My spine goes rigid in an instant. I don't like where he's going with this.

"I hope you enjoy your *one* evening with her." He walks away, leaving me reeling.

I don't care about Persephone. Not in the way Zeus is implying, anyway.

So why the hell do I feel like he's about to obliterate my world?

PERSEPHONE

I don't know what I should be feeling, but it's definitely not this strange calmness. I'm about to be sold to the highest bidder, after all. Maybe it's because I don't recognize myself as I stare in the mirror. The woman looking back at me is a polished and buffed stranger.

My hair has been tamed into beautiful waves, and the designer dress fits me like a glove, highlighting my best features. I hate the silver color. It should have been red to mirror the rage I know I'll feel once the deed is done.

I'm in a luxurious waiting room but not alone. There's a security guard stationed in front of the door. I glance at him, but he doesn't meet my eyes. He looks like a statue until he presses his finger to his right ear. He just received a message through his earpiece.

Then he looks at me. "They're ready for you."

In silence, I follow him down a wide corridor. It feels like I'm heading to my execution. Just as I'm about to face the crowd of disgusting, rich men who are willing to pay God knows what to take my virginity, the nerves finally get the better of me. I'm shaking from head to toe, and there's a pang of regret in my stomach.

I can't let them see that I'm terrified. I curl my hands into fists, digging my long nails into the softness of my palms. The pain helps a little, but nothing could have prepared me for the feeling of unworthiness that settles over my shoulders when I walk onto the stage and all eyes focus on me.

My ears are ringing, and I can barely register what the

emcee is saying. I just know the auction has started when different masked men start to raise their hands. I make a point to not look at any of them directly—until a familiar voice breaks through my numbness.

"Five million," he says.

I glance at him, and even with the mask, I recognize that arrogant jawline. But he's not looking in my direction. He's staring across the room.

I follow his line of sight and see another tall and imposing blond man. His mask is grotesque, but it doesn't hide his resemblance to Hades. That must be Zeus, who looks like he's about to commit murder. Masks can't hide their eyes, or the ill intentions in them.

The noise in my ears ceases, and there's nothing blocking me now from noticing the eerie silence that has descended over the room. It's like everyone is waiting for something to happen with bated breath.

"That's five times the amount of the last bid. Do I hear six?" the emcee asks, but his voice doesn't have the confidence I'd expect from someone in his line of work.

"This is absurd!" a man with tanned skin and pitch-black hair blurts out. "I did not come here to be humiliated in this manner."

He throws a murderous glance at Hades first, then at Zeus before turning on his heel and storming out of the room.

My feelings are all over the place, but confusion is the predominant one. *Did Hades bid five million dollars for me?*

"If there aren't any more offers, the lovely Persephone Flores is now sold to Hades Godaire."

I guess that answers my question. Hades bought me, and I'm not sure if I just traded a bad outcome for something far worse.

11

PERSEPHONE

My mind is spinning like a top, and my heart is thumping so hard against my rib cage, it hurts. Hades just bought me at an auction for five million dollars, which is more money than I've ever dreamed of. I have no idea why he did it, but my imagination makes up for it, and nothing I can conjure up is good.

The emcee escorts me to the backstage room and tells me to wait.

Before he leaves, I ask, "What's going to happen now?"

"Now you'll wait for Hades Godaire to come for you." He stares at me for a moment in silence, making me anxious.

"What?" I ask.

"You're lucky, you know?"

"Lucky?" My voice rises an octave. "I don't think so."

"Trust me."

I frown. "Why? What do you know?"

He shakes his head as if he regrets making that comment. "Never mind."

A second later, he walks out, leaving me alone for the first time. There's no security guard standing in front of the door. I bet he's outside, although I don't know why they bother guarding my exit. I don't even know where I am, and I don't have anything on me, no cell phone, no wallet, basically no means to get home or call for help.

If the emcee thinks being sold to Hades is a good outcome, then what would have happened if another man had won the auction? A shiver runs down my spine, and suddenly I feel weak. I take a seat, resting my head in my hands.

What the hell have I done?

Someone walks in, and I get up. Hades is standing there, more imposing than I remember, making the room feel smaller. He took off his mask, but his face is still unreadable to me. His blue eyes are cold and unyielding. We stay locked in a staring contest for I don't know how long, but I refuse to look away first.

"Are you ready?" he finally asks.

Swallowing the lump in my throat, I stand up. "As ready as I'll ever be."

His eyes travel the length of my body, and I fight the urge to cross my arms over my chest.

"You don't look like yourself."

I mentally snort. *You think?*

"I don't feel like myself. Perhaps that's for the best."

He tilts his head, narrowing his eyes. "Why did you do it? What does Zeus have hanging over you?"

I could tell him that Zeus doesn't need much to coerce a little nothing like me to do this bidding, but I don't owe Hades any explanation.

"The five million dollars buys you a fuck, not the right to question me."

"Is that so?" His lips curl into a sardonic grin. "Who told you that?"

My spine becomes taut. "I.... My virginity was the deal."

He walks over and stands in front of me. I have to crane

my neck to hold his stare, but being this close to him is not working in my favor. He smells like a day at the beach with a cocktail in hand, an image I've always associated with paradise, not someone like him. It must be the citrus scent in his aftershave. Either way, it's making my heart beat out of control.

"Yes, but I can collect my prize any time I want." He lifts his hand and runs the tips of his fingers down my arm. Goose bumps follow. "And there are many things I can do to you before the deed is done."

Fear pierces my chest like an arrow. Unfortunately, it's not the only emotion swirling there. There's a hint of excitement too.

"Did you just buy me so you could torture me at your own pace?"

He smiles, and a glint of amusement shines in his eyes. "Maybe."

"Aren't you afraid that if you don't get what you paid for, it won't be around when you finally decide to do it?"

Like I'd ever risk sleeping with someone else or be inclined to do so.

He chuckles. "No, darling. I'm not afraid that'll happen." He leans closer and whispers, "I don't plan to lose sight of you until I collect what I'm owed."

Trying to ignore what his warm breath against my skin is doing to me, I step back. "What's that supposed to mean?"

"It means that until I'm ready to fuck you, you'll stay with me."

My eyes go round. "You're out of your mind. I'm not moving in with you."

"You speak as if you have a choice."

I want to scream that I *do* have a choice, but he's right. I don't. I have to think about Perseus, who's the reason I agreed to this insanity in the first place. If I refuse Hades, he can back out of the deal, and then I'll be indebted to Zeus again. That sounds like the worst of the two outcomes.

"Do I have time to collect my stuff first?"

"It's being taken care of."

"How?"

He pinches my chin between his fingers and then runs his thumb over my lips. I shiver in pleasure, and I'm pretty sure he notices. *Hell and damn.* This man has no right getting such a reaction from me. He's the devil. Why is my body betraying me like this?

"Don't worry about it."

I lean back to break free from his hold. "You bought my body, not my mind. You can't tell me how to feel."

He works his jaw, watching me through slitted eyes. "You talk too much."

I mirror his expression. "You haven't seen anything yet."

There's a knock on the door, and Hades turns toward it. "What?"

It opens, and a dark-haired guy sticks his head in. "Hey, just checking how everything's going."

Hades snorts. "Yeah, right. You just want more gossip."

Unbothered, the newcomer opens the door all the way and walks in. His hazel eyes seem to miss nothing. Like Hades, he's wearing a sharp suit, a golden-winged sandal pinned to the right lapel.

"Maybe, but I also came to warn you that you should leave the premises sooner rather than later. Salas Ciriano is still here, and he doesn't like to lose."

"Tough shit for him."

"He'll be a problem, mark my words."

Hades laughs. "Not to me."

"No, not to you." He looks pointedly at me. "But to Persephone certainly."

I bristle. "Why?"

He casually shoves his hands in his pockets. "That I can't say."

"He *won't* say unless someone pays for the information," Hades interjects.

The guy grimaces. "No, this time I really can't say, and it pains me to admit that I don't know what's going on between him and my father."

"Find out," Hades tells him.

He smirks. "Sure thing, *Uncle Dearest*."

Shit. He's another Godaire, and since Zeus is the only one in the family who procreates like a rabbit, this dude is one of his sons.

Hades glances at me. "Let's go. I don't like to deal with unpleasant situations unprepared."

I follow him out of the room, and his nephew brings up the rear. We take a different way than the one that led me to the stage, and soon I get lost in the maze of corridors. When we finally exit the building, Hades's shiny Batmobile is parked nearby, the only car in the area. I don't know where we are, but I have a feeling this isn't the main entrance.

I try to keep my jaw from dropping. This car is more badass from up close than I thought, and I'm not gonna lie and say I'm not keen about riding in it.

Hades walks around it and glances at me. "What are you waiting for? A formal invitation? Get in."

His tone aggravates me. If this is how it's going to be, he'll regret ever buying me. I do as he says, though, because I don't want to spend another minute in this place. But I make sure I hold his stare, glowering the entire time. He slides behind the steering wheel, and from the corner of my eye, I can tell he belongs in that seat. He probably looks even sexier driving the damn car.

Oh God. When did I start to think Hades is sexy?

Folding my arms, I slouch against the supple leather, trying to become smaller. Since I have to sleep with him at some point, it *will* be easier if I'm attracted to him, but that puts a damper on my determination to keep hating him.

The rumble of the engine makes me jump in my seat. I feel Hades's stare burn a hole through my face.

"What's the matter, Flores?"

An unpleasant feeling ripples through me. People used to call my father Flores. I flick my gaze to him. "Don't call me that. My name is Persephone."

"It's too long. You must have a shorter nickname."

"I do," I grumble.

"You're not gonna tell me?"

"No. Only my friends call me by my nickname."

He puts the car in gear. "Suit yourself. I'll keep calling you Flores, then."

That won't do. Resigned, I say, "It's Seph. You can call me Seph."

"Hmm."

"'Hmm'? Is that all you have to say?"

"I'm not sure I care much for your nickname. I'll think of something else."

I throw my head back against the seat. "God, why don't you just call me 'hey, girl'?"

He peels his eyes from the road for a moment to look at me. "Is that supposed to mean something?"

With a sigh, I glance out the window. "Never mind. If I have to explain common pop culture references to you, what's the point?"

"You have an attitude. We'll have to work on that too."

"Why? How long do you plan on keeping me captive?"

He cuts his icy stare in my direction again. "For as long as I want."

"I'm not a thing you own. I have a life. What about my brother?"

"What about him?"

"He'll worry if I don't come home tonight, for starters."

"You can tell him you're with me. It's not a secret."

I clamp my jaw shut. Fat chance of me telling Perseus I sold my virginity to Hades. I don't want him thinking less of me, or worse, feeling responsible for my decision. And he wouldn't believe me if I told him I'm dating the guy.

"I'll think of something," I murmur.

We don't speak for the rest of the ride, and I purposefully keep my gaze on the landscape passing by, even though I sense Hades glancing at me a few times. I should be worried about what he has in store for me, but right now, I'm just too sad and tired.

12

HADES

Something I said deflated Persephone's sassy attitude like a balloon, and I don't like it. I can bully someone who isn't afraid to stand toe-to-toe with me, but I can never be mean to a person who's already defeated.

It was the topic of her surname that changed her demeanor. She didn't speak a word after that, and I have a suspicion that it relates to her last name. Why was she so adamant that I not call her that?

Hercules filled me in on the general information about her. Persephone's father passed away when she was eight. He was a truck driver who died of a heart attack, leaving his family in a bad financial situation, which wasn't helped by her mother's drug addiction. Persephone had to grow up fast and take care of her younger brother, Perseus, something I could relate to but for different reasons. I could tell Hercules was sympathetic to the girl when he was giving me the report, and that irritated me, because hell, I was too.

She doesn't make a peep when the solid steel gates to my property open. She's either lost in her own head, or she's trying to appear unaffected; no one who comes here for the first time isn't taken aback by the design of my house. You can't see anything from the street thanks to the tall wall that surrounds the property. I made sure it looked imposing and miserable at the same time to discourage visitors. I like my privacy. But once the gates are open, it's another story.

The house stands on a small hill, and the illuminated driveway at night just makes the house seem more glorious with its sharp edges, large glass panels, and all the lights coming from inside. They turn on automatically because I hate coming to a home shrouded in darkness.

It's only when my headlights show a ghost figure standing in front of the guesthouse that Persephone lets out a gasp, making me chuckle. I should have known Hecate wouldn't let me bring a *guest* home without showing her face.

"Who's that?" she asks.

"Hecate."

Persephone twists her neck to keep staring after I drive past her. "Does she live here?"

"Yes, in the guesthouse. Don't worry."

She whips her face to me. "Worry? Why should I?"

"No reason."

It's cruel to not warn her about Hecate, but I'm curious to see how they're going to interact, and if I tell Persephone anything, that might alter their first meeting.

I keep driving until I enter the underground garage, which is also lit up. I get out of the car first, but then I wait for Persephone instead of heading up the stairs. Her jaw is slack as she takes in her surroundings. She gives the entire space a cursory glance, making me curious about what's on her mind. Another first. I usually don't care about what others think. I have an impressive car and motorcycle collection, but the few girls I've brought home were only interested in the dollar sign attached to it.

"Are you compensating for something?" One of her brows arches.

I smirk. "Oh no, honey."

She blushes and then avoids my gaze. Her embarrassment pleases me more than it should. I'm beginning to question my sanity by not taking what I paid for immediately and sending her away. But even as the thought crosses my mind, I reject it. I guess I'm a glutton for punishment.

She follows me up the stairs, and the first thing I do as I reach the landing is call Cerberus. He barks once but doesn't come running as usual all thanks to her. Immediately, I'm reminded of the reason I shouldn't be nice to her. She maimed my dog.

"How is he?" she asks.

"His leg is broken. What do you think?" I stride to the living room where Cerberus's crate is.

He wiggles his tail and presses his nose against the grid. I hate seeing him trapped like that, but I'm also glad I crate trained him; otherwise, he'd think he was being punished.

"Why is he in a cage?"

"It's not a cage. It's a crate. And he needs to stay there to limit his movements."

I crouch in front of the crate before opening it, knowing Cerberus will try to jump on me in his excitement. He does exactly that, but in this position, I keep him from moving too much. He licks my face, making me laugh despite the company.

"I've missed you too, buddy."

Persephone drops into a crouch next to me. Cerberus is usually wary of strangers, but he turns to greet her with a wet kiss too. Her laughter echoes in the room as she scratches his head.

"I'm so glad you're okay," she tells him.

"You should be," I snap and then get up.

I don't know why I'm in a bad mood again. I veer for the

open kitchen and grab Cerberus's medication from the counter.

Persephone follows me. "What's that?"

"Aren't you full of questions?"

"Well, if I'm going to stay here for an undetermined length of time, I'd like to help take care of your dog."

I turn to her so she can see my glare. "I don't want you near Cerberus. You've done enough damage."

Her green eyes sparkle with anger. "How many times do I have to tell you it was an accident? He came out of nowhere."

"Right. And your attention was one hundred percent on the road." Guilt replaces her anger, igniting my own. "Were you texting?" I growl.

"No! I'm not an irresponsible driver. But if you must know, something did distract me for a second."

"You admit it was your fault, then."

She throws her hands up in the air. "I never said it wasn't. But it wasn't deliberate. I feel like shit, okay? And my guilty conscience is worse than any punishment you might have in store for me."

"I doubt that."

I circle her and walk over to Cerberus.

"Are you going to lock me in a dungeon and chain me to the wall?"

I look over my shoulder. "If you keep talking, I might consider that possibility. Just go to your room already before I bend you over that kitchen counter and spank your ass."

Her eyes grow larger, and once again, a blush spreads through her cheeks. It's only then that I realize how fucking hot that scenario is, and now I want to do exactly that. But if I fuck Persephone now, I'll be denied weeks of fun.

She turns on her heel and disappears down the hallway. I almost follow her, but then Cerberus barks, breaking the lust spell that had taken hold of me.

I scratch the back of his ear. "Thanks for the save, buddy."

13

PERSEPHONE

Who does that jackass think he is? I was just trying to help, but he had to go and be a big asshole. I walk away fuming without any sense of where I'm going. He told me to go to my room as if I were a child. Never mind that this place is huge and he didn't show me where I'm supposed to stay.

All the lights are on, and the desire to turn them off is immense. It's the always-counting-pennies mentality ingrained in me. Obviously, Hades doesn't have to worry about money. He just blew five million dollars to sleep with me, after all. It proves how demented he is. Who would pay that much money to fuck someone they hate?

I just want to get this over with. The longer I stay under his roof, the more anxious I'll become about the inevitable.

I open the first door I pass in the hallway. It's an office with a big glass desk in the middle of the room, a leather couch pushed against the wall, and a breathtaking view from the panoramic windows. I'm sure this is off-limits, and for a second, I consider closing the door, but my rebellious side wins, and I leave it open. Let him know I was snooping here.

The second door is locked, so I move on. Immediately to my right, I come across another set of modern stairs. It's the open kind without any railing, and I can't imagine going down them wearing high heels. I'd fall and break my neck.

There are still a few more doors to be tried on this level, but I find myself going up. On the second floor, there are only two doors. I veer for the one on the right.

Before I can turn the knob, a woman says, "Wrong one."

I jump on the spot, pressing a hand against my chest. "What the hell!"

It's the girl I saw standing outside. Hecate. Now that I see her without the glare of the headlights, she doesn't look ghost-like. She's not pale as I thought she was, but her straight, long hair is jet black, and it shines like silk. I'm getting serious hair envy right now.

She tilts her head and watches me with her ember-colored eyes that I suspect are contact lenses.

"So, you're the famous Persephone Flores."

I straighten my spine. "I'm not sure about famous, but yeah, I'm Persephone."

She takes a step forward and offers me her hand. "I'm Hecate."

Shaking hands with her is surreal and so businesslike. I wonder what her deal is with Hades. Why does she live in his guesthouse?

"Nice to meet you," I say.

Her eyes have a deranged glint in them as she smiles. "Don't say that yet. Anyway, if you're looking for your bedroom, this is the one." She points at the door she just walked through.

I frown. "What were you doing in there?"

And most importantly, how did she get here without us seeing her? There must be another way into the house.

"Just checking for booby traps," she replies with a straight face. In any other circumstance, I'd assume she was joking, but I can't be sure. "The room you were about to enter is Hades's. I'd stay clear of that one if you want to live."

I narrow my eyes to slits. I know when I'm being manipulated. Hades is awful, but I've been in enough life-threatening situations before to recognize this isn't one. Still, it'll be unpleasant as hell to spend time with him, no denying it.

"Thanks for the tip." I step forward, making my intentions clear. But she won't move aside to unblock the way into my room. "Do you mind?"

She finally gets out of the way, keeping her curious gaze on me. But I'm done being ogled for one evening, so I shut the door in her face without an ounce of remorse. Unfortunately, there isn't a lock.

All the lights are on here as well, and there's a nice scent in the air. It makes me think of dark-green leaves, hyacinth, and jasmine. This room is three times larger than my bedroom, and there are huge windows offering amazing views of the ocean. The house sits atop a cliff, a prime real estate spot.

The king-size bed has an off-white duvet cover and so many pillows I could bury myself under them. I bet the mattress is divine, but looking at it makes me think of the reason I'm here. Will Hades take what he paid for on that bed? A funny feeling unfurls in the pit of my stomach, and I don't know if it's nervousness or something else. Surely it can't be giddy anticipation.

I continue my inspection of the room, finding first the en suite bathroom, which is the best part of my new accommodations. There's a Jacuzzi-style tub and a separate rain shower with dual heads. I've never had a bubble bath before, and right now, I want very much to take off this stupid dress and soak my weary body in the tub. But before I succumb to the crazy impulse, I need to figure out my clothing situation. I'm not going to take this dress off and then parade around naked.

I open the cabinets and find towels and toiletries. Hanging

on a hook behind the door is a plush bathrobe. Okay, I could potentially walk around in that, but I'd still be naked underneath. Reluctantly, I forget the bathtub for now and continue my perusal. I find the closet, and lo and behold, some of my clothes are in there on the fancy hangers. I open the drawers and find more personal items. Mortification makes my face hot. Someone went through my underwear, packed them, and then organized them neatly.

"I see you found your stuff," Hades says, making me jump.

I turn, finding him leaning against the closet door.

"What's up with you and your friend trying to send me to an early grave by giving me a heart attack?"

"My friend?" His eyebrows shoot up. "Ah, so you've officially met Hecate."

"Yes, she was here making sure my room didn't have any nasty surprises. Was she the one you sent to my house to collect my stuff?"

He chuckles. "No, I'd never ask her to do that. She'd punch me in the throat if I did."

I watch him through slitted eyes. "What's your deal with her?"

His good humor changes in an instant, and his gaze darkens. He straightens his back and walks over.

Fuck. I'm trapped with no way out. My pulse accelerates as my brain tries to think of how I could best Hades physically in case I need to escape. He looks predatory, feral. *Is he going to collect now?*

He stops just short of invading my personal space. "You don't get to ask the questions here, darling."

"Bullshit," I grit out. "I want to know why you bid so high for me. And why are you intent on being an asshole?"

He presses forward, resting his hands on the shelves behind me and bringing his face inches from mine. "I said you don't get to ask questions. Are you incapable of following orders?"

"You're not my boss. Why should I?"

He grabs my neck, making my heart jump up to my throat and get stuck there. *Shit, maybe I'm not as safe as I thought.* He doesn't squeeze, but his hand is possessive.

"I *am* your boss for as long as you're in my house. Get used to it."

"Release me," I hiss.

His eyes flash with emotion, but I can't tell if I angered him more or not.

"Make me."

I'm shaking now—a mix of fear and anger. I try to remember the self-defense lessons I took with Helen freshman year, but none of the moves seem applicable. Also, there's the fact that I haven't practiced in a while, and self-defense is all about muscle memory.

A crazy idea pops in my head, but I don't stop to think about it. I reach for his crotch, but not to squeeze him into agony. I cup his dick as if I plan to give him a hand job. His eyes widen, and he pulls back a little.

"What are you doing?" he asks through clenched teeth.

"Accepting your dare."

He grows larger against my hand, and now I get his comment about not compensating for anything.

"You're playing with fire," he murmurs as his eyes turn soft with desire.

"Am I?"

I slide my hand over his erection and watch him try to remain in control. His breathing is definitely shallower now.

"I thought you were a virgin," he replies in a voice tight with need.

"So? That doesn't mean I'm a saint."

He narrows his eyes, and his hold on my neck tightens. "I see what you're doing. I won't fuck you tonight."

"Why not? You clearly want to."

And if I'm honest with myself, I want that too. My nipples are hard and pushing against the fabric of my dress, and the yearning within me feels like liquid fire in my veins.

Suddenly he steps back—more like jumps back—releasing me, and then strides out of the closet without uttering another word.

I don't move from the spot, my body frozen while my mind is spiraling like a top. *What the hell just happened here?* I can't believe I rubbed Hades's junk. My emotions are all over the place. I'm caught between relief that he let me go and disappointment that he didn't fuck me.

In a daze, I walk out of the closet and notice my purse in the middle of the bed. Hades must have brought it when he came in. In a rush, I grab it, looking for my phone. The battery is low, and I don't see a charger in there. I bet whoever packed my things didn't think to include it.

There are a couple of messages from Helen, but none seem important. I call Perseus before my phone dies. I left him a vague message before I left the house, but I never said I wasn't coming home tonight.

It rings and rings, and I fear he won't answer, but finally his annoyed voice comes through. "What is it?"

"Hey, I'm just calling to check in." I hear voices in the background, which doesn't give me comfort. "Are you having a party?"

"No, jeez. I just have some friends over."

"Did anyone come by the house earlier?"

"Uh, no? Why?"

"Are you sure?"

"I think I'd know. But I've only been home for an hour."

Son of a bitch. Then whoever Hades sent broke into my house. I suppose he needed to be sneaky, but still, I'm mad as hell.

"I'm not coming home tonight."

"Are you staying at Helen's?"

The fact that that's his immediate conclusion and not that I'm with a guy is telling. But it's better this way.

"Yes. So please behave."

"Yes, *Mom*. I'll see you tomorrow."

He ends the call, not leaving me any chance to discuss why our mother isn't around anymore. When he figured out her stuff was gone the morning after I kicked her out, he simply shrugged it off and then headed to school. I didn't see him before Deimos's minion took me to the auction, and now I don't know when I'll get the chance to have a proper conversation with him.

A blanket of sadness drapes over my shoulders, making me feel bone tired. Still wearing the stupid gown, I lie in bed, clutching my phone. I feel like I should cry, but my eyes are dry. I close them for a moment, and Hades's image comes to the forefront of my mind. I fall asleep with him in my head, and for some weird reason, thinking about him gives me comfort.

14

HADES

I'm glowering when I reach my living room. Naturally, Hecate is still there, nursing a glass of whiskey and looking smug. One glance in my direction and she seems to guess exactly what transpired between Persephone and me. Curse her witchy ways.

"What are you still doing here?" I make a beeline for the bar to pour myself a generous dose of spirits.

"You can't expect me to walk away when the show is getting good."

"I'm not here to entertain you," I bark, immediately berating myself for letting Hecate get to me.

"I like her. She's feisty."

I turn around too fast, spilling some of the drink on my shirt. "She hurt Cerberus. You aren't allowed to like her."

She raises an eyebrow. "Oh, but you are?"

"I don't like her," I grumble, then take a large sip of the whiskey, enjoying the smooth burn down my throat.

"Right, so you just have a roll of coins in your pocket."

I choke on my drink, which causes me a fit of coughing.

"Are you okay there?" she asks, and I can hear the amusement in her tone.

Once my airway is cleared, I wipe my mouth with the back of my hand. "You'd better make yourself scarce before I tell Dio he can move in with you."

Her mirth vanishes in a flash. "You wouldn't dare. You'd have blood on your hands because I'd kill that pest."

I shrug. "He's resourceful. He wouldn't be easy to kill."

With a huff, she stands up. "Fine. I'll leave you alone with the skull princess."

"Skull princess?" My forehead crinkles.

"Oh, didn't you know? She's obsessed with them. Just check her underwear drawer." She smirks and then literally skips away as if she were a child.

I throw my head back, swallowing the last of my drink in one gulp. I'm far from relaxed, so I refill my glass and go sit in front of the fireplace. Cerberus is snoring in his crate, and finally, after a full day of twists and turns, I'm utterly alone and have to deal with my thoughts.

Persephone occupies them mostly, but I can't ignore my brother and what he was planning to accomplish with Salas Ciriano. And why was Persephone part of the deal? Tomorrow, I'll ask for Hercules's report on her, and if he doesn't provide satisfying information, I'll have to put pressure on Hermes. Though I don't like relying on my nephew too much for information. That gives him too much power over me.

I lose track of time, but judging by the amount of alcohol I've consumed, I can tell I've been sitting here a while. When I get up, the room seems to spin. Grinding my teeth, I focus on finding my balance. Then I head upstairs with every intention to call it a night, but instead of veering for my room, I end up in Persephone's. It's my fault for giving her the guest room next to mine. I should have let her take the one downstairs.

The lights are still on. She fell asleep wearing that stupid gown. My better judgment is telling me to turn around and leave, but my reckless, drunk brain ignores the warning. I walk over to the bed and hover, staring at her like a fucking creep. She's so beautiful it hurts. That's the first thing I noticed about her when we met, and probably the reason I held on to my annoyance. Visceral reactions are never good. It makes me vulnerable.

It's so much easier to appreciate her beauty when she's not defying me. The high cheekbones, the bee-stung lips that beg to be kissed. The strain in my pants is more obvious than ever. I can have her now if I want to. Then it would be over, and she'd leave. But then what would I do with all this hate—no, that's not the right word for it. I don't hate her.

I run a hand through my hair. Hell, I'm losing my mind.

Just a couple more seconds and I'll go.

She stirs and then mumbles, "Hades..."

God, my name on her lips makes me crave her even more. Is she dreaming about me? And if so, what am I doing to her there?

She gasps and says my name again. Her legs rub together as if she's trying to ease an ache between them. *Fuck me.* I have to leave now or I'll end up turning her dream into reality.

Before I can follow through, she opens her eyes.

Busted.

I expect her to scream, not stare at me with hooded eyes. "Is this still a dream?"

"No." My voice comes out like a growl.

"Were you staring at me while I slept?"

"Yes." There's no point in denying it.

"Why?"

"I don't know."

Her eyes drop to my crotch. I don't try to hide the obvious. She swallows hard before she brings her eyes back to my face.

"Are you ready—"

"No."

She seems disappointed that I don't want to fuck her right this second, even though my body is one hundred percent on board.

"I was dreaming about you."

"Is that so?" I raise an eyebrow, pretending I didn't already know that. "What kind of dream?"

Danger, Hades. You're already hanging on by a thread.

A blush spreads through her cheeks, but she holds my stare. "The naughty kind."

I sense a trap, but I can't stop following the lure. "What were we doing in that dream?"

"You were...." Her face is even redder than before. "Never mind."

"Was I touching you?" I sit on the edge of the mattress and run my fingers over the back of her hand.

She trembles beneath my touch, and her skin breaks out in goose bumps. "Yes," she hisses.

"How was I touching you?"

She closes her eyes. "Your fingers... were between my legs."

My cock twitches in my pants. There's nothing I'd like more right now than to dive into her folds.

I'm about to succumb when Cerberus's whining reaches my ears. I remember then why I can't fall for her seduction games. I jump to my feet and fix my pants.

Her eyes fly open. "Where are you going?"

"Nice try, darling. You aren't as irresistible as you think."

I stomp out of the room, not looking back, and then bang the door shut for good measure.

I know exactly what I'm doing right now—going to take a very cold shower.

15

PERSEPHONE

I'm bleary eyed when I wake up, and at first, I don't recognize my surroundings. But then a heavy feeling sets in my chest, almost caving it in, and all the memories flood my brain. With it comes mortification. Hades turned me down twice in the span of hours. I had an excuse for throwing myself at him the first time. I was trying to escape him. But the second time, I did it because I was turned on as hell and I wanted him. I didn't even care that he was spying on me Edward Cullen style.

I glance at my phone, but the screen is black. *Fuck*. It's dead. I have no idea what time it is, but it can't be too late because the sky has the pink tinge of dawn. I push myself to a sitting position and run my fingers through my hair. I can't believe I'm still wearing the stupid auction gown. I should tear it to pieces despite it being so pretty. I never want to see it again. It's just a reminder of the lowest point in my life.

I jump to my feet and yank it off before I head to the bathroom. I don't have an early class, so I can indulge in that bath after all. But then I remember I have no means to get to school. Petunia is still parked in front of my house. My stomach clenches with worry. Perseus had better not take advantage of my absence and borrow her. If I hurry, I might catch him before he leaves for school.

A shower it is, then.

I try not to moan when the hot, powerful jets hit my skin. My old shower has no pressure, and washing my hair takes forever. I wish I had time to enjoy the luxury, but sadly, I don't.

All too conscious that my door has no lock, I put the bathrobe on before stepping out of the bathroom. I cringe when I pick a pair of skull undies to wear, knowing a stranger packed them. I don't think I'll ever feel better about it.

At least it wasn't Hades.

I get ready fast, choosing whatever items of clothing I see first—a basic long-sleeve T-shirt that unfortunately has a plunging neckline and an old pair of boyfriend-style jeans. Before I head downstairs, I grab my purse and check my wallet. I have twenty dollars, but my card will most definitely be denied if I try to use it. Once again, I think about all the money Hades paid for me and get angry. The debt was only twenty-five grand. Why the hell did that fucker Zeus have to keep it all?

Thanks, Mom.

I have to think about the silver lining, though. At least now her debt is paid many times over, and I don't have to worry about his henchmen hurting Perseus or me.

My plan is to sneak out of the house and see if there's a bus stop nearby. I don't expect to bump into a sweaty, half-naked Hades in the kitchen. I stop in my tracks and must have let out a gasp, because he turns to me with a glass of orange juice and a raised eyebrow. He's wearing boxing shorts, and his hands and wrists are wrapped with a red cloth. He has so many tats, it's impossible to tell the individual designs apart. I wonder if I'll get the chance to appreciate every inch of inked skin when he finally gets his prize.

I remember the scorching-hot dream I had of him last night, and my pussy throbs, reminding me that I never got any relief. I hope he can't tell that I'm turned on again. He might think I'm a nympho.

He doesn't say a word as he finishes his drink, but his eyes are glued to my face. They're veiled though, revealing nothing.

"I didn't know you were up already," I say.

"Were you hoping to escape while I slept?"

I bristle. "If I wanted to escape, I'd have tried last night."

"Hmm." He crosses his arms, leaning his hip against the counter.

Do not look at his washboard abs, Persephone.

"Is there a bus stop nearby? I need to go home."

He quirks an eyebrow. "You aren't going home."

"Not to stay. I need a few things that your minion didn't pack."

"Whatever you need, I'll get it for you."

I copy his stance, crossing my arms. "You can't expect me to not go home during my captivity stint here. I have a younger brother. I have a life!"

He sets his glass down and walks over. *Oh dear. I poked the beast.* Is he going to grab me by the throat again and invade my personal space? My pulse accelerates, and it isn't fear that's causing it.

"You'll stay here for as long as I want, and you won't say a word to complain."

"What are you going to do if I *do* complain? Spank me like you promised?"

He narrows his eyes. "You'd like that, wouldn't you, *Skulls*?"

I take a step back, widening my eyes. "Why did you call me that?"

He runs his index finger down my side, making me shiver, and then slides it underneath my waistband. I can't breathe but also can't stop the shakes that are wreaking havoc through my body. I don't know what Hades intends to do until he hooks his finger under the side of my panties and pulls the strap up.

"Because you love them." He stretches the fabric to the max and then releases it with a loud snap.

I glower. "You went through my things?"

He smiles like an imp and then turns around. "Tell me what you need, and I'll ask Hercules to stop by your house again."

My face couldn't burn more from embarrassment. So Hades's giant employee was the one who packed my things. *Kill me now.*

"I need Petunia, and to check on my brother. He can't help me."

Hades's forehead crinkles. "Petunia?"

I sigh. "My car. I call her Petunia."

He chuckles and shakes his head. "You don't need your car."

"How am I supposed to get to school?"

"You're coming with me."

My eyebrows shoot up to the heavens. "Oh, so now you're my jailer *and* chauffeur?"

He watches me through narrowed eyes. "Careful, Persephone. Pissing me off won't help you."

"Maybe it'll make you claim your prize faster."

His eyes flash with annoyance, and then he growls, "No."

Bullshit. I bet if I pushed his buttons hard enough, he'd snap. But do I seriously want my first time to be rough, hate sex?

My pussy clenches again.

Damn it. Maybe I do.

"I also need my phone charger," I say.

"You can borrow one of mine."

I cross my arms. "I want to see Perseus before he goes to school."

"Not today. Now, there's food in the fridge. Help yourself."

He walks around me and heads toward the stairs. I wait until I hear his door close to go into his garage. He's insane if he thinks I'm going to obey his orders. I'm hoping he keeps the keys to his many cars inside the vehicles. I aim for the less ostentatious option, a black Escalade SUV. The door is unlocked, and a quick look at the storage under the armrest proves me right. There's the fob, and the clicker for the gate is right next to it.

"Jackpot."

I turn the car on, and the rumble of the engine makes me jump in my seat. It's too noisy. I expect Hades to come running in any second now, or maybe his weird friend Hecate. But neither shows up before I put the car in gear and drive out.

The outside gate opens automatically as I approach it, and I use the car's navigation system to get my bearings. It says I'll make it to my house in fifteen minutes. That should be plenty of time to catch Perseus at home.

I've never driven a car with juice, and it'd be fun to see how fast it goes, but I'm mindful of keeping the speed limit. I might be driving Hades's car, but I'm not him, and I don't want issues with Johnny Law.

I didn't realize how tense I was until I begin to relax. I turn on the radio and find a good station with pop songs I can sing to. Dua Lipa's "Don't Start Now" comes on, and I crank the volume up.

I'm distracted for maybe a minute and don't see the flashy sports car gaining on me until it passes me and blocks my way ahead. *Fuck!* It's Hades's Batmobile. I stomp on the brakes, hoping I can stop the car before I crash into him.

The tires screech loudly, and my seat belt digs against my chest. My heart is beating too fast, making my breathing come out in bursts.

"What the actual fuck!"

With trembling hands, I release the seat belt and step out of the car. Hades is already coming my way with murderous intent shining in his eyes. He's not the only one who wants to kill, though.

"You ass!" I yell. "I could have wrecked your car."

He grabs my chin with his big, calloused hand and forces my gaze to his. The roughness of his touch sends a thrill down my spine, and mixed with the rage in my blood, that's a dangerous combination.

"You stole my property and disobeyed my orders. I told you there'd be consequences."

"I'm not your property."

He pushes me against the SUV's side and cups my pussy with his free hand. "This belongs to me, and until I use it, you'll obey me."

"Just take it already before I decide to offer it to the first guy I come across."

His blue eyes darken as he applies pressure down below. *Oh my God*. The friction is already making my legs feel boneless.

"Shall I take you here, then, out in the open for anyone who drives by to see?"

A whimper escapes my lips, and I hate that it's obvious how turned on I am. I expect him to step back—he never continues when he believes I'm trying to seduce him—but instead, he rubs his thumb over the seam of my jeans and slants his mouth over mine. His tongue is possessive and takes without mercy. Closing my eyes, I clutch his biceps, needing the support because now my entire body is on fire and melting. This is the most savage kiss I've ever had, and the fucking best too. One more second and I'll shatter under his fingers.

But Hades is gone before he sends me over the edge. My eyes fly open, my lips still tingling from the rough kiss. Hades stands in front of me, but he's no longer invading my space. His breathing is shallow, and he seems caught in a daze. His expression darkens in the next moment, and the hard mask falls back in place.

He grabs my arm and drags me to his Batmobile.

"What are you doing?" I ask.

"I'm taking you to see your damn brother."

My head spins. I don't know what to do with that information. He's giving me a win, though I can't imagine one kiss would make him change his mind.

"What about the Escalade?"

"Fuck the Escalade. Now get in the damn car before I change my mind."

16

PERSEPHONE

Hades remains silent the entire ride to my house. My body is still under the effects of his lips on mine, and my mind is spinning like a top. *Why did he kiss me like that? To show me how puny I am in his hands? How I'm all bark and no bite?*

I wish I could say his kiss was inconsequential, but I know it'll be imprinted on my mind forever. Hades ruined all other kisses for me. Is it going to be the same when he finally fucks me?

When he parks in front of my house, he doesn't comment on the faded walls or the peeling paint on the shutters. At least the garden is pretty. Petunia is still parked in the driveway, and I let out a breath of relief. Perseus didn't borrow her, but is he still home? I glance at the clock on the dashboard. It's early. We have twenty minutes before the school bus comes.

"I assume that's Petunia," Hades says in a smooth voice, cool as a cucumber.

It seems he's already forgotten he had his tongue deep in my mouth and his hand between my legs. I turn to him and find him staring ahead. His square jaw is locked tight. His face is so angular and perfect; I could cut myself on those sharp edges. Damn, the man is beautiful.

Probably sensing my stare, he looks at me. "Did you forget how to speak?"

"No," I grumble. "That's my car."

I get out before he can throw more insults at me. I'm halfway to the front door when I notice he's following me.

"What are you doing?" I ask.

"I don't feel like waiting in the car. Plus, I'm *dying* to meet your brother."

Sarcasm duly noted, buddy. I'm unhappy about this, but it's futile to argue with him.

"Fine. But fair warning, Perseus is a dragon in the morning."

"In case you failed to notice, so am I."

I glance at him again. His tone was lighter, but I don't think he was attempting to be humorous. "Yeah, that was the first thing I noticed about you."

I fish my key out of my purse to unlock the door, but it isn't even closed all the way. My heart jumps up to my throat, and fear paralyzes me.

"What's the matter?" he asks.

"I... the door."

Hades walks ahead of me and pushes it open. His body is coiled tight, ready to spring into action. "Wait here."

I only give him a few seconds of a head start before I follow him. This is my house, and my brother is inside. I won't sit on the sidelines and let him deal with the situation.

No sooner do I step foot inside than I smell the stench of beer and junk food going bad. Hades is staring at the mess in the living room with his hands on his hips. Without looking at me, he says, "Didn't I tell you to wait outside?"

"You should know by now that I don't follow orders well."

He whips his face to mine, sporting a glower.

"Yeah, yeah. Save the death glare for another time. I have to kill someone first."

I march down the hallway, avoiding looking too closely at the mess Perseus left in the living room. From my periphery, I see all the empty beer and soda cans, discarded chip bags, and pizza leftovers. Would it kill him to ask his douche friends to help clean up? And judging by the chaos, he had way more than just a few people over.

I push his bedroom door open hard, and it hits the wall loudly. Perseus jolts to a sitting position, looking scared shitless before he realizes I was the one who made the noise.

"What the hell, Persephone!"

"Don't even start." I walk over to him. "I left you alone for one evening, and you trashed the house."

His eyes go rounder. "Oh shit. I forgot about that. I was gonna clean up this morning, I swear."

"Oh really? You need to be on your way to school in twenty minutes, and unless you're the Flash, I fail to see how you would accomplish that."

His brows are scrunched together, and I know a retort is on the tip of this tongue, but his gaze travels past my shoulder a second before I notice Hades's presence behind me.

Fucking great. He followed me.

"Who are you?" Perseus asks.

Hades steps into the room and gives the messy place a cursory glance before focusing on Perseus's broken arm.

"How did you get hurt?" he asks.

Perseus gets a panicked glint in his eyes and turns to me, rekindling my anger at Zeus and my mother.

"You can thank your big brother for that," I tell Hades.

He turns his face to mine, not hiding the fury in his blue gaze. "I see. Well, get what you came for already. I don't have the whole day."

He walks out, and then I hear the sound of the front door shutting hard.

Why did he *get bent out of shape? We're the ones suffering for our mother's mistake.*

"What are you doing with Hades, Seph?"

Fuck. I *so* don't want to tell Perseus about my sordid deal with Zeus, but I have to say something.

"Mom owed a lot of money to Zeus, and Hades paid her debt."

Perseus's eyebrows shoot to his hairline. "Why?"

I shrug. "I don't know. Probably to piss off his brother. He hates him."

He narrows his eyes. "That doesn't explain why he would help us. I didn't even know you knew him."

"We're friends... sort of." I can't believe I didn't choke on that lie.

His jaw drops. "Oh shit. You're sleeping with him."

My face becomes as hot as lava in zero point two seconds. "I'm not!"

He tilts his head and studies me. "Maybe not yet, but you want to."

"Shut up, Perseus. Just get ready for school. And clean the house."

"Fine," he grumbles. "But it'll take me double the time with only one good arm."

"That's not my problem. Don't try to guilt-trip me into helping you. Call your friends to assist."

"You're in a mood today. I'm the one who was beaten up."

Now *that* does make me feel guilty. And I won't be around for God knows how long.

I throw my hands up in the air. "Ugh! Fine! Just get in the shower, and I'll start cleaning."

"What about Hades? He said he was in a hurry."

"Well, no one is asking him to wait."

The front door opens again, and immediately I assume it's Hades coming back to hurry me up. But when I hear female voices instead, I go investigate. There are two ladies already making themselves comfortable in my kitchen.

"Who are you?" I ask.

One of them glances at me. "Oh, hello, miss. We're with Express Cleaning Service."

"I didn't call you."

"I did," Hades replies from the front door.

"What? Why?"

"Because I knew you would want to do it yourself, and I wasn't going to wait until you finished."

I put my hands on my hips. "Your controlling ways are getting out of hand. And how did they get here so fast?"

"We live only two blocks away, miss," one of them replies.

"I called them when you went into your brother's room," Hades adds. "Now, did you pack what you need, or do I need to do it myself?"

I'm caught between feeling angry about his high-handed way and grateful that he cared enough to hire help. He could drag me out of the house and forbid me from cleaning if he wanted to. But I won't let him see that. He's still my jailer, after all.

"I can manage on my own."

I veer to my bedroom and first locate my phone charger. That's really the only thing Hercules forgot to pack. My wardrobe and drawers are empty.

Jesus, how long does Hades intend to draw this out?

I spot my old copy of *The Iliad* on the floor, hidden partially by my nightstand. I've lost count of how many times I've read it. It belonged to my father, and it has his annotations in the margins. I decide to bring that with me too.

The last item I grab is my car key. Maybe I can convince Hades to let me drive it.

When I return to the living room, Perseus is in the open

kitchen, eating a bowl of cereal. The cleaning ladies already cleared all the trash from the floor and coffee table.

"You got lucky," I tell him.

"Tell Hades thanks for me." He smiles.

I fleetingly glance at the women and then pull up a chair next to Perseus. "I wanted to talk to you. I didn't have a chance to ask how you were after your ordeal."

"It sucks that I'm gonna miss football season."

"I know. I'm so sorry, Persi."

He sets the spoon down and meets my gaze. "Hey, don't feel sorry, okay? It wasn't your fault. Besides, I'm getting loads of female attention thanks to my broken arm." He wiggles his eyebrows up and down and smiles.

I roll my eyes. "Like you didn't get enough female attention before."

He shrugs. "The more the merrier. But seriously, don't worry about me."

"I can't. That's my job as your older sister."

He picks up the bowl and drinks the rest of the milk, then wipes his mouth clean with the back of his hand.

Classy.

"Are you coming home tonight?" he asks.

Remorse pierces my chest. "I can't."

"You're staying with Hades, aren't you?"

I drop my gaze to the table, afraid Perseus will read the truth in my eyes. "Yes. It's part of the deal I made with him."

"He isn't asking you to do shit you don't want to, right, Seph?"

I flick my eyes to his. "No, of course not. I'm helping him with his dog. Some lunatic ran him over with their car."

His eyes widen. "Oh shit. That's horrible. How's the dog?"

"Broken leg."

A throat clearing interrupts our conversation. Hades is once again standing by the front door. He doesn't look angry, per se, but he isn't happy either.

"Okay, I'd better go. Please, no more parties, okay?"

"I'll try." Perseus smirks.

I get up and then kiss the top of his head. "I'll call you later."

Hades's eyes don't leave my face as I walk toward him. They're a pool of mystery; I can't even begin to imagine what's going on in his head. I hold his stare, though. He looks like a statue—no, a boulder, unmovable. I wonder if he's going to force me to shove him aside, but he finally moves out of the way at the last second, allowing me to walk out first.

I play dumb and make a beeline for Petunia. He's next to me in a flash, gripping my wrist before I can open the driver's door.

"I said you don't need your car."

He's much too close, and all I can think about is his mouth on mine.

"Our schedules aren't the same." I try to be reasonable by appealing to logic since butting heads with him gets me nowhere.

He pries Petunia's key from my hand. The contact sends a ripple of pleasure up my arm.

"You let me worry about logistics," he replies in a timbre a little lower than his normal tone, almost as if he's having trouble getting the words out.

He steps away and veers for his Batmobile.

"What's your game, Hades?"

He pauses slightly before glancing at me. "I can't tell you."

"Why not?"

"Because when you figure it out, you win."

17

HADES

My original idea was to force Persephone to tag along for every single appointment and class I have today, but it seems when she's involved, I can't expect things to go according to plan. It's also unfair to make her miss her classes. I really didn't think things through. She made me lose control, and I caved. I kissed the damn woman, and I would have gone further if a moment of sanity didn't pierce through my lust-infused brain.

I park in front of the main library and say, "Get out."

"Are you serious? I don't have class until after lunch."

"I don't care."

I keep my eyes focused ahead, but I can feel her glare burn a hole through my face.

"You're an asshole. I hope that when you do decide to fuck me, it sucks as much for you as it does for me."

She gets out in a huff and slams the door. Unable to resist the temptation, I watch her stalk toward the library's entrance. I hate that I'm insanely attracted to the woman, and I doubt fucking her will be a bad experience for me. I'll make damn sure she has a good time too. Ruining her for other men is the perfect final punishment.

A sudden irritation comes out of nowhere, and it takes me a second to realize the idea of her with another guy is what's triggering my foul mood now.

Fuck. I can't develop any type of attachment to her.

More annoyed than before, I peel away from the curb and go find a place to park. My agenda is full today, and Persephone already occupied too much of my time.

My phone rings, and the dashboard shows it's Hermes's number.

"What?" I bark.

"Good morning to you too."

"I'm not in the mood for idle chat. Get straight to the point or I'm ending this call."

"When are you ever in the mood to shoot the shit? I'm calling because I have news regarding our friend Salas Ciriano."

That makes me sit straighter in my seat. "I'm listening."

"He wasn't the target. He was a means to an end."

I grind my teeth. Hermes and his need to draw out a simple story is not what I want to deal with right now. "Just get to the point already."

"Jesus, you *are* in a foul mood. I guess you didn't fuck Persephone yet, huh?"

"Do not speak about her," I grit out.

"Fine, I won't. Anyway, Zeus wants to strike a deal with Salas's brother, Dimas."

I pass a hand over my face, annoyed that I didn't come to that conclusion myself. "Makes sense. Let me guess, Dimas blew him off, so he was hoping to butter his younger brother up to get an in with the head of the family."

"Exactly. Only his plan backfired because you interfered. Instead of gaining an ally, he got a pissed-off loose cannon. He's still in town, by the way. I'd watch my back if I were you."

I roll my eyes. Like I'm afraid of vermin like Salas. "Thanks for the tip. You can send me the bill later."

"Hold on. I don't want money this time."

Fuck. What could he possibly want instead?

"I want a date with Hecate," he answers my unspoken question.

I laugh. "You must be out of your mind."

"I'm not joking. That's my price."

"You should have laid your terms before you gave the information away, dumbass. I'm not going to force my friend to go out with you."

"Hell, you make it sound like I'm a loser who can't get girls."

"If the shoe fits. If you want to ask her out, man up and do it. She'll probably carve you up like a turkey, though."

"Thanks for the pep talk. And for your information, *jackass*, I already asked her out, and she said no."

"There you have it. Why are you trying to involve me in your shenanigans?"

"Because this deal with Persephone isn't over, and if you want me to keep feeding you information, you'd better help me out."

I pinch the bridge of my nose and say through clenched teeth, "As I said, I can't force Hecate to go out with you."

"Fine. Let's go on a double date, then. You, me, Hecate, and Persephone."

I reject the idea immediately. "Yeah, that's exactly what I need."

"You may not need it, but you *want* it. I'll text you the details."

The call goes silent before I can say "Hell to the fucking no." I can't go out on a date with Persephone. That's not our arrangement.

Fuck. Hermes and his idiotic ideas. I bet he only wants Hecate because she turned him down. Idiot.

A couple minutes later, I receive another call, this time from Hercules. "Please tell me you aren't calling with more bad news."

"I'm afraid I can't say that, boss. The funeral home was vandalized last night."

Groaning, I let my head fall back. "How come the security company didn't alert me there was a break-in?"

"Because there wasn't one. They just trashed the front of the store with spray paint. It looks like the work of punks."

I grip the steering wheel tighter. "I doubt it. I want eyes on Salas Ciriano at all times. He's still in town and apparently looking to get even."

"You got it. Should I tag him?"

"No, I want you to cover Perseus Flores. I won't put it past Zeus to send his goons after the kid again. Put your other men on Salas's trail."

"Copy that. What should I do about the storefront?"

"The funeral director can handle it."

I keep driving toward the economics building, but a nagging feeling keeps telling me I should veer back to the library. I want to ignore the sixth sense, but just as the economics building comes into view, I make a U-turn and speed back to Persephone.

I'm not sure what's propelling me, but there's a sense of urgency in the air now. It's possible I let Hermes's and Hercules's news influence me and this strange sensation is just a figment of my imagination. But if it isn't, then Persephone might be in danger. Both scenarios are horrible. They prove that no matter how much I fight it, I can't escape the hold she has on me.

PERSEPHONE

With hours to kill and no car, my best option is to stay in the library and get some studying done. If only my mind wasn't stuck on Hades. I'm still angry as hell, but there are other feelings more worrisome than that. The memory of our kiss keeps playing in my head on a constant loop, and I can't concentrate on the book in front of me.

Frustrated, I shut the heavy tome with a bang, and the noise earns me a few pissed-off glares from the students nearby.

Yeah, yeah. It wasn't that loud.

I turn my computer on, and when it pings as it starts, someone shushes me.

"Bite me, jerkface," I snap.

The annoyed girl stands up in a huff and walks away.

Good riddance.

The first thing I check is my inbox. At the top sits an email from Prof. Cashore.

Great. That's exactly what I need to perk me up.

There's no point in ignoring it, so I might as well see what that douche wants.

I look over his message twice to make sure I didn't misread it. He wants to discuss a possible way for me to make up for the test I missed over coffee. *Fucker*. Why can't he just tell me in the email how I can earn my extra credit? I want to tell him to go to hell, but then he will flunk me, and then it's bye-bye bachelor's degree.

Not knowing what to do, I text Helen. I haven't talked to her since the auction, which feels like eons ago. I wait and wait, and she doesn't reply. She's not in class—I have her schedule memorized. That means she might be with Paris, and if that's the case, it could be a while.

I stare at Prof. Perv's email, drumming my fingers on the

desk. I don't know what to say to him, so I decide to not answer right now.

I can't study, I can't reply to emails, so what the hell am I going to do in this library? My stomach grumbles, reminding me that I skipped breakfast. I remember the twenty dollars in my wallet and decide to splurge on coffee and a donut. I won't get paid until next week—that is, if I still have a job. With Hades's insane rule that I need to be attached to his hip, I might not be able to work.

Fuck that. He won't keep me from earning an income.

Now I'm back to being annoyed. It seems my existence with him will be made of ups and downs and sudden drops like a damn roller coaster.

I shut my laptop, pack my things hastily, and leave the library. The earlier sunny sky has been replaced by angry clouds, and the gust of strong winds warns me a storm is approaching. Fantastic. I'm sick and tired of getting caught in the rain without an umbrella.

I hurry toward the café closest to me, and just as I'm a couple steps from the entrance, the first droplets of rain fall. It's my stupid bad luck that the damn place is closed. There's a sign that says the entire staff got the flu.

"You've got to be kidding me."

I glance back to the library building, judging if I can sprint there before I get drenched from head to toe. The rain is getting heavier, and with the wind, staying under the café's awning will do me no good.

The bad weather cleared the people from the park, and despite it being early morning, the whole place looks eerie now, like a ghost town. A shiver runs down my spine. I don't know why I'm getting this weird feeling that something dreadful is about to happen.

Yeah, I'm not staying put. I guess getting wet it is.

Holding my backpack close to my chest in the hope of

avoiding water damage to my laptop, I break into a run, keeping close to the building. It offers me little protection, though.

I have to pay extra attention to where I step, because with my track record, I'll twist my ankle and fall on my ass if I'm not careful. With my eyes on the ground, I don't notice that someone stepped in front of me before I almost collide with them.

"Sorry." I jump back, lifting my chin.

My heart squeezes tightly as if there were a vise wrapped around it. The man standing in front of me is the same one who got into a bidding war with Hades and got furious when he lost. If that wasn't enough to make my adrenaline level spike, the cruel glint in his eyes means it's obvious he didn't come here to chat.

"Hello, beautiful," he greets me with a sly smile.

I move to turn around and run, but he grabs my arm and pulls me closer. "Oh no. I'm not losing you again. You were meant to be my prize, and I intend to collect."

"Let go of me, you freak, or I'll scream."

He sneers. "And who's going to come to the rescue?"

I don't care that there's no one around. I scream at the top of my lungs as I try to break free. If anything, maybe I can damage his eardrums.

"You stupid bitch."

He pulls his arm back to deliver either a slap or a punch, but someone grabs his wrist and twists it savagely. He bellows in pain and lets go of me completely. I stagger backward, still clutching my backpack, and watch Hades deliver a knockout punch that sends the motherfucker straight to the ground.

He tries to get up but seems too stunned to do so.

"You're going to pay for this, asshole," he mumbles.

Unfazed, Hades kicks him in the ribs a few times and then bends over to lift him up by the lapels of his jacket. "You stay the fuck away from what's mine. Do you hear me?"

"Mine." He didn't say "stay away from Persephone," he said "stay away from what's mine," and that makes me unbearably sad. Not angry, sad.

I let that realization sink in. I want him to see me as a person, not property. It's a stupid wish. He paid a lot of money for me; of course he'll see me as something that belongs to him.

I'm more upset about that detail than almost being kidnapped, and the display of violence. Maybe my fucked-up upbringing desensitized me.

As much as I'm glad that Hades came out of nowhere to save me like a hero from the movies, I turn around and walk away from him. I barely feel the rain against my skin now; I'm too numb, either from the shock or the cold. I can still hear Hades's grunts as he punishes Salas further.

When I'm almost across the park, Hades calls, "Persephone, wait."

I stop, but I don't look back.

He walks around to block my path, then pinches my chin between his thumb and forefinger, lifting my gaze to his.

"Are you okay?" He sounds concerned.

"Don't worry. Your property is still intact."

His eyebrows furrow, and his lips become nothing but a thin line. "You're drenched. I'm taking you home."

I could point out that he's also wet, but I don't have it in me to be sassy. I just want this day—this *week*—to be over.

18

HADES

Persephone doesn't utter a single word on the way back home. I glance at her several times, but she seems lost in her thoughts. I want to console her, but I don't know how. It's crazy that I have the need to make her feel better when I was intent on making her suffer only a few hours ago. I don't understand all the contradictory feelings swirling in my chest.

I'm blowing off class and work to make sure she's okay. I probably started a war with a family of murderous bastards, and yet I have no regrets.

She gets out of the car the moment I park in the garage and stalks up the stairs. I don't move from my seat for a couple beats; I need to get my head straight before I follow her.

My phone rings, and I'm surprised to see Ares's number flash on the dashboard.

"What do you want?" I bark.

"I see you haven't gotten rid of the aggression yet."

"What are you talking about?"

"I heard about your altercation with Salas Ciriano."

I let my head fall backward and close my eyes. "Good news travels fast."

"And bad news even faster. Do you know the clusterfuck you caused?"

"I can imagine, and I don't give a fuck. That son of a bitch tried to take what's mine, and he got what he deserved."

"I hope you're prepared to keep an eye on your prize twenty-four seven, then. Salas is a crazy psycho, and he's obsessed with her, a fact my father is exploiting to the max."

I scowl. It doesn't surprise me that Zeus would try to win that douche back. He must really want a partnership with Dimas, and I can guess he promised Salas my head on a platter.

"I don't intend to let her out of my sight."

"She was that good of a fuck, huh?" He laughs, but I'm not amused.

"You'd better watch your mouth, punk," I grit out.

"Damn! It seems my dear uncle has caught feelings."

Caught feelings, my ass.

"If you don't have any more useful information, then I'm hanging up."

"Touchy. I *do* have something else to say. You'd better make sure Persephone's family is safe too."

"I've assigned Hercules to keep an eye on her brother."

"What about her junkie mother?"

I pass a hand over my face. *Damn it.* I forgot about that good-for-nothing woman. She was more than happy to sell her daughter off to save her own skin. I couldn't care less about her fate. My intel told me Persephone kicked her out, but that doesn't mean she no longer cares about her mother.

"I'll look into it."

He snickers. "Yeah, not whipped, my ass."

"Fuck off, Ares."

I end the call before he can say more aggravating things. In hindsight, I should have thanked the fucker for giving me the heads-up. I do have terrible social skills—a fact Hecate loves to point out. I snort at the thought. Like she's Miss Congeniality.

I finally get out of the car and head inside the house. I expect to find no trace of Persephone in the main living area, but she has Cerberus out of his crate, and he's currently curled up on her lap while she runs her fingers down his back. She didn't change out of her wet clothes, but maybe she didn't want to be alone.

I can't forget that she deliberately ignored my order to stay away from Cerberus, but I also can't summon an ounce of anger at the sight. Instead, warmth spreads through my chest, and I find myself watching the scene like an enamored fool.

Walk away, Hades. Walk the fuck away.

My phone rings, alerting Persephone of my presence. She whips her face to me with eyes that are round and startled. I don't look at the phone before I press the button to ignore the call.

"I.... He looked sad, so I let him out," she says.

Holding her stare, I walk over and sit next to her on the floor. Cerberus lifts his head and glances at me but clearly has no intention of moving from her lap to mine. I wouldn't either.

"It's fine." I scratch him behind his ear.

She faces the fireplace again. "Is that guy going to come after me again?"

I clench my jaw tight, hating that I can't say she doesn't need to worry about him anymore. "Probably."

"What am I supposed to do, then? Look over my shoulder for the rest of my life?"

"I won't let anything happen to you."

She glances at me. "Because I'm your property."

I narrow my eyes. "No. Because I don't want to see you get hurt."

"Ah, of course. Only you can hurt me."

I cup her cheek and run my thumb over her luscious lips. Damn, I want to kiss her again.

"I don't know what to do about you, Skulls."

Her gaze hardens. "You can fuck me so I can get back to my life."

I drop my hand and look away. "You can't go back to your old life."

"Bullshit I can't!"

"Salas isn't going to leave you alone. Even after I fuck you, he'll still come for you."

She laughs. "That's just great. I have a stalker now. You should have let him win at the auction. At least my nightmare would have been over by now."

I drop into a crouch in front of her, holding her face between my hands. "Do you think he'd be satisfied with having you for only one night? I wouldn't."

Her eyes widen, and I realize my mistake. I'm a second away from making another one when I hear loud footsteps echo in the hallway.

"Hades, I'm going to fucking kill you!" Hecate bellows.

I don't know if I should thank her for the interruption or curse her ill timing. She can't find me this close to Persephone, though, so I jump back to my feet.

"What now?" I ask when she walks into the living room.

She flicks her gaze at Persephone first, and I'm shocked when she doesn't comment on her wet look—or mine.

"You told Hermes we would go out on a double date?"

I groan. "That fucker. I never agreed to anything."

She puts her hands on her hips and intensifies the glower. "Well, he just told me he made reservations for us tonight at Pantheon."

That gives me pause. Hermes wouldn't have chosen that specific location if he wasn't up to something. "Hmmm."

"Why aren't you cursing his name like I am?"

I glance at Persephone and find her frowning. She must have a thousand questions running through her head. I face Hecate again. "We should do it."

Her eyebrows shoot to the heavens. "You wanna have dinner at one of Zeus's restaurants? Why?"

"I have my reasons."

She looks over my shoulder. "What do you have to say about that, girlie?"

I turn and catch Persephone shaking her head. "It doesn't matter what I think. Hades will do whatever he wants anyway."

Her comment feels like a dagger of guilt sliding into my chest. She got embroiled in my family's twisted games through no fault of her own, and I've been giving her hell since I met her. The worst part is I'm not done making her life harder.

"You can tell Hermes it's on," I say to Hecate.

She watches me through narrowed eyes. "I know you're planning something to piss off your brother, and it's for that reason alone that I'm going to follow along. But you owe me big-time."

"Come on now. Hermes isn't that bad." I smirk.

"I'll pretend you didn't say that." She pivots with a flair and strides back the way she came.

"It's time for your medication, sweet boy," Persephone tells Cerberus in the softest tone.

Hell, why does she have to be so nice to him? It's like she knows all my weaknesses.

"You don't need to trouble yourself with him," I say.

Her eyes flash with annoyance. "I want to help. Are you still intent on keeping me away from your dog?"

"It's not that. You've been through an ordeal and you're in wet clothes. I don't want you to catch a cold."

"Oh, I see. You don't want your trophy to get sick or else you can't parade me around tonight."

Fuck, she's twisting all my good intentions into something

perverse. The bitter realization drops like a bomb. She can't make the distinction between Zeus and me. We're probably made of the same cloth in her eyes, and I've done nothing to prove the contrary.

Maybe it's for the best that she thinks I'm just as bad as him. Hate can work as a weapon and a shield, and she'll need both tonight.

19

PERSEPHONE

Another day, another class I missed because of my mother's mess. That creep coming after me is entirely her fault. If I keep this up, I'll lose my scholarship faster that I can say, "Do you want fries with that?" The job at the flower shop is rewarding, but it doesn't pay well enough to cover rent. I need the stipend my scholarship provides.

Helen didn't reply to my text until after lunch, but then I didn't feel like texting her back. She called, and I ignored it. I'm in a funk, and since I can't tell her the reason, it'll make our conversation stressful. She'll be able to tell I'm hiding something, and she'll get hurt.

I've never been to Pantheon, but I've heard about it from Helen. It's one of the most expensive restaurants in Olympus Bay, and now I know Zeus is the owner. I got the impression Zeus and Hades don't get along based on Hades's exchange with Hecate, so I can only deduce that he's using me to annoy his brother. It goes hand in hand with him believing I'm his property.

Tough luck for him, because I have nothing to wear. I'll look like I don't belong, hardly a prize. I pick the most outrageous skull underwear I own. They're boxer-style panties with huge rainbow-colored skulls that shoot lightning bolts from their eyes while they fly around in a neon-pink sky. Sadly, there's no matching bra. No one will see I'm wearing it, but it makes me feel rebellious just the same.

I get dressed in a simple tank top and denim skirt and pair them with my secondhand cowboy boots. The leather is scuffed in places, but it's supple and comfortable. While I wait for Hades to show up, I decide to finally reply to Prof. Perv and agree to meet him for coffee. My life is already an asshole parade fest; what's adding one more to the mix going to change?

The knock on the door is a surprise.

"Come in," I say.

Hades enters, and I immediately gravitate toward him. I'm glad I'm sitting at the desk, because once again, I'm taken aback by his presence. It ought to be illegal for someone so horrible to be that gorgeous. Next to him, I look like a reject from *Yellowstone.*

"Are you ready?" he asks.

"Yep." I stand and wait for him to criticize my attire.

He gives me an elevator glance—painfully slowly—and then quirks an eyebrow. "Interesting choice."

I cross my arms. "It's the best I can do."

His lips curl into a grin, and then he's moving. *Shit.* He's coming over, and I have nowhere to go. *What's he going to do now? Push me against the desk for a repeat of what happened on the road?* My heart races in excitement at the prospect. My own body is betraying me. *Son of a bitch.* I want to seduce Hades and get this ordeal over with, but I don't want to do it this very second.

Standing in front of me now, he leans down and whispers in my ear, "Are you wearing a pair of your skull panties?"

A shiver of desire runs down my back, curling at the base of my spine. And why does he have to smell so damn good?

"Why do you care?" My reply is weak, almost vapor.

He chuckles, and his warm breath fanning against my neck gives me goose bumps. I fight not to shut my eyes and whimper like a kitten.

"Maybe I'll get lucky tonight and see them for myself."

Alarm bells sound in my head. Is he flirting with me? He's never been this open about wanting to see me naked.

I lean back and look into his eyes. "Are you drunk?"

He squints. "Stone-cold sober."

I sidestep him and manage to put some distance between us. His proximity is messing with my ability to think clearly. "You're acting weirder than normal."

He straightens his jacket and schools his expression into the cold mask he likes to wear. "Let's go. Hecate will kill me if I make her wait at the restaurant alone with Hermes."

"She isn't coming with us?"

He gives me a droll look. "Of course not. This is a date, darling."

I tense. "No, it isn't. This is a business transaction."

He tilts his head. "Aren't all dates business transactions? You pay for food and drinks in the hopes to fuck your date in the end."

"You've already paid plenty for the guaranteed fuck. I don't know why we have to go through this charade."

"Take off your clothes, then."

My stomach bottoms out. "What?"

His gaze hardens, devoid of the previous amusement. "You heard me. If you don't want me to treat you nice, then I'll fuck you like a whore."

Whore. That's what I am, isn't it? There's no other name for a woman who gets paid for sex, only I won't see a dime of that fortune.

My eyes burn, and I hate myself for letting him get to me. I curl my hands into fists, digging my nails into my palms and hoping the pain will stop me from crying in front of him.

"Hecate is waiting for us. You can fuck me like a whore after dinner." I turn around and march out of the room.

My body is shaking, and I know I'll need something strong to calm me down. Hades doesn't follow me right away, so I make a beeline for his bar and help myself to one of his top-shelf drinks.

I barely have time to take a sip when he finds me. "What are you doing?"

"Getting ready," I say after I drink the whiskey as a shot.

It burns, almost making me choke. I rarely drink, and when I do, it's usually beer.

"I'm sorry about what I said," he tells me.

His face looks remorseful, but lies can be heartfelt too.

HADES

I can't believe I fucked up again. I'm an idiot who can't seem to find the right thing to say when I'm around Persephone. I assume she was expecting to be told off because of her outfit. She looks like she's going to a rodeo, not an upscale restaurant, and I love that. It's a big "fuck you" to what the Godaire name represents. Yes, it's a shame I'm included with the bad, but it doesn't stop me from enjoying her rebellious act.

She's not a whore, and I've never thought about her in those terms. She's a fiery minx who has the ability to get under my skin and make me lose control. I'd turn this car around and take her back to the house if I thought she'd welcome me into her bed. When I do fuck her, I want her to want me as badly as I do her. Just thinking about it is giving me a boner.

"You look very pretty tonight, by the way," I say to break the glacial silence that's threatening to smother me.

She snorts. "Flattery will get you nowhere."

"I see."

I curl my fingers tighter around the steering wheel and vow to keep my eyes on the road. My foot on the gas pedal becomes heavier, and the car's speed increases exponentially.

"What are you doing?"

"Driving."

"You're going at—" She gasps. "Almost two hundred miles per hour. Are you insane?"

"No, I'm a very good driver."

Going this fast, I don't dare take my eyes off the road. When she whimpers, I ask, "Are you afraid, Skulls?"

"Of dying? Absolutely. Can you please slow down?"

"All right." I drop down to a hundred twenty, which is still far above the speed limit. But everyone in Olympus Bay knows my car, and the chance of getting pulled over is zero.

"Thank you."

Her reply doesn't have a bite, so I decide on a different approach.

"When did you decide to work with flowers?"

"Is this a trick question?"

I flick my gaze to her. "How would asking about your interest be a trick question?"

She bites her lower lip, and I have to look away because damn, that was too much temptation.

"Since I was a little girl. My father was into gardening, and we used to spend time together deep in the dirt."

"Do you miss him?"

"Very much." Her voice is tight. The hurt in her tone is undeniable.

On an impulse, I reach over and grab her hand. She doesn't try to pull away. I count that as a small victory.

"How about you?" she asks.

"What about me?"

"Do you miss your father?"

I laugh without humor. "No."

"I'm sorry."

"Why would you be sorry? He was an asshole."

"I'm sorry you didn't have someone to love when you were a kid."

She's wrong. I did have my rescue pets, but they were ripped from my life in the blink of an eye, leaving me hollow.

"You didn't ask about my mother," I say.

When she doesn't reply right away, I glance at her. She's biting her lip again.

God, give me strength.

"I know she died when you were a baby," she says softly.

"Are you saying you Googled me?" I can't help the smile that tugs at the corners of my lips.

"Of course. I needed to know who I was dealing with."

"And did Google clarify that for you?"

She snorts. "No. You're still a mystery, Hades. Don't worry."

I laugh. "You can ask me questions. I won't bite your head off."

"Riiight. Says the guy who vowed to make me pay for sins I didn't intend to commit."

"Touché. But tonight, I'll make an exception. Any question is fair game."

"Is that so? Okay, then. What's your deal with Hecate?"

I was wondering when that question would come up. "She's a friend."

"She acts like she's more than a friend."

"If you want to ask if Hecate and I were ever involved romantically, just say it, Skulls."

She pauses for a couple beats. "Fine. Were you?"

I shake my head. "No. Never. She's like an extremely annoying younger sister."

"Oh."

Maybe I'm imagining things, but it seems there's a bit of relief in her reply. "Can I ask you another personal question?"

"Sure."

"How come you're still a virgin?"

I cringe hearing the question out loud. *What a fucking stupid move, Hades.*

She laughs, but I can't tell if it's out of amusement or derision.

"Guys suck, and I always thought my first time should be with someone worthy."

I grind my teeth. I'm sure I don't qualify. If I were a better man, I wouldn't collect the debt, but it seems I'm already so deep into whatever is going on here, I can't let go of her yet.

"I'm sorry about what happened to you," I say.

"Me too."

We're approaching Pantheon now, which stands on a hill and looks impressive with its white Greek columns and strategically placed lights that change from blue to purple. There's already a line of cars waiting for the valet. I refrain from asking more questions. It's time to erect my shield and face the music.

I put the car in first gear and pull the handbrake before I turn to Persephone. "Are you ready?"

"I'm not sure what I should be ready for."

"You might see some familiar faces inside."

"Familiar faces?" She furrows her brows, but a moment later, her eyes widen. "Oh, I see."

"I'm sorry. I should have warned you sooner."

She glances out the window. "It's fine. I barely saw the faces in the crowd last night. I only remember you and the bastard who tried to kidnap me today."

Her mention of that son of a bitch yanks my protectiveness

level up several notches. I pinch her chin and turn her face to mine. “He’ll never put his hands on you again. You have my word.”

“I appreciate the sentiment, but you can’t promise me that.”

“The hell I can’t.”

I cup the back of her head and shorten the distance between our mouths. She tenses for a second, but when I pry her lips open with my tongue, she doesn’t resist. Like before, I’m on fire, melting from the inside out.

I almost forget where we are until a loud horn brings me back to reality. I end the kiss with regret, but when I notice how soft her eyes are, I grin like a fool.

20

PERSEPHONE

My stomach is still turned upside down, and my lips tingle. I barely notice getting out of the car or the people I pass by as I walk into Pantheon with Hades by my side. He kissed me again, and damn if it wasn't better than the first time.

His arm is hooked with mine, and all I can feel is his presence, how I want to move closer and meld myself to his frame. The anger is still there, simmering low in my gut, but the butterflies are louder.

Despite my daze, I don't miss the wanton look the hostess gives Hades. It's like I'm not even here. *Bitch.* My fingers curl on reflex, tightening my hold on his arm while I glare at the woman. Out of the blue, he kisses me on the cheek, sending my pulse skyrocketing. The sweetness of his gesture makes my heart soar, and for a moment, I forget why I can't get attached.

The hostess finally sees me, and the jealousy shooting from her eyes makes me grin. "Your party is already waiting for you," she tells Hades through a forced smile. "I can ta—"

"No need. I know the way. Thank you."

Her face falls, and I'm assaulted by the urge to stick my

tongue out at her. But Hades steers me into the busy restaurant, and I'm saved from the childish impulse.

He chuckles, making me curious. "What's so funny?"

"You are."

"What did I do?"

He shakes his head. "Never mind. There are Hermes and Hecate. Let's hurry. I think she's a second away from stabbing him with the butter knife."

I follow Hades's line of sight and spot the pair. Hermes is leaning close to Hecate, looking all enamored, while she's clutching the knife in a vicious hold.

Despite their opposite expressions, I say, "They look good together."

"What makes you say that?"

I shrug. "I don't know. A hunch."

"Don't ever tell Hecate that." He laughs.

The woman in question lifts her gaze to us, and relief is evident in her eyes. "Finally. What took you so long?"

"Distractions." Hades gives me a lust-infused look that makes my knees go weak.

Hecate scowls. "Please spare us the details."

"Speak for yourself." Hermes leans forward, resting his chin on his linked hands. "Tell me everything."

"You're a child." Hecate leans back in her chair, folding her arms.

"No, he's just a savvy businessman who's trying to get information for free." Hades pulls out a chair for me.

Faking outrage, Hermes presses his hand against his chest. "You wound me."

"Yeah, yeah." Hades takes the seat next to mine, moving the chair even closer. His hand immediately finds my thigh, and the touch is electrifying. Hell, how am I supposed to hold on to a conversation when all I can think about is how I want his hand to disappear underneath my skirt?

Hecate picks up the menu and asks, "Have you ever been to Pantheon before, Persephone?"

"No." My voice comes out as a croak, which makes her raise an eyebrow.

I drop my gaze to the menu, but it takes me a couple tries to actually be able to read the offerings. Hades is making small circles against my skin with the tips of his fingers, which has a direct link to how fast my panties are soaking through.

"The oysters are to die for," Hermes pipes up.

"I don't like oysters," I reply.

My face is burning up, so I keep my eyes on the menu, hoping my hair will hide how furiously I'm blushing.

Hades leans closer and whispers, "You won't need oysters tonight anyway."

If I don't put a stop to it, I'll burst into flames. I push his hand off my leg and try to concentrate on the menu for real.

A waiter approaches our table to take our drink orders. It'd be the smart thing to just stick to water since I drank that shot of whiskey earlier and I'm a lightweight. But it seems tonight I'm throwing caution to the wind, because I order a dirty martini instead. I'm surprised when Hades sticks to water, though.

He catches me staring, and maybe my expression shows I'm surprised because he explains, "I never drink when I'm driving the Bugatti."

"That would be suicidal," Hecate chimes in.

I bite my lower lip, "Maybe I should drink water too."

"Why?" She whips her face to mine. "Only one of you is driving. Have fun. Hades is paying anyway." She smirks at him.

"Am I now?"

"Wasn't this Hermes's idea?" I ask. "I think he should pay." Now everyone is looking at me like I said something outrageous. "What?"

Hades's face splits into a radiant smile that sends the damn insects in my belly into a frenzy. "I agree with Skulls."

Oh my God. Why did he have to call me that in front of his friends? I want to disappear through a hole.

"Aw, look at you, already calling her by a cute nickname," Hermes replies. "What do you call him, Skulls?"

Hades makes a noise in the back of his throat that sounds like a growl. "Only I can call her that. It's Persephone to you."

His eyes grow larger. "Whoa. Don't let anyone else see how protective you are of her."

The atmosphere changes in an instant, becoming charged with tension. *Why would Hermes's comment piss him off?*

Hades's expression is closed off as he scans the menu. I try to ignore it, but it takes me a while to be able to read the food options.

When the waiter returns with our drinks, I'm fucking glad I didn't change it to water. I don't wait for a toast before I take a large sip. As I set my glass down on the table, Hades returns his hand to my thigh. I let him have that because his touch is soothing.

A few minutes later, the waiter comes back, but he addresses Hecate first. I'm grateful because I still don't know what I'm having. What I really want is Hades's hand to inch farther up my leg.

I cross them, and that serves two purposes—keeping Hades from granting my secret wish and giving me some relief. My clit is throbbing, begging for attention.

"And you, miss?" The waiter turns to me.

Drat. "Uh, I'll have the... steak."

"Which one?"

Shit. There's more than one? I look at the meat options again.

"She'll have the beef Wellington," Hades answers for me. I glare at him, but his attention is still on the waiter. "I'll have the same."

Once everyone places their orders, Hecate pipes up. "A little high-handed there, friend."

"What do you mean?" He reaches for his glass of water and takes a sip.

"I can order for myself," I grit out.

His eyes widen innocently. "I know you can, but you seemed a little lost. Besides, the beef Wellington is what meat lovers come here for."

"He's right," Hermes chimes in.

I drink more of my martini, hoping it'll keep me from kicking someone's shin under the table.

"I prefer the lobster." Hecate grabs a piece of bread.

I follow her example, not wanting the alcohol to go to my head too fast. I spread some of the creamy butter on it, and when I take a bite, I moan out loud. *Jesus, that's fucking good butter.*

"Please don't do that," Hades tells me in a low voice.

Since I'm still chewing on a little piece of heaven, I can't ask him right away what he means. Surely he doesn't think my reaction was bad.

"Hell, it took him long enough," Hermes says under his breath.

I turn to see what got his attention and immediately tense up. It's Zeus making a beeline toward our table. Hades's hand slips off my thigh, and I miss the connection in an instant.

"My, my, I couldn't believe my eyes when I saw you lot in my restaurant," the asshole says.

No polite greetings, just straight for the barb.

"I don't know why you're surprised, Dad," Hermes replies calmly as he leans against his chair and casually throws his arm behind Hecate's. "This is the best restaurant in town, and we're celebrating."

Zeus's shrewd eyes narrow, not missing the gesture.

Hermes's hint that Hecate is his date was obvious, and it's clearly pissed off his father.

"Celebrating what, exactly?"

My stomach coils tightly. If Hermes mentions celebrating Hades winning at my auction, I might throw up.

Hermes shrugs. "Anything and everything. We don't need a specific reason to enjoy life."

Zeus turns to me, and I try not to flinch. I'm keenly aware of him paying attention to my simple attire.

He looks at Hades. "I'm afraid your date isn't dressed accordingly. I'll have to ask you two to leave."

Kill me now.

"Really, asshole? That's the best you can do?" Hecate complains.

People sitting at the tables nearby are staring, and I don't know what to do myself. My clothes are simple, but I didn't think they were inappropriate.

Hades laughs without humor. "Don't worry, Hecate. Being creative has never been Zeus's strength. He'd rather use idiots with big egos to do his dirty work. How is Salas, by the way?"

"You're an imbecile if you believe this has anything to do with Salas. You dared to bring a whore to my restaurant and couldn't even bother to at least have her dress appropriately."

Tired of the humiliation, I stand up. "If I'm a whore, then what are you? The pimp?"

The surprised rage in his eyes almost makes me take a step back, but I hold my ground. A vein throbs on his forehead. Does he want to strike me? I bet he does, but Hades steps between us, protecting me from his vicious brother.

"Tell your new friend that if he comes close to Persephone again, it'll be the last thing he does in his miserable life."

Zeus smiles, pleased with himself. "You'd better enjoy your whore while you can, little brother."

Hades curls his right hand into a fist and flexes his arm as if he intends to punch Zeus in the middle of the restaurant.

I pull him back. "Don't. He's not worth it."

He looks over his shoulder, and the dark storm brewing in his eyes is intense but not scary—but only because I know his anger isn't aimed at me.

"Way to be a party pooper, Dad," Hermes pipes up.

My gaze is still locked with Hades's when Zeus curses loudly. "What the fuck!"

I see my martini glass in Hecate's hand, and it's empty. Zeus is furiously wiping the front of his slacks while Hecate watches the scene, a wicked smile on her face.

I think I love her.

"Oops," she says.

Hades's arm snakes around my waist, and then we're walking away. It seems the entire restaurant is looking at us now, and I wonder how many overheard Zeus calling me a whore. What does it matter? I bet half the people here were at the auction and know exactly who I am. But it was nice to pretend for a moment that a sickening deal hadn't linked me to Hades.

Outside, he doesn't need to utter a word to the valet; one glance from him has the young man hurrying to bring the car around. Hades still has his arm curled possessively around my waist, which makes me think about Hermes's earlier comment. He warned Hades not to show anyone his protectiveness toward me, and he ignored the advice and did exactly that.

I'm missing a big piece of the puzzle, and I intend to get to the bottom of it. It seems I'm a pawn in this game, but I refuse to be played like that.

Hades's Batmobile comes up the ramp and stops in front of us. As I slide inside the vehicle, I spot Hermes and Hecate making their way, but I shut the door before they reach us.

The engine roars loudly as Hades accelerates. My back flattens against the seat, and my fingers curl automatically, turning into fists in my lap. He's not going that fast yet—he can't until we're out of the restaurant's driveway—but the acceleration was too sudden. I risk a glance at his profile. His jaw is locked tight, and his brows are scrunched together in a deep *V*. I have no idea what he's thinking, but I don't dare ask.

I keep my mouth shut as he reaches the highway and then forgets there's a speed limit. The speedometer once again gets close to the two hundred mark, but this time, I refrain from asking him to slow down. It doesn't take a genius to know the encounter with Zeus set him off. I didn't get out of it unscathed. In fact, I was the only one he offended, but it seems I'm handling the aftermath better than Hades.

At a certain point, I decide it's best if I close my eyes and hope not to die. In hindsight, if he does crash, going this fast will probably mean an instantaneous death. It's only when I feel the car slow down that I open my eyes again. But we aren't back at his place yet. We're in line at an In-n-Out drive-through.

"Burgers for dinner?" I ask.

"Yes. I'm starving and don't feel like going to another restaurant."

My stomach grumbles, agreeing with his choice. "I prefer a cheeseburger over a fancy steak dinner anyway."

His eyes are softer when he smiles. "Me too."

My heart does a backflip, and immediately the common-sense voice in my head screams, *"Nooooo!"* which I promptly ignore.

Shit. I'm so screwed.

21

PERSEPHONE

If I didn't already know Hades was the devil, he proves it tonight by forbidding me to eat my cheeseburger in his car. When we finally return to his mansion, I'm hangry as hell.

"There. We're home. You can stop crying about it."

I try not to feel anything about his usage of the word "home." It makes it sound like we live together and this is *our* home. Unfortunately, the alcohol made my barriers flimsy, and not even my aggravation at being denied food keeps my stupid heart from swelling with emotions it has no business feeling.

I'm the first out of the car, and I stomp like a child in my old cowboy boots all the way to the kitchen. When Hades catches up with me, I'm already chewing a mouthful of burger.

"Did you leave any for me?" He pulls the greasy bag toward him and fishes out the fries.

"Hey! Those are mine," I say with my mouth half-full.

He takes a bite of one. "I paid for them."

His comment rubs me the wrong way, probably because it reminds me that he believes I belong to him too.

"Fine, eat them all. I hope you choke on them."

I take another aggressive bite of my cheeseburger but keep glaring at him.

Hades remains unaffected by my temper tantrum. He leaves the bag alone and walks to the bar in the living room.

I wish he had yelled at me. Now my mean outburst sits heavily in my stomach, making me lose my appetite. I set the burger down and go look in the fridge for a bottle of water.

Hades returns to the kitchen, carrying a bottle of tequila and two shot glasses.

"What's that for?"

"I think we both need drinks."

I furrow my brow, ready to argue, but think better of it. I didn't have the chance to finish my martini, so I think I can handle a shot of tequila without losing my mind. Maybe it'll help me release all this pent-up aggression. If I don't, I'll lash out at Hades, and I'm not sure if he deserves all my rage tonight.

"Yeah we do."

He fills both glasses and then slides one toward me. Then he raises his, and we drink them at the same time. I forgot to ask for the lime and salt and almost choke when the tequila leaves a scorching path down my throat.

"God, this stuff is strong," I say.

"You've never had tequila before?"

I shake my head. "No. All alcohol does is help people make stupid decisions."

He chuckles. "You're not wrong. It's probably why you're still a virgin."

Heat spreads through my cheeks. "Do you have to keep reminding me of that?"

"Don't get mad. I didn't mean to offend you."

I drop my eyes to the counter. "I know. It's just… if I wasn't a virgin, I wouldn't be in this situation."

Hades walks over. "Please don't regret your life choices because of it."

"I don't." I lift my chin, and our gazes collide.

A powerful yearning hits me then. I want to forget about everything that happened tonight and get lost in one of his kisses. I don't take the initiative, though, too afraid that if I do, he'll reject me again. I don't know if he still wants to take his time with me or if his earlier taunt means he's ready to collect.

"One more." I lift my glass.

He fills mine and then his, and once again, we drain them at the same time. All the tension in my body slowly evaporates. Tequila is magic. Hades seems much closer to me now, and when he cups my cheek, I know he's indeed in my personal space.

"I don't think you're a whore," he murmurs.

"I sold my body for sex. That's the definition."

He shakes his head. "I didn't pay for sex."

That confuses the hell out of me. "What did you pay all that money for, then?"

"For you." He rubs his thumb over my lips, making me shiver.

"I'm not a thing that can be bought."

"I know. I couldn't bear the thought of you being sold like that. I just wanted to keep you safe."

His eyes widen just like mine do. It's almost as if he's surprised by his own confession.

"Damn it, Skulls. Why do you make me so unraveled?"

I have no chance to reply before he crushes his lips to mine, prying them open with his possessive tongue. I don't even pretend I don't want him, just throw my arms around his neck and rise on my tiptoes. I taste the tequila, and also something much more intoxicating. It's like I'm kissing a savage god, and I want to drown in him.

Without breaking the kiss, he lifts me off the floor, and I latch on to him like a damn monkey. My skirt rises as I hook my legs around his hips, and his erection presses against my bundle of nerves. The fear is gone. I want him to be my first regardless of any contract. I want to be his even if it's only for one night.

Maybe that's the tequila talking. Alcohol just helps people act on their impulses, right? Or help them make mistakes? I don't know anymore, and I'm way past caring.

He goes up the stairs with me glued to him, and then we're in my bedroom. I'm already tugging at his shirt before he sets me down on the bed, but he leans back and stops me by grabbing my wrists.

"No," he says gruffly. "Not tonight."

"But—"

He presses his finger against my lips. "I'm going to earn this moment, Skulls."

My mind is spinning. I want to scream that he's earned it, that I'm ready, but I'm not sure if that's the truth either. Is this just pure lust, or is there more?

He kisses my chin, then trails down my neck and between my breasts. He doesn't stop to play with them, though. He continues until he reaches my belly button and then glances up.

"Will you let me see what you're wearing under this skirt, darling?"

I nod, unable to form the actual words.

He pushes my skirt up and stares at my bright underwear. A chortle escapes his lips, and then he kisses me right above my panty line. I'm shaking, wondering what he's going to do next.

He unfurls from his crouch, leaving me completely disappointed and confused.

"Where are you going?"

He runs his hand through his hair, messing it up in a deliciously sexy way. I'm gonna die if he doesn't come back to bed.

"I think it's best if I go."

There's a sudden pang in my stomach. Here he goes rejecting me again.

"Says who? It's fucking cruel to turn me on like this and

leave. Unless that's what you want to do, torture me until I go insane."

His eyebrows rise. "You think it's not torture for me?"

He hasn't walked away yet, so I reach for his slacks and rub my hand over his erection. He sucks his breath in, but he doesn't stop me. I unbutton his pants and pull the zipper down. I'm a virgin but not a useless person in the bedroom. Holding his stare, I free his cock, wrapping my fingers around it.

"What are you doing?" he hisses.

"What does it look like?" I lean forward, but once again, he stops me.

"If you put your mouth on me, it's over, Skulls. I'll plunge my cock so deep and fast in you that you won't have time to ask for mercy."

"Was that supposed to scare me?"

"You should be afraid of me, and if you aren't, that's the tequila talking."

"How many times must I throw myself at you before you finally fuck me into oblivion?"

He narrows his eyes. "Is that what you truly want? To shatter into pieces? To come so hard you forget your own name?"

"Yes," I whisper.

He drops to his knees in front of me and opens my legs wide. "I don't need to fuck you for that."

I watch him pull my panties down and toss them aside. His eyes remain glued to mine when he licks my clit in a long and sensual stroke. Leaning on my elbows, I throw my head back and gasp.

"Look at me while I eat your pussy, Skulls."

My face is blazing, but I do as he says. He dives into my folds, first licking and sucking my bundle of nerves without mercy. I've never let a guy go down on me before, and I'm wholly unprepared for the sensations that keep building up faster than a hurricane. My pulse is beating loudly in my ears, and my breathing is coming out in bursts. I know I'm about to come, but I fight it because once I do, he'll most likely leave.

I buckle when the first wave of pleasure hits me. Hades holds my legs tighter and works his tongue as if he's on a mission. I couldn't stop this even if I wanted to. I scream from the top of my lungs as he sends me shooting across the sky in a million pieces. He groans and fucks me with his tongue harder. I climax again within seconds, and now I'm truly, one-hundred-percent obliterated.

It's official. Hades has ruined it for all men.

22

HADES

It takes an extraordinary amount of self-control to taste Persephone's sweetness and walk away from it without taking more. I'm shaking as I stand up and step back, zipping up my pants.

She leans on her elbows and looks at me with hooded eyes. "Where are you going?"

"I can't be here," I grit out.

She sits up and drops her eyes to my crotch. "But… what about you?"

"Don't worry, Skulls."

Her brows furrow, and a glint of determination shines in her eyes. I'm trying to do the right thing here, but it seems she won't let me escape without a fight.

"Stop telling me what I should feel." She jumps to her feet and shortens the distance between us.

My heart is hammering faster than I drove my Bugatti earlier by the time she stops in front of me.

"Fine. I won't. But you're under the influence, and I've already done more to you than I should have."

"So it's okay for you to go down on me, but I can't return the favor?"

My cock twitches inside my slacks. *No. I can't succumb to the temptation.* If I let her do that, I might not be strong enough to stop.

"I already told you that if you put your mouth on me—"

"You'll ravage me. I heard you. But that's a risk I'm willing to take." She drops to her knees and unzips my pants again.

"Persephone...."

Her eyes are defiant when she ignores my plea and wraps her luscious mouth around my cock. I hiss, reaching for her hair. Her fingers curl around the base while she swallows my entire length slowly. God, it almost feels like I'm fucking her pussy. My balls are tight, ready to explode, but I can't yet. I wrap my fingers around a fistful of her hair and yank at the strands.

"Damn it." I throw my head back, closing my eyes.

She releases me with a loud pop and says, "Eyes on me, Hades."

I look down, and only when our gazes are locked does she resume her work. Letting her set the pace is torture—she's working me provocatively slow. It's the only reason I haven't come yet, but hell, I'm done with it. I hold her hair tighter, forcing her head to remain in place, and then I release all my restraint. I fuck her mouth hard, pushing my cock all the way to the back of her throat. Her eyes water, and for a second, I think maybe I should slow down, but the defiant glint in her gaze is still there. I don't think she wants me to go easy on her.

"Fuck!" I yell as I come in her mouth, and don't stop pumping in and out until there's not a single drop left in me.

After a moment, the lust-induced frenzy recedes, leaving me alone with the sordid realization of what I've done. I pull out, and then Persephone drops to the floor, sitting on the backs of her legs. Her face is flushed as she wipes the corner of her mouth. Guilt rams into me, making me feel like the scum of the earth. I knew I should have walked away.

"I'm so sorry," I say.

"For what?"

Jesus, she's too innocent to know. I lean forward and help her to her feet, but she feels unsteady, so I keep holding her.

"I shouldn't have done that to you."

Her forehead crinkles. "I'm not a porcelain doll. You think I didn't like it, don't you?"

"Did you? Don't lie to me."

"It was rough, but I did enjoy it." She tilts her head. "Does that make me a depraved person?"

I caress her cheek. "Not at all, darling."

She steps back and laces her fingers with mine. "Come to bed."

I almost let her steer me toward it. Sleeping next to her would be the perfect ending to an evening that didn't start out great. My body is more than on board with the idea, but my mind stops me in my tracks. "I can't."

"Can't or don't want to?"

I release her hand and step back. "Both. Good night, Skulls."

I turn around before I can see the effect my words had on her. I was harsh, no denying it, but if I lie next to her, there won't be sleep of any kind for a while. I'm not taking her virginity tonight. When that happens, I want to be absolutely sure she wants it.

Out in the hallway, I debate heading downstairs. Sleeping in my own bed might be a bit too close to her. But I also need a cold shower, so in the end, I decide I can be strong enough and not sneak into her room in the middle of the night.

It doesn't occur to me then that *she* could be the one doing that.

PERSEPHONE

Sleep eludes me. I've lost count of how many times I've tossed and turned, making a mess of the sheets, without any hope that Mr. Sandman will visit me anytime soon. I don't know what's going on with me. I thought sex was supposed to make people relaxed, so how come my double orgasms have done the opposite?

There's only one explanation for it. I won't be satisfied until Hades fucks me. I don't understand his hesitation. Does he think he's unworthy of me? If I had said I was waiting for love, then I could pin his reluctance on that, but that's not the case.

I get out of bed and head to the kitchen. Maybe drinking warm milk will do the trick. Or I could just sit in front of the fire. Even if I don't fall asleep, it's better than the agony of not sleeping when Hades is probably snoring in his bedroom without a care in the world.

I'm careful to not make a sound. On my tiptoes, I go down the stairs, but I don't make it halfway down before a bloodcurdling scream almost makes me lose my footing and tumble down the rest of the way.

It's Hades. The scream came from his room. Cerberus howls in his crate, probably sensing he's in trouble.

I rush back up the stairs, worried someone has broken into the house and Hades is in serious danger. I burst into his room, but I don't see any intruder. Hades is jerking on his bed, though. He's having a nightmare.

I run to his side and shake his shoulder. "Hades, wake up."

"No, no. Don't hurt them. Please!"

"Hades!" I shake him harder.

His eyes fly open, and then his right hook follows. It hits my jaw hard, sending me to the floor on my back. Pain flares where he hit me, and I can't do anything but stare at the ceiling and hope the sting will ease.

Damn it. It hurts.

"Persephone! Oh my God."

He turns on the lamp and slides off the bed, pulling me into his lap to stare at me with the most pitiful expression I've seen.

"I didn't know it was you. I'm so sorry."

I wiggle my jaw, hoping it's not broken. "Damn. I can't believe people do this for fun."

He touches my chin softly. "We need to put ice on it."

"Yeah." I begin to get up, but Hades lifts me off the floor and sets me on his bed.

"I'll get it. You stay here."

He runs out of the room before I can say anything. But it's best if I don't move. My head is still ringing from the hit, and I know that wasn't the full strength of his punch. I'm sure my jaw would have shattered if he'd put all his might behind it.

Hades returns a moment later with a bag of ice. He sits on the edge of the mattress and gently presses the cool surface to my throbbing face.

"Ouch."

"I can't tell you how sorry I am that I hit you. I'll never forgive myself for that."

"It was an accident."

He shakes his head. "It doesn't matter."

"Hades… come on. You were having a nightmare. You were probably still in the throes of it when you attacked me."

He winces and then turns away. "I've never laid a hand on a woman before. That's not who I am."

I touch his hand. "I know that."

He whips his face to mine. "How can you? We've just met, and I was horrible to you from the start."

God, he looks so pitiful and remorseful. It breaks my heart.

"The first impression wasn't great, but I'm a pretty good judge of character. I know you're not an asshole."

"I *am* an asshole. I'm forcing you to stay with me because I don't want you to go."

I push the bag of ice aside and sit up. My jaw is numb enough that I barely feel any pain.

"Why don't you want me to go?"

He looks away. "I don't know."

I cup his cheek, and he leans against my caress, closing his eyes for a moment.

"What were you dreaming about?" I ask.

He looks at me, but he doesn't answer right away.

"It's okay. You don't have to tell me," I continue.

"I was reliving a nightmare," he murmurs, his shoulders slumping forward.

My heart constricts painfully, and then I remember what he said about his father. I already know his older brother is an asshole. I start to picture what growing up was like for Hades, and now I don't want him to tell me. It's probably too painful.

I pull him into a hug, resting my cheek against his shoulder. "It's over. You're not in the past anymore."

He hugs me back and then kisses the top of my head. "Sometimes I feel like I'm still there."

I ease back so I can look into his eyes. "I get what you're saying. It's the same for me as well. But right now, you're with me, and the bad memories can't get to you. I won't allow it."

He doesn't say a word as he stares deep into my eyes. I sense when a deeper connection forms between us, making my stomach flip and my heartbeat take off in a mad race.

"I don't deserve you, Skulls," he whispers right before he kisses me, robbing me of the chance to offer a retort to his silly statement.

He keeps it brief, probably afraid to hurt me more. I press my forehead to his and say, "You're wrong. You do deserve me."

"Please don't say things like that. Not when I just punched you."

I laugh. "This was nothing. Perseus got me way worse as kids."

He kisses the tip of my nose. "All the times I said no to you, it wasn't because I didn't want you. I hope you know that."

"Why, then?"

"I want you to be sure of what you're doing."

"Maybe before, I was only trying to get our deal over with, but now, it's different. I do want you, more than I've ever wanted anything in my life."

He traces my collarbone with a featherlight touch. "I'm not sleeping with you tonight, Skulls, no matter how much I want to. I just can't when I can see the damage I did to you."

I touch my jaw and sigh. "Okay. I'll go to my bed now."

He holds my wrist. "No. Please stay."

"Are you sure?"

"Yes. I'll behave. I promise."

I smirk and regret it immediately. Maybe I should put more ice on my wound. I reach for the bag. "You don't need to behave completely."

He smiles. "Not even a punch to the face will kill your libido, huh?"

"Nope. I have a few years of celibacy to make up for."

"I'll get you some painkillers. Maybe that will help."

"If you're trying to make me fall asleep, your fingers would be more helpful."

He shakes his head and then lies in bed next to me. "I suppose I can't deny your request. Not after I gave you that shiner."

I snuggle against him, loving the feel of his chest against my back. I'm already relaxed and he hasn't done anything to me yet.

Who knew I'd find peace in Hades's arms?

23

PERSEPHONE

An arm is wrapped around my middle, and my legs are trapped under a heavy leg when I wake up. Still caught in the fogginess of sleep, it's a miracle I don't freak out. But it's like my body knows exactly who's spooning me even if my brain hasn't caught up with it yet.

Hades's hand is between my legs—I don't know if he put it back there or never moved it from his playtime last night. He nuzzles my neck and flicks my clit with his finger, making me moan.

"Good morning, babe," he whispers.

"Hmm, are you sure it's morning already?"

Another swipe of his finger makes my toes curl. "Yeah, unfortunately."

"What time is it?" I open my eyes and search for a phone or a clock.

I find Hades's phone on the nightstand. I not only see that it's already past eight, but there's also a message from a girl called Aphrodite flashing on the screen. Jealousy takes hold of me, making me tense.

"What's wrong?" he asks.

"Nothing." I slide his hand off me and sit up.

"Let me see your face."

I almost snap, thinking he wants to see if I'm lying, but then remember that he probably wants to check the damage from his punch. So I look at him, and he winces.

"God. I got you good." He touches my jaw with the tips of his fingers. "Does it hurt?"

"No, I barely feel a thing," I lie, because I don't want him feeling guiltier than he already does. "We should get going. It's late, and I have class in an hour."

Another notification flashes on his phone. This time it's a missed call from Aphrodite. His phone is set on Silent. *Hell, why is she bothering him this early in the morning?*

Annoyed, I hand him the device. "Someone is trying to reach you."

He frowns as he stares at the screen, then sits up. I watch as he unlocks his phone and reads her text. Then he glances at me. "You should probably get ready."

My stomach bottoms out. I feel like a fool. Of course Hades would have a parade of women at his disposal. I don't know why I thought I was the only one in his life.

I get up and stalk out of his room. I'm hurt beyond belief, but it's my own damn fault for letting Hades breach my defenses.

When I glance at my reflection in the mirror, I wince. My jaw is purple, and I'm not sure there's enough makeup in the world that will cover it. Helen will demand to know what happened to me, so I'd better think of a good excuse. There's no way I can tell her Hades punched me by accident. Even if she knew I was staying with him—which I have no intention of telling her—the story sounds like the half-baked excuse someone who's enduring domestic abuse would give.

I shower quickly, put on whatever clothes I find first, and then layer on foundation and concealer. You can still see the purplish hue, but it's better than it was before. I'll just say I slipped and fell if people ask.

When I make it to the kitchen, I find Hecate there. She's almost done eating her bagel. I wonder if she eats here a lot.

"Wow, Hades wasn't kidding when he said he got you good."

"Wait, you spoke to Hades this morning?"

"Yeah. He had to leave in a hurry and asked me to drive you to school."

If the feeling of loss wasn't already crippling me, now it feels ten times worse. He left without saying a word to me.

"This is absurd. If he'd let me bring my car here, I wouldn't need to be driven around."

"Hades can be ridiculous sometimes. But hey, if you give me your car keys, I'll pick it up for you."

"He would see it parked in his garage and throw a fit."

She smiles like an imp. "Yeah, one more reason to do it."

I reach for a bagel and break it into small pieces. "Did he tell you where he needed to be this early?"

"Yep." She brings her giant coffee mug to her lips and watches me over the rim.

"To see Aphrodite."

Hecate is smiling when she sets her mug down. "My, my. Are you jealous?"

I cross my arms and glower. "No. Of course not. Why would I be jealous of Hades with another girl? He's not my boyfriend."

She shakes her head and laughs. "It's so funny to watch you two deny the obvious. But whatever."

"You're delusional. There's nothing going on between us. Once he fucks me, I'm out of here."

Her eyebrows shoot up to the heavens. "He hasn't popped your cherry yet?"

My cheeks heat. *Who the hell still uses that expression?*

"No."

"Why not? You were almost fucking each other with your

eyes last night."

Oh God. She must have seen Hades's hand on my thigh. This is not the type of conversation I look forward to first thing in the morning with a veritable stranger.

"Don't know. You have to ask your *bestie*." I shove a piece of bagel in my mouth even though I'm not really hungry.

"I can guess. Hades likes to project this image that he's lethal and mean, but he's a big softy. He won't do anything until he's certain you want to fuck his brains out too."

"He knows I do."

Shit. Did I really say that out loud? It wasn't my intention to give Hecate more ammunition to tease me.

"Maybe, but he's like a mule sometimes, stubborn as hell. You need to give him a couple shoves to get him moving in the right direction, if you know what I mean." She wiggles her eyebrows up and down.

"Yeah, I get your meaning."

"Don't worry about Aphrodite. There's nothing going on between them."

I shrug. "Don't care if there is."

She laughs. "Please, don't ever try to gamble. Your poker face is a disgrace." She wipes her face with a napkin and stands. "Are you ready?"

"I just need to grab my backpack. I'll meet you in the garage in a minute."

HADES

I park at the back of Playground, the upscale nightclub owned by Aphrodite Loveless. Unlike most of the powerful players in this town, she's not originally from Olympus Bay. She arrived a few years back with her younger brother Eros in tow, paid in cash for one of the biggest oceanfront properties for sale at the time, and, a few months later, opened Playground. No one knows much about her past or where her fortune comes from. She's a mystery Hermes has been trying to solve all these years without any luck, much to his chagrin.

I hate that I had to leave the house in a hurry without telling Persephone why. She saw who the message was from and must be thinking the worst right now. It couldn't be helped. I didn't want to worry her needlessly.

The security guard at the back entrance nods when I approach and silently opens the door for me. I enter a dark corridor illuminated only by low blue lights. If I follow this path directly, it'll lead me to the main room of the club, but I turn left at the first intersection and then knock on the door at the end of the corridor.

Another security guard opens the door, and I finally enter Aphrodite's private room. The atmosphere is dark and seductive when the club is open, but right now, all the lights are bright, which takes away from the ambience.

She's speaking in hushed tones with two men I don't recognize, but they're tall, muscular, and carrying concealed weapons under their jackets. I only pay attention to them for a moment before my eyes land on Dionysus, sprawled on one of the luscious couches, looking like a lion chewed on him and spat him out. His clothes are in tatters, and there are bloodstains everywhere. He has an ice pack over his eye, and his lips are busted.

I stalk toward him and drop to a crouch so I'm at eye level with him.

"Hey, Hades. You came." He cracks a smile, or tries to.

"Dio, what the fuck happened to you?"

"I think I pissed off the wrong crowd. I don't know. The details are a bit hazy."

Aphrodite approaches and hands over a bloodied note. "This

was stapled to his chest when we found him in the back alley."

My nostrils flare when I read the contents of the note. It's from Zeus. I crumple it into a ball so tight it almost cuts my palm.

"What's going on, Hades? Why is your family feud staining my domain with blood?" she asks.

I unfurl from my lower position. "Because my brother is a piece of shit, and he wants to get to me at any cost."

"I didn't ask for the obvious answer. I know very well who your brother is. But he's never dared to involve me in his affairs before."

"This has nothing to do with you."

Fire blazes in her green eyes. "He cornered one of my best patrons and beat the shit out of him behind my club. Tell me how this has nothing to do with me."

I pass a hand over my face. "I didn't mean it like that."

"Playground is successful because my clients know it's safe to come here. Shit like this"—she points at Dionysus—"is bad for my business."

"Why are you telling me this? I didn't order my friend to be beaten up. Your issue is with Zeus. Go complain to him."

She steps forward and pokes my chest. "No, Hades. My issue is with you. You're the reason Zeus is acting more recklessly than usual. You interfered in the auction. Salas Ciriano was guaranteed to have Persephone."

I narrow my eyes to slits. "Guaranteed? What do you know about Zeus's deal with that scum?"

"Don't get your panties twisted in a bunch. I know what everyone with a functioning brain does. Zeus is desperate to find a way to break into the European market, but he doesn't have a secure route. You're not cooperating, so he turned to Dimas Ciriano and his cargo fleet."

I let her insult slide. I had already figured out that much about Zeus's plan.

"That's not what I'm asking. Why was Persephone part of the deal?"

Aphrodite blinks fast and then looks over my shoulder. When she answers, it's in a much lower tone. "This isn't information I can vouch for, but it seems there's a link between Salas Ciriano and Persephone's late father, Walter Flores. If you want to know the truth, I'd start there."

"Hey, guys. Not to be a burden, but when can I go home?" Dionysus whines.

"Do I need to take you to a hospital?" I ask.

"My physician has already checked him. He doesn't have any broken bones," Aphrodite replies.

"Good," I say when nothing truly is. Zeus couldn't punish me, so he went after one of my closest friends.

I call Hercules immediately, fearing that he also sent his goons after Perseus.

"Good morning, boss," Hercules answers in a surprisingly cheerful tone.

"Where are you?"

"Uh, I'm at my post, watching the kid."

"Hey, I'm not a kid," Perseus complains in the background.

"Wait. You're inside the house with him?" I pinch the bridge of my nose.

"Eh, yes. He caught me stalking the house, so I had to come clean or he'd call the cops on me."

That's a load of crap. Hercules is the stealthiest guy I know. He wouldn't get caught unless he wanted to. But I don't have time to get to the bottom of this right now. I have to take care of Dio first.

As I help him up from the couch, Aphrodite warns me, "This is just the beginning. Zeus won't allow you to mess up his expansion plans. I hope Persephone is worth the hassle."

"She's not worth the hassle," I state matter-of-factly. "She's worth the war."

24

PERSEPHONE

Miraculously, I don't miss my morning class. Hecate drives like a maniac, just like Hades does, and I arrive at school with minutes to spare. Concentrating on the lecture is a different matter, though. I'm still riding on the jealousy train despite Hecate's assurances that there's nothing going on between Hades and Aphrodite.

I keep checking my phone, stupidly hoping for a text from Hades. For someone who promised he wouldn't leave my side, he sure dropped me like a hot potato at the first chance. I'm so lost in my head that I have no idea if my makeup did a good job at concealing the bruise on my chin. But when I meet with Helen after class, I have my answer.

"Seph, what the hell happened to you?"

"What do you mean?" I play dumb.

"Your face. How did you get that bruise?"

"Oh, this?" I touch my jaw. "I slipped and fell yesterday. You know what a klutz I am."

She narrows her eyes, scrutinizing me. Maybe Hecate is right, and I can't lie to save my life.

"Where did you fall?"

"Near the library. I was caught in the rain and tried to run for cover. You know me, I can never win a fight against a wet floor." I smile, hoping she doesn't see the deception through my bad joke.

The frown doesn't disappear from her forehead, though. When she puts her hands on her hips, I know I'm in trouble.

"I have a bone to pick with you."

I widen my eyes innocently. "What did I do?"

"You never told me you were dating Hades."

Whoa. Where did that question come from?

"Uh, what?"

"Don't 'what' me, Seph. You were seen at Pantheon with him last night."

My mortification returns with a vengeance. Did Helen's source also tell her about the words exchanged? If she ever finds out I allowed myself to be sold at an auction, I'll never be able to look her in the eye again.

"I'm not dating him. It was dinner with friends. Hecate and Hermes were also there."

"*Friends?* I'm your best friend, and I've never heard about those people before. What's going on? I thought Hades hated you because of the accident with his dog."

Fuck. Maybe I should have told her I'm dating him, but then I'd have to lie again and pretend to be upset when we part ways.

Sadness pierces my chest. I won't need to pretend that part. I'll be crushed when that happens.

Damn it, when did I let Hades take over my heart like that?

"He clearly no longer hates me." I start walking toward my next class.

"Fine, let's say I believe you aren't a couple. But do you think there's a chance the situation might change?"

Ugh, I forgot how relentless Helen can be when the subject is my love life.

"I don't know. I can't predict the future. But speaking of

relationships, is everything okay between you and Paris? I noticed a certain tension during the underground fight."

Her expression closes off. "There was no tension. Sometimes when you've been dating someone for that long, they get on your nerves."

"But isn't that a sign that things aren't going well?"

I expect her to refute my argument, but instead, she grows quiet. Her gaze is downcast, making me feel guilty for broaching the subject only to deflect her questions about Hades. I'm a sucky friend.

I throw my arm over her shoulder. "I'm sorry, hon. I didn't mean to upset you. What do I know about relationships? I've never had a steady boyfriend."

She stops suddenly and turns to me. Her eyes are filled with anguish, which makes me worried. "What if I did something to screw up everything with Paris?"

"My first question would be 'Is it that bad, or are you just making a storm out of a glass of water?'"

"Oh, Seph. It's really bad."

Helen is getting ready to spill the beans in the middle of the hallway, which isn't the best place for this type of conversation. I'm about to suggest we go somewhere more private when Prof. Cashore approaches. He sees me, and I swear his lips curl into a sly grin. It sends shivers of disgust down my spine.

"Hello, Persephone. I'm looking forward to our chat later," he says and then continues down the hall.

My blood is ice cold now. I forgot about my meeting with the man.

"What was that all about?" Helen asks.

"Ugh. He wants to meet at a café later to discuss how I can make up for missing the test."

Her eyes grow larger. "Is he for real? And you said yes?"

"I don't have a choice. I can't flunk his class."

"He's up to something. You should wear a wire and record the meeting."

I laugh without humor. "You've been watching too many spy movies. Where would I get a wire?"

"Fine. Record the conversation with your phone, then."

I think about her suggestion. "I probably should do that. But knowing me, I'll end up screwing things up."

"What time is the meeting? Maybe I can be there."

"He knows who you are."

"I can be in disguise."

The hopeless glint she had in her eyes a moment ago is gone, and I'm glad about that. But I also curse Prof. Perv's ill timing. Helen was about to tell me something important, and now I don't think she will. I'll have to wait for another time to try to get her to open up.

"I'm meeting him at two o'clock at Ida Café."

Her eyebrows shoot up. "Why there? It's old and dingy, and no one likes that place."

"Probably the reason he chose that one. Less chance of being interrupted by people I know."

She squints. "I'll be there, Seph. It's high time we deal with that disgusting man."

Relief washes over me. I'm so grateful that I pull her into a bear hug. "Thank you."

I can't tell her about every fucked-up thing that's happening in my life, but at least she can help me with this problem.

"You're welcome." She pulls back and then glances at a point over my shoulder. "Shit! I'm late for a group meeting. I gotta run."

I watch her sprint down the hallway in her high-heeled boots and laugh out loud. Helen is always running late somewhere. At least she can run wearing those shoes without falling. I've always envied her dexterity.

On my way to class, I text Perseus to check on him, not

expecting a prompt reply. Color me surprised when it comes through right away.

PERSEUS: Everything is fine, Seph. Stop worrying.

ME: It's my job to worry. I'm your big sis, remember?

PERSEUS: How can I forget? You remind me all the time.

ME: Ha ha.

PERSEUS: How's your boyfriend?

I grumble out loud. He had to speak of the devil I'm trying to forget.

ME: He's not my boyfriend.

PERSEUS: Say hi to him anyway. And remember to use protection.

My face bursts into flames. *Why couldn't I have had a little sister instead?*

I'm only a couple of steps from the classroom when I hear a comment that sets my teeth on edge.

"That's the one who was kicked out of Pantheon last night."

"And she was Hades's date?" another girl asks.

"Yup. Don't know what he sees in her. Total white trash."

I had every intention to ignore them, but fuck those bitches. I spin around. "Who are you calling trash, bitch?"

Ah hell. I recognize one of them. It's the hostess who was drooling over Hades. They widen their eyes, and then their gazes focus on my bruise.

The hostess sneers, "My bad. I guess you aren't trash, just a common whore."

I curl my hand into a fist, ready to give her a matching shiner to mine when someone steps next to me.

"Did you just call my friend a whore?"

The hostess blanches. "Hermes, I—"

"Don't waste your breath. I heard you loud and clear. You'd better go update your résumé."

Her face turns stark white. "I… you can't fire me."

He puckers his lips and taps his finger over them. "I can't? Hmm, the last time I checked, my last name is Godaire."

The girl has tears in her eyes now, and I feel bad. She was awful to me, but what if she needs the job? I know too well what it's like to live paycheck to paycheck.

"That's not fair. I was just repeating what your father said," she whines.

"Not my fault you're a brainless bimbo without an original thought in your head. Now get out of my sight. You're a waste of space."

Damn. I never knew Hermes could be so vicious with his words.

Both girls scurry away and disappear around the corner.

"You don't need to fire her," I tell him.

His gaze is still hard and locked in the direction they went when he replies, "I know. But I want to."

"What if she needs the money?"

He gives me a quizzical look. "You were about to bitch-slap her, and now you're worried about her finances?"

"I'd rather give her a black eye than make her homeless."

Hermes shakes his head. "Don't worry. She's not poor. Besides, I'm fairly certain she's sucking my father's dick. She'll be fine,—that is, until he gets bored of her."

I don't even balk at his crude words. I guess hanging out with the gods of Olympus Bay has desensitized me to depraved things.

"Well, thanks for the save, I guess." I start for the classroom.

"Uh, it was self-serving," he says with a straight face.

"Why am I not surprised? What do you want?"

"Nothing crazy." He rubs the back of his neck, losing a bit of his cockiness. "Could you maybe talk me up to Hecate if you have the chance?"

My jaw drops, and I wait for the punch line, because he's clearly joking.

"We're still on this?"

"I can't help it. The heart wants what the heart wants. You of all people should know that."

I glower. "What's that supposed to mean?"

"Come on, Persephone. My job is to gather information, read people. You're in love with Hades. Don't try to deny it."

The hell I am!

I cross my arms. "You're mistaking attraction for feelings."

"I'm not. Don't worry. He feels the same way about you." He smirks, then walks away, leaving me standing there with my jaw hanging to the floor.

25

PERSEPHONE

I spend the better part of my day obsessing about Hades and all the things his friends told me. I refuse to believe they're right, though. Hades doesn't have feelings for me. Best-case scenario, he's developed a bit of an obsession, probably triggered by the fact that another man wants me.

It's almost time for my meeting with Prof. Cashore, and the sunken feeling in my stomach has turned into an ache. My phone pings with a text message, and I totally expect to see Helen's name on my screen. But it's Hades wondering why I'm not in the economics building where I should have been.

Oh, the nerve of that man! My class was canceled, so I went to the library to kill time. He must have memorized my schedule and went there to pick me up as if he were my boyfriend.

I ignore his message. I don't owe him an explanation, and I'm still angry about him ditching me this morning without a word. Ida Café is right in front of me anyway. I have to prepare to deal with Prof. Perv and can't worry about Hades now.

My palms are clammy as I open the door and search for the creep inside. There's barely anyone here, and it's not surprising. It seems the place has gotten worse since the last time I came.

It's dark, and it smells funky. The tables and chairs have seen better days. Some of the fake leather upholsteries are torn in places, and the tiled floor has multiple cracks. I'm not sure why this place hasn't been renovated or sold to someone who can do a better job at managing it. I'm sure it isn't profitable.

I spot the jackass in a booth all the way in the back. He had to pick the most private spot in the joint.

I don't see Helen anywhere, so I check my phone for any messages. Nothing.

ME: Where are you?

HELEN: I'm sorry. I'm running late.

I grumble. I should have known. It seems I'll have to try to catch the perv in action on my own. I press the Record button on my phone before I shove it back in my purse, then head over to his table. He smiles from ear to ear when he sees me, making me nauseous. He's approaching his fifties, and it shows. Balding hair, deep bags under his eyes, and those yellow, crooked teeth that make him look like a troll. But it's the way he stares at me as if he's picturing me naked that makes my skin crawl.

"Hello, Prof. Cashore." I slide across the booth seat opposite his.

"Hi, Persephone. I was beginning to think you were going to stand me up."

"Uh, I'm only a couple minutes late."

And this isn't a date, asshole.

"Well, I'm here," I continue. "What do I need to do to make up for the test I missed?" I get straight to the point, not wanting to spend a second more than necessary in his company.

He furrows his brows. "What's the hurry, honey? You just got here. Have some coffee first, maybe a slice of pie. You like sweets, don't you?"

Oh my God. He's not even trying to hide his intentions. My skin crawls just from sitting across from him. But he hasn't said anything inappropriate yet besides calling me "honey," so I have to suffer his presence for a little longer.

He flags the waitress, who takes her time coming over. *Hurry the fuck up, please.*

"What would you like to drink, Persephone?" he asks me when the woman stops by our table with notepad in hand.

I honestly don't want anything, but I have to pretend I'm not on the verge of throwing up. "I'll have an espresso."

"Same for me," he tells her.

The waitress nods. "All right. Would you like to see the menu?"

I say, "No," at the same time he says, "Yes."

He chuckles, and I don't know what he finds so amusing.

"I'll have the menu. Thank you," he replies.

He rests his elbows on the table and leans forward. I do the exact opposite, leaning back as far as I can, flattening my back against the fake leather seat, and crossing my arms. When he stretches his legs, brushing them against mine, I slide my feet back, and my muscles tense, preparing to flee.

"Listen, Prof. Cashore. I appreciate you taking the time to meet with me, but I have to be at work in half an hour," I lie. "Could you please tell me how I can make up for the test? If it's an assignment I need to write, just tell me the subject."

"You really don't know why I asked you to meet with me here, do you?" He shakes his head and smiles slyly. "I thought I was being pretty obvious, Persephone."

Oh God. So he wasn't even trying to hide how creep-tastic he was?

"Uh, I'm confused." I play dumb, hoping he'll see that I'm not in the least interested in him and back off.

The waitress returns with our order, and he straightens his posture as if he doesn't want her to notice his interest in me.

I don't think I can drink anything with the way my stomach is unsettled. But it's better to focus my attention on something other than the sleazy man in front of me. I load the espresso with sugar, then glance at the door while I stir the coffee, praying Helen will come in.

He takes my momentary distraction and grabs my free hand, making me jerk. I try to pull away, but he holds it tighter. His touch is repulsive, and I already feel the need to shower.

"You're young and gorgeous, and completely out of my league, but I'm a hopeless romantic anyway. If you come away with me for the weekend, I promise you won't have to worry about any grades."

"Let go of my hand," I grit out.

"It's just a weekend, honey. We'll have fun, I promise." He rubs his thumb over my knuckles, making bile rise up my throat.

I should get him to spell out what he wants from me in exchange for a passing grade, but I can't bring myself to push for that confession. I'm on the verge of tears already, and that makes me feel like a loser. I'm not a damsel in distress, I could throw my coffee in his face and get out of here, But I'm frozen in shock. *Why does this shit keep happening to me?*

"I'm not going away with you. This is preposterous." I finally get my hand free and immediately slide out of the booth.

Prof. Cashore is already halfway out when a presence stops him short. His pasty face grows even paler, and his beady eyes widen. I don't need to turn to know who's standing next to me.

"You piece of shit," Hades says in a dangerously low tone before he pulls Prof. Cashore up by the lapels of his jacket. "How dare you try to coerce one of your students into sleeping with you?"

"I… that's not what happened here. I wasn't coercing anyone." He looks at me pleadingly. "Tell him, Persephone."

"I'm sorry, Prof. Cashore, but I won't tell lies."

"You little b—"

Hades grabs him by the neck, cutting him off.

"Go on. Insult her in front of me. I dare you."

His eyes bulge as he begins to turn purple. Hades shows no sign that he intends to stop squeezing his neck. He's going to strangle the man in front of all these witnesses. I can't let him get in trouble because of this scum.

"Hades, please. Let him go."

He narrows his eyes and applies more pressure to the creep's neck. It seems my plea had the opposite effect intended.

"Hades!" I pull his arm back with a jerky movement, and Prof. Cashore staggers backward, wheezing. Hades turns to me, looking incensed, so I say, "He's not worth it."

The rage in his eyes doesn't dim, and it's now aimed at me. He grabs my arm and barks, "Let's go."

I don't make eye contact with the few people in the café as I let Hades steer me out of the place. He's too angry, and I don't want to cause a scene. I'm too tired of having embarrassing moments in public.

He doesn't release me as we cross the main park on campus at a rapid pace, and then I see his Batmobile sitting in a no-parking zone. He opens the door for me, then stalks around the front of the car, looking like he's possessed. Only when he's on the other side do I get in.

He doesn't drive right away. He's gripping the steering wheel hard and glaring at the windshield. I rub the sore spot his tight hold left on my arm as I swallow the huge lump in my throat. He's angry with me, and I don't know why. All I did was try to get my academic life back on track. It's not my fault Prof. Cashore is a horrible man.

Hades whips his face to me. "Did I hurt you?"

"No."

"Don't lie to me," he says through clenched teeth.

"I'll live."

He looks away and passes a hand over his face. "I'm a fucking menace."

"Don't say that."

He doesn't reply or look at me, just turns the car on and drives off.

I don't know what to say, so I just bite my tongue and remain quiet during the trip, but my mind is whirling nonstop. My chest is tight, and my stomach still hasn't recovered from my meeting with Prof. Cashore. I hate feeling like this, untethered.

I receive a text message and see it's from Helen. I also remember that my phone is still recording everything. I stop it, then reply to her before she freaks out, telling her the situation has been taken care of. The three dots appear, but I shove my phone back in my purse. I don't have enough emotional spoons to text her back and forth.

My phone rings a moment later, which I also ignore. It stops when it goes to voice mail.

Hades remains quiet. Good. I don't want to talk to him either.

When the tall walls that surround his property come into view, I feel relieved. I can maybe escape to my room and not have to feel his wrath.

I'm the first out of the car, which has become a habit of mine. I sprint up the front stairs, going up two steps at a time. I don't make it past the living room before Hades grabs my arm and spins me around.

"What the—"

His mouth slants over mine, cutting me off.

He kisses me like he's drowning and I'm the air he needs. Caught in his vortex, I grab his face between my hands and meet his claim stroke for stroke. I can't remember anymore why I was supposed to be mad at him.

With our lips still fused together, he lifts me off the floor and sets me on the kitchen counter. My head is spinning, unable to hold on to any thoughts. All I care about is the man who's devouring my mouth. He leaves my lips to run his hungry tongue down the column of my neck. I arch my back, offering him anything he wants to take and more.

He cups my breasts over the T-shirt, and I wish our clothes were gone.

"Hades," I whisper.

"What is it, Skulls?" He looks up, leveling me with a heated glance so intense, it sets me ablaze.

"You're the one I've been waiting for. I don't care about how we came to be together. I want you, just you."

He watches me with his penetrating gaze for a couple of beats before he sweeps me off the counter and carries me up the stairs to his bedroom. It seems like forever ago since I woke up in his arms on his bed. I was more than ready for him then, and now I'll claw out of my own skin if he doesn't make me his.

He sets me down in the middle of the mattress and steps back. He remains silent as he stares at me, eating me with his eyes. My insecurities decide to make an appearance, and I'm hit with the urge to cover myself—and I'm not even naked yet. I'm shaking, and my heart seems like it's going to explode out of my chest.

"God, you're breathtaking," he murmurs.

"What I am is lonely in this huge bed."

Did I really say that out loud?

Hades's eyes widen a fraction before his lips curl into a grin. He reaches for the back of his shirt and takes it off. My mouth waters as his inked chest comes into view. I already knew he was sculpted perfection, but seeing him in broad daylight solidifies the emotions in my chest. He's beautiful, mercurial, and savage, but also kind and loving. The realization hits me like a cannonball. I never stood a chance; I was destined to fall for this man no matter how hard I fought.

He gets rid of his jeans and boxers next, and I try not to whimper. It's desire that's turning my head upside down, but I don't want him to think I'm afraid to continue. He needs to know I'm one-hundred-percent sure of my decision.

Following his example, I take off my T-shirt, lobbing it to the side. I'm wearing a black bra with tiny skulls, and that clearly pleases him. His smile is broader now, wolfish.

"Shall I help you out of those jeans?" He drops to his knees and reaches for the button before I can say yes.

Leaning back on my elbows, I watch him unzip my pants and then peel them off my legs painfully slowly. He leaves my panties on. With a chuckle, he parts my legs, then toys with the seams of my underwear. I never knew a simple touch could cause such a maelstrom of sensations in my body. I'm panting, so desperate for him to inch his fingers closer to my center that it's almost an ache.

"I love your choices in underwear, sweetheart." He presses a kiss to my pubic bone over the fabric.

"Hades, please…."

"Please what?" He kisses me again, lower this time, but not quite where I need his mouth to be.

"I'm dying here."

He laughs again, blowing hot air over my sensitive skin. I gasp, caught by surprise when the first tendrils of orgasm hit me.

"Make that sound again, beautiful."

"Please touch me. I'm begging you."

He licks my clit over the fabric, and my hips buck. "Oh my God."

With a groan, he slides the fabric aside and sucks my clit into his mouth. I scream louder, completely overwhelmed by the wave of pleasure that rips me apart. My back arches as I press my head against the mattress. My fingers are curled around the cover in a vicious hold because it's the only thing anchoring me to this reality. I don't know if I'm flying or falling.

Hades's tongue is everywhere: over my clit, inside my pussy.

I can't keep track. He leans back to finally get rid of my panties, then slides his finger inside me, making me tense a bit.

"I love how wet you are already, babe. Does this hurt?"

It's a strange sensation, but it doesn't hurt. I shake my head. "No."

"Good." He puts another finger in and gives me a sample of what's to come soon—at least I hope so.

I close my eyes and moan, "This feels good."

"It'll feel even better in a second." He pulls his finger out, and when he doesn't replace it with his tongue, I open my eyes.

He's standing in front of the nightstand, looking for something in the drawer. When he turns, I see the foil packet between his fingers. I swallow hard. This is finally happening.

"Do you want to help me put it on?" he asks.

"I…." Blush creeps up to my cheeks. "I'm afraid to screw it up."

He rips the packet and pulls the condom out. "It's easy. You'll do it next time." He pinches the top and then rolls the condom down his shaft. Then he gets on his hands and knees on the mattress and lowers his mouth to my belly. Goose bumps form where he draws his tongue along my skin, going up until he finds my breasts. He teases one nipple, flicking it mercilessly until it turns as hard as a pebble, while he kneads my other breast with his hand. It's a sensory assault that's making the room spin.

He's keeping his body hovering over mine, but I need more of him. I bring my knees up and cross my legs at the ankles behind him, forcing him to come closer. He releases my nipple with a soft pop and inches his way up until his sexed-up face is in front of mine.

"Hello there." He smiles lazily.

"Hi." I smile back.

He traces my hairline with a featherlight touch. "I've never met anyone more beautiful than you."

I bask in his compliment, but a part of me can't believe a guy like him would think that about me.

"Have you looked at yourself in the mirror lately?" I joke to hide my insecurity.

He kisses me softly and slowly, but it still has the same devastating effect on me. The butterflies in my stomach are awake and wild. I think if my heartbeat accelerates any more, I might die of a heart attack.

The tip of his erection presses against my entrance, and I know he's holding back, because I'm slick as hell and one tiny movement will do the trick.

I run my fingers down his back and then grab his ass, digging my nails in. He slides a little farther in.

"Skulls, I don't want to hurt you," he whispers against my lips.

"You won't. I'm ready, babe. Please make me yours."

"Damn it, woman. You know exactly what to say to drive me wild."

With a single thrust, he fills me completely. There's a sharp pain at first, which I hope I was able to hide from him.

"Are you okay?"

I nod and then kiss him hard. He mimics my enthusiasm with his hips, moving in and out in a delirious rhythm. My initial discomfort soon vanishes, and I'm able to enjoy every bit of pleasure from this moment.

Hades leans back and lifts one of my legs over his shoulder, which allows him to penetrate much deeper. And just when I thought this couldn't get any better, holy hell. It's not only the new angle that's toe-curling, it's watching his muscles flex, his hooded gaze as he looks at me, that's already melting my bones.

"Your pussy feels so good, babe." He rubs his thumb over my lips while his face shows exactly how much he's enjoying fucking me.

I suck his thumb into my mouth, making him hiss. He

increases the tempo of his thrusts, and then he hits a secret spot inside me that has me seeing stars. I release his thumb and gasp loudly, not daring to believe this earth-shattering orgasm is real.

"That's it, beautiful. Come for me."

He's moving so fast now that the headboard is banging against the wall. He seems to grow larger inside me, or maybe I'm squeezing him somehow. He lets out a roar and then returns to the position we started in so he can claim my lips again. He doesn't stop or slow down, not even when I scratch his back or gently bite his shoulder.

With a final, deep thrust, he stills and then collapses completely on top of me. He's blocking my airway, but I don't want him to move an inch. I'm loving the weight of his body over mine. Breathing hard, he slides to the side, allowing me to breathe properly again.

"That was... wow." He laughs.

"I'll take your word for it."

He turns his face to mine. "What do you mean?"

"I have no previous experience to compare."

He snakes his arm around my waist as he rests on his side. "And you won't have any experiences with anyone else if I have anything to say about it."

My heart soars at his comment, but then my brain reminds me that he bought my virginity, and now our bargain is fulfilled.

"Hades...."

He silences me by placing his forefinger over my lips. "Shh. Don't let your pretty head put a damper on our happiness."

"I can't help it. You got what you paid for. There's no reason for me to stay."

His face twists into a scowl. "Yes, there is. I *want* you to stay."

He's saying everything I want to hear, but why does my chest still feel like it's being crushed?

"I don't belong to your world."

"You belong with me. And that's all that matters."

With me, not *to* me. My eyes prickle with the tears that are forming in them. If I bawl them out in front of him, he'll get the wrong idea for sure. But I don't want to keep talking about a future that most likely won't come to pass.

Smiling, I cup his cheek and say, "You were worth the wait."

26

HADES

Persephone fell asleep a while ago, and I haven't been able to leave her side. Never mind that I have a million things to take care of, and one of them includes dealing with Zeus. But the world can burn for a little longer while I take my fill of her.

I vowed to never let myself become consumed by anyone. I wasn't prepared for her, and now I can't bear the thought of letting her go.

It was by sheer luck that Hermes saw Persephone enter Ida Café and texted me. I see red again when I think about that fucking perv trying to force Persephone into sleeping with him for a passing grade. He'll never teach again if I have anything to say about it.

Voices coming from downstairs tell me my time is up. I don't want my visitors to wake Persephone, so reluctantly, I slip out of bed, get dressed, and head down to tell Hecate and Dionysus to shut the fuck up.

Not surprisingly, I find him sprawled on my couch while she raids my fridge. He lifts his head when I walk into the living room, still looking as dreadful as a few hours ago. My annoyance simmers down. He's messed up like that because of me.

"The god of doom and gloom finally emerges." The pest grins despite his busted lip.

"What are you doing here? I thought you were dying." I crouch in front of Cerberus's crate to let him out.

"Don't blame me. Hecate was the one who dragged my ass up here."

I turn to her, and she pouts. "You bet your ass I did. I didn't sign up to be a nurse."

I can't fault her for the sour mood. I did dump Dio at her doorstep after I picked him up from Playground, and then I went to see Hercules to discuss increased security for Perseus. It's been hours though. I'm surprised she waited this long to complain about her "guest."

Cerberus jumps on me as soon as I open the crate, licking my face in happiness. Few things can brighten up my day when I'm feeling down, and he's at the top of the list.

I laugh and scratch his back. "How are you, buddy? I'm sorry I neglected you earlier."

"Where's the guest of honor?" Hecate asks.

"She's sleeping, so be quiet." I get up and head for the kitchen.

Cerberus trails after me despite his broken leg. I can tell he wants to jump up and down on Hecate but can't. Poor thing. A few days ago, that sight would make me mad as hell and blame Persephone. It's crazy how I don't anymore. She still unravels me and makes my head spin, but in a good way.

"Sleeping, huh? Does that mean it's done, then?" She raises an eyebrow.

I grumble, not in the mood to discuss what happened in my bedroom with her, or anyone for that matter.

"I'm not gonna tell you anything."

"Can you guys speak louder? I can't hear a word," Dio complains from the couch.

Neither of us acknowledges him. I grab something to eat from the fridge and try my best to ignore Hecate's scrutiny.

"I'm happy for you, Hades."

I frown, opening my mouth to reply, then think better of it.

"Why are you sulking? You've been pining for Persephone since you brought her home," she adds.

"That's a lie. I didn't like her then." I start cutting veggies to make a salad, but if I'm not careful, I might end up losing a finger. Hecate is getting to me.

"Oh, so touchy. Anyway, I assume you aren't sending her home."

I set the knife down and look at her. "More than ever, I can't send her away. It seems Salas's obsession isn't new, and until that scum is dealt with, she'll stay where I can protect her."

"What about Zeus? You can't let him get away with what he did to Dio."

"I heard my name. Now I demand to know what you guys are talking about," he chimes in.

I forget the salad and return to the living room. I didn't have a chance to ask a lot of questions about his attack, so I might as well do it now while Persephone isn't around. I don't want to make her more worried.

"Did you recognize the guys who cornered you?"

"No. They weren't any of Zeus's goons. They had accents, though. Greek is my guess."

"Probably Salas's men." Hecate snorts. "Zeus is not only a coward but a lazy one."

"I don't understand why they came after me. I've always tried to stay out of Zeus's path."

I make a fist, wishing Zeus was in front of me so I could flatten his face. "You're my friend. That's enough."

"And who is this Salas guy?"

"Someone Zeus wants as an ally badly."

Dio scratches his head, frowning. "I'm still confused."

Hecate joins us in the living room. "Basically, Zeus promised Persephone to Salas, and then Hades swept in and took her for himself. Now both are pissed at him."

I glower. "That's an oversimplification of things."

She gives me a droll look. "I have to explain things to Dio as if he were five."

"Hey! I take offense to that," he complains.

Narrowing my eyes, I tilt my head and watch him closely. I can't tell if he's annoyed for real, but hell, it doesn't matter.

"Aphrodite heard rumors that Salas's connection to Persephone may go back to her late father," I say.

"How old was she when he died?" Hecate asks.

"Eight, I believe."

A glint of sheer horror shines in her eyes, and her face becomes paler.

"What is it?" Dio asks.

She shakes her head. "Nothing."

I stare at her, trying to guess what memory gave her that horrified look. Hecate had a rough childhood. When I met her, she was running away from people who had hurt her terribly. I never learned the full details of her ordeal, only enough to know she needed protection. I wonder if there's a connection between her past and what I said about Persephone's father.

"Doesn't Persephone have a mother?" Dio asks. "Why don't you ask her about her husband?"

I rub my face and sigh. "She's a junkie, current location unknown. And even if I knew where she was, she isn't the most reliable source."

"What do you want with my mother?"

My stomach sinks as I turn. I didn't hear Persephone approach at all. She looks too pale for my liking, and most importantly, not one bit happy.

Damn everything to hell.

PERSEPHONE

I wake up and find the bed empty. Disappointment and sadness compete for space in my chest as I wonder if everything that happened between Hades and me up until this moment has been nothing but a dream. He got what he paid for; there's no need for him to pretend any longer.

No, I didn't misread the emotion shining in his eyes. And he said he wanted me to stay. Maybe I should give him the benefit of the doubt. Maybe not all men in my life are only interested in one thing from me.

The sky is more orange than blue, meaning the sunset isn't far away. I get up and collect my clothes scattered on the floor. A smile tugs at my lips when I pick up my skull-print underwear. Who knew I'd find a man who would go nuts over them?

I don't want to wear the same clothes as before, and I need a shower, so I decide to go back to my room and use my own bathroom before I go look for Hades. But conversation coming from downstairs stops me in my tracks. I recognize Hecate's voice, but there's a male voice I can't place. It's not Hermes. Showering is out of the question now. I'll just get dressed quickly.

My hair is a bit of a mess, and my face is red around my mouth. It's a ghastly combination with the bruise that's now purple and yellow. I resemble a painter's palette, but I'm too curious about what's going on downstairs to bother putting makeup on.

I walk on my tiptoes, not wanting to announce my presence prematurely. It's the right decision to make, because I'm the topic of conversation. I shouldn't eavesdrop, and yet here I am. It's not the worst sin I've ever committed, though.

It wasn't my plan to reveal my presence so suddenly, but when they mention my parents, I can't stop myself.

"What do you want with my mother?"

Hades's expression is guilty as hell as he turns to me. I cross my arms and wait for an explanation. He looks like he'd rather have a root canal than give me an answer.

"I gained some information about Salas that I need to verify with your mother," he replies.

I squint. "What kind of information, and where did you get the intel?"

His posture is tense, guarded, making me afraid of what's going to come out of his mouth.

"It seems there's a connection between your father and Salas."

I immediately reject the idea. Shaking my head, I say, "That's impossible. My father was a good man. He'd never get involved with someone like Salas. Who told you that?"

Hades clenches his jaw and doesn't seem inclined to reveal that either.

Jesus, this conversation feels like pulling teeth. Why is he so tight lipped when the matter involves me and my family?

"Aphrodite told him," the man lying on the couch replies.

I forgot he was in the room, and now that he has my attention, I see how badly injured he is. His face is a mess of bruises and cuts. He looks worse than me.

But his answer trumps my need to know who he is and what happened to him. I'm back at being angry that Hades left me earlier to see that woman.

"She's wrong," I tell him through clenched teeth.

"It's possible that she's wrong," Hades replies. "She said she couldn't vouch for the information, but it's a rumor worth investigating."

"The hell it is!" I yell, letting my emotions bubble to the surface.

I don't want anyone digging up my father's past. I'm afraid I'll discover he wasn't as perfect as I believe him to be, and I can't handle another parent disappointing me.

"Girl, you'd better calm down," Hecate pipes up.

"I don't want to calm down!" My face is hot and wet. Damn it. I can't believe I'm crying in front of these people. "I'm going home."

I turn around and stalk to the stairs. I'm totally acting like a drama queen, but I can't stop. The dam that kept my emotions in check broke, and now there's no stopping them from rushing out and destroying everything in their path.

Hades is following me, but he doesn't grab me or try to stop me. He waits until we're in my room and the door is closed before he speaks. "You're not serious about leaving."

"I'm damn serious. I've fulfilled my end of the bargain. You can't keep me here."

He crosses his arms and watches me through slitted eyes. "Tell me what this is really about, Skulls."

Him being calm is not what I expected or wanted. I need him to yell at me so I don't feel bad about acting like a psycho. He doesn't even seem angry.

Deflated, I sit on the edge of the bed and hide my face behind my hands. A moment later, the mattress dips next to me, and then Hades wraps his arm around my shoulders.

"Is this only about your father, or are you mad about something else?"

Since I'm already making a fool of myself, I might as well tell him everything.

"You left this morning in a hurry after reading a message from her."

"Are you upset because I went to see Aphrodite?" There's genuine surprise in his voice.

I turn to him and let him see the pitiful woman I truly am. Blotched face, for sure red eyes, and probably a deranged glint in my gaze too.

"Yes," I murmur.

He gently wipes the moisture from my cheeks with his thumb. "I didn't say anything to you because I didn't want to worry you. Aphrodite is a friend, and she called me about Dionysus."

"Who?"

"The man you just met downstairs."

"Oh."

"He was attacked near her club."

My eyes widen as remorse spears my chest. "Why? Do you know who did it?"

He nods. "My brother. He didn't like that I brought you to his restaurant. As a punishment for showing up at Pantheon last night, and for kicking Salas's ass, he decided to go after someone I care about."

"That's awful."

"He used Salas to do his dirty work, which means he must have offered the man something he wants terribly. My guess is he promised you."

I wait for the fear to strike, but it doesn't come. Remorse is the most prevalent feeling swirling in my chest. Ashamed, I drop my gaze. I spent my entire day mad at Hades, consumed by jealousy, when he'd just been trying to shield me from the ugliness of this situation.

He places his finger under my chin and forces me to look at him again. "You have no reason to be jealous of anyone, Skulls. You're the only woman who has ever made me feel...."

He seems at a loss for words, so I press. "Feel what?"

A shuddering breath escapes his lips. "Alive."

Impulsively, I throw my arms around his neck and press my mouth to his. He takes charge, kissing me so deeply that I don't know anymore whose air I'm breathing. His tongue is like a spark, turning me into flames. I never knew kissing someone could make me feel this way, as if I'm the queen of the world. I'd kiss him forever if I could.

Unfortunately, he eases off and presses his forehead against mine. My lips tingle, yearning for more.

"As much as I want to keep savoring your mouth—and the rest of you—there are issues I must take care of."

I pull back. "Like finding my mother."

"Among other things."

He's acting mysterious again, and I won't have it. "Please don't leave me in the dark. This is about me, and I have the right to be involved."

A thought occurs to me that makes my blood run cold. Perseus. I've been so wrapped up around my own personal drama that I didn't stop to consider that he's in danger too.

"We need to get my brother. He can't stay by himself in our house. What if—"

Hades cups my cheek. "He's fine. Hercules has been keeping an eye on him since you moved in with me."

I stare at him dumbfounded, not knowing if I should smack him or kiss him. "You knew Perseus wasn't safe, and you didn't tell me or bring him here?"

"I didn't want to uproot his life. It was bad enough that I did yours."

I can't help thinking that Hades had a choice. He could have slept with me on the first night and let me be. But then I wouldn't have gotten to know him. I wouldn't have fallen in love with him.

I look away, afraid he'll read the truth in my eyes.

"This is too much," I whisper.

He pulls me against him and kisses my temple. "I won't let anything happen to you or him. I swear it on my life."

27

HADES

"Okay," she says. "Then let's go get him."

"Are you saying you're not leaving?" I almost added "me," but that would sound too needy.

She bites her lower lip, and I nearly lose my mind. She needs to stop doing that. It's like a shot of libido straight to my cock.

"Hades… I can't stay with you forever. Eventually, I have to go back to my life."

"What if I want you in mine?"

Her pretty eyes widen. "I can be part of your life and live in my own house."

That idea has zero appeal to me. Even if there weren't a couple of bastards trying to take Persephone from me, I'd fight her idea tooth and nail.

"But my house is so much nicer." I smile and immediately realize my error.

Persephone's gaze darkens right before she stands up. "Good for you, but it's not *my* house," she grits out.

I get up too and rest my hands on her arms. "I'm sorry. That came out wrong. I didn't mean to diss your place."

She steps back, crossing her arms. "Well, you did. Besides, I don't even know what's happening between us. You bought my virginity, and you got it. Our deal is over."

A dark feeling spreads through my chest like a disease. I don't like the direction this conversation is going. But a knock on the door prevents me from pressing the issue.

"Hades, your phone has been blowing up," Hecate tells me.

Ah hell. What now?

I open the door and find Hecate with my phone in hand. "It's Hercules."

I jerk the phone from her and call him back. He answers on the first ring.

"What's going on?" I ask.

"You're not going to like this, boss. There's been a fire at Persephone's place."

"What? Tell me everything. Don't spare any details."

My gaze connects with hers, and guilt rushes through me. If anything happened to her brother, I'll never forgive myself. Not wanting to uproot the kid was just an excuse. I didn't want anyone getting between Persephone and me, and having her brother stay with us would definitely have put a damper on my initial plans.

"Someone set her car on fire while we were in the house. I rushed outside, but the bastard had already gone. I'm sorry, boss."

"It's not your fault. How's the kid?"

"Pissed off and wanting heads to roll."

Despite everything, I laugh.

"What's going on?" Persephone asks with anguish in her eyes. That sobers me up pretty quickly.

I cover my phone and say, "I'll tell you in a sec, darling." Then I resume my conversation with Hercules. "I'll be there as soon as I can. Have Perseus pack whatever he needs. He's moving out."

"Will do, boss."

No sooner do I end the call than Persephone asks frantically, "It's Perseus, isn't it? Something happened to him, didn't it?"

"Calm down, babe. Nothing happened to him."

"But something *did* happen."

I nod. "It's your car. Someone set fire to it."

Her face drains of color, and she steps back, hugging her middle. "They burned Petunia?"

"I'm afraid so. I'm sorry."

I'm not surprised by her reaction. No one would name their car if they weren't attached to it.

"But Perseus is okay. You're sure?"

"That's what Hercules told me. Get ready. We're going over there to pick him up."

"And where are we going after?"

Not this again.

Frowning, I invade her space. "You'd better stop trying to run away from me, from what's happening between us. I don't want you to move out. I need to fall asleep and wake up with you by my side every night and day."

"Do you really mean that, Hades? Because if you don't, if this is just a game—"

I frame her face with my hands and capture her lips, trying to pour everything I'm feeling into the kiss. I'm not good with words, so I have to show her what she means to me through actions. When the fire between us threatens to take over my senses completely, I release her. But my breathing is out of pace, erratic, and my heart is beating so fast it might break through skin and bones and take off.

"How many times do I have to say that I want you before you believe me?"

She chuckles. "I don't know. A million?"

I kiss the tip of her nose. "You're a silly, painfully beautiful girl. The question is do you want me?"

Her eyebrows arch. "You don't know?"

"I'd like to hear you say it. I won't keep you here against your will."

"I *do* want you. It's terrifying how much."

I slide my thumb over her lip. "We'll take the plunge together, then. Now get ready. I don't want to explain to your brother and Hercules why your jaw is bruised."

"I get you not wanting to tell Perseus you decked me, but why would Hercules care?"

A humorous laugh escapes my lips. "He'd be the first one to give me an ass-whooping if he knew I punched you, even if by accident."

"Jesus. I can't anymore with all this sugar. I probably turned diabetic just from listening to this conversation," Hecate complains from the hallway.

I forgot she was around. *Shit*. And she witnessed the whole scene with me practically begging Persephone to stay. She won't let me live that down.

"No one forced you to eavesdrop on it," I grit out.

"Eh, you left the door wide open. It was too much of a good opportunity to pass up." She shrugs. "Are we going to get Persephone's brother or not?"

"You don't need to come," I say.

"I know I don't, but I want to." She smiles like the devil she is.

"It's fine, Hades. I don't mind if she comes. I'll go get ready." Persephone disappears into the bathroom, and I turn around to stalk past Hecate.

I veer straight to my office downstairs.

"What are your plans for retaliation?" Her voice no longer has any mirth. She's all business now.

"First, I make sure Persephone and her brother are safe." I press the button on the wall next to the couch that reveals the safe hidden behind the only painting in my office. After a thumbprint and retina scan, the lock releases.

"And then what?" she asks.

I pull the Glock from inside and set it on my desk. "Then I go to war."

Hecate rests her hip against the desk and glances at the gun. "You're going to need way more than that to take on Zeus and his new friends."

"I know."

"Who are you calling to help? Surely not Hermes."

I meet her gaze. "Don't let your prejudice get in the way. There's no love lost between Hermes and his father."

"Hermes is a self-serving son of a bitch. He's only loyal to himself. You said so many times."

"True, but I think he might want to finally pick a team." I smirk.

She narrows her eyes. "Because of me? I'm not going to sleep with him so you can gain an ally!"

"I'm not suggesting that. In fact, I don't expect you to do anything about him. If you're not into him, then that's your choice. But he'll help me because of his feelings for you whether you reciprocate them or not."

She snorts. "He doesn't have feelings for me. He just wants to fuck me."

I pinch the bridge of my nose. "I don't have time to argue whether Hermes has real feelings for you or if he just likes the chase. I have bigger fish to fry, if you haven't noticed."

She crosses her arms. "You don't need to bite my head off."

Persephone walks in, saving me from this idiotic conversation.

"I'm ready." Her gaze drops to the gun, and she pales. "Is that really necessary?"

I tuck the Glock underneath my waistband in the back. "I'm afraid so, Skulls. Zeus and Salas aren't kidding around."

She swallows so hard that I can hear it. "Is there anything I can do to help?"

"Yes, let me protect you to the best of my ability."

"Oh, I don't know. That sounds too passive and damsel-in-distress-like," Hecate chimes in.

"I'm not going to shove a gun in her hand!" I bark at her.

"Hades, please." Persephone touches my arm, and it's like she has magical powers. My anger begins to subside.

"I'm sorry." I shake my head. "We should go before I blow a fuse."

"I think it's already too late for that," Hecate retorts.

I swallow my angry reply, but I don't miss the glare Persephone throws at her.

Pride swells in my chest.

That's my girl.

28

PERSEPHONE

I try not to cry when I see Petunia's charred carcass. The fire licked away every inch of color on my beloved car, and now all that's left is a pitch-black, mangled skeleton. A sob bubbles up my throat. I cover my mouth and look away.

"Is she crying over a car?" Hecate whispers to Hades.

"Petunia was more than a car to her," he replies.

I glance at him, surprised that he would know that. His eyes are soft and kind, shining with a compassion I didn't think I'd ever see from him. When I met Hades, I pegged him to be an arrogant and cruel man, but he's proven me wrong time and time again.

Despite the sadness, there's another feeling occupying my chest, filling the gaping hole. I'm in love with Hades, which seems impossible. We just met, but matters of the heart don't need to make sense.

The front door opens, and out comes Perseus. He looks grim but not distraught.

I shorten the distance between us and pull him into a hug. "Are you okay?"

"Yeah. I'm sorry about Petunia."

We break apart and stare at what's left of her. "I'm glad the fire didn't reach the house."

"We saw the flames from the living room and called the firefighters right away."

It's only then that I notice the absence of onlookers, and there's no heat coming from Petunia. The fire was put out a while ago.

"When did this happen?" I ask.

"In the morning," a giant man who I assume is Hercules answers.

"And you only called me now?" Hades takes a step forward, his body tight with tension.

Hercules's expression crumbles. "I wanted to have the situation under control before I let you know."

"I don't care about what you wanted," he grits out.

Hecate steps between them and says, "It's over now, Hades, and Hercules was right in handling the situation himself. Think about what wouldn't have happened otherwise." She gives him a meaningful look that makes my cheeks burn.

How does she know about what happened? Did he tell her?

If Hercules had called about the fire earlier, Hades and I wouldn't have finally succumbed to our feelings. He would also not have put the fear of God in my asshole professor. There's a silver lining here.

Out of the blue, I hug the tall man. "Thank you for keeping my brother safe."

He tenses and doesn't hug me back, but it's okay. I didn't expect him to.

I step back and turn to Perseus. "Did you get everything?"

"Yeah. But where exactly am I going?"

"You're staying with me," Hades replies.

Perseus's eyes bug out. "Really? That's awesome and all, but how far is your house from my school?"

"Don't worry about that. Hercules will drive you."

Perseus glances at the giant, rubbing the back of his neck. "Eh, do you think I can still go to the game tonight?"

I don't miss the familiarity with which Perseus addresses Hercules, and I raise a brow. They've only known each other for as long as I've known Hades, after all.

He doesn't answer right away and seems concerned about the situation. He flicks his gaze to Hades first, then me. I have no idea what's going on.

"What game?" I ask.

"Jesus, Seph. Football. Remember? I used to play before this happened." Perseus raises his cast.

Now I feel like an ass and a horrible sister. I've been too embroiled in my own problems and forgot all about my brother.

"I don't—" Hades starts, but I cut him off.

"Yeah, it's fine. I'll come too."

"Cool! We should get going, then. The game starts in a couple hours."

When I look at Hades, I know he disapproves. But I didn't have the heart to tell Perseus he couldn't do the one thing he cares about.

Perseus and Hercules head over to the big-ass SUV parked across the street, which I assume belongs to Hercules. Now it's only Hades, Hecate, and me standing next to dead Petunia.

"You shouldn't have agreed to let him go to a game," Hades says.

"It's important to him. You can't expect us to stay locked behind your walls forever."

"I can while Salas is still on the loose," he grumbles.

"He's not going to kidnap me in the middle of a high school football game crowd."

At least I hope he won't be crazy enough to attempt it. He only came for me on campus when it was deserted.

Hades passes a hand over his face. "I don't like this."

"I'll go too if that makes you feel better. Plus, Hercules will be there," Hecate pipes up.

"That's not enough manpower. I need more people to cover the area."

"We'll be at a high school. They have security there," I say.

He gives me a droll look. "Not the kind that will keep Salas away."

I cross my arms. "Then you should come too."

His eyes widen a fraction, and his jaw tenses. I remember the gun he's packing and wonder what he'd planned to do tonight. My stomach twists into knots thinking about it. I don't want Hades dealing with that vermin Salas alone. It's clear he's a sneaky bastard who wouldn't think twice about stabbing someone in the back. Hades could very well be walking into a trap.

"I—" He starts.

"Yes, Hades," Hecate cuts him off. "You should go to the game. Zeus and Salas will be expecting a prompt retaliation. By not going after them now, you'll have the element of surprise."

"That's not how I operate."

She smiles. "Exactly. They've been taunting you, expecting you to blow."

He glances at me, defeated. "I'll come, but only because I don't trust Hecate to keep you out of trouble."

"Uh, rude much?" she complains.

"Yeah, that was uncalled for." I cross my arms. "When do *I* go looking for trouble?"

He cups my cheek. "You don't need to look for it. Trouble finds you, Skulls."

I can't refute that argument. Since I met him, it seems I can't get out of the house without something happening to me.

"Ugh, I can already tell tonight is going to be torture watching you two lovebirds," Hecate whines.

"There's a solution for that," I say.

"You keeping your PDA to a minimum?"

I shake my head. "We can invite Hermes to come."

Her jaw drops to the ground, and then she glares at Hades. "You recruited her to the Hermes cheer team, didn't you?" Hecate's eyes spark with annoyance, but I suspect it's half-hearted.

Hades widens his eyes. "I did no such thing."

Hercules honks once and then drives away. It's our cue to leave. My gaze flickers one more time to Petunia, and I sigh. *So long, dear friend.*

Hades throws his arm over my shoulders, pulling me flush against his body. "Zeus is gonna pay for that too, Skulls. You have my word."

29

PERSEPHONE

Hades, with his brooding attitude, is sticking out like a sore thumb in the crowd. The atmosphere is electrifying and vibrant, and the entire school came out in force to support their team. He, on the other hand, looks like he has a storm cloud above his head.

The game tonight is a big deal for the Pegasuses, Perseus's team. They're playing against their rivals, the Titans. It's heartbreaking that he can't play, but he's cheering them on from the sidelines with all the enthusiasm he can muster. Hercules is down on the field, keeping a close eye on him. How the man managed to get permission to be there is a mystery to me.

Hades is tense and not paying any attention to what's happening on the field. I wish he'd relax, but I can't give him any grief over it either. These are stressful times for all of us.

Hecate is wearing a matching gloomy expression, but why she's unhappy, I don't know. She's the one who volunteered to come tonight, after all.

I lean closer and ask, "What's the matter?"

"Nothing." She crosses her arms and pouts, not meeting my gaze.

"You and Hades are a pair," I joke.

"Hecate is mad because Hermes didn't come," Hades chimes in without relaxing his stance. He reminds me of a watchdog, tense and ready to attack at any sign of trouble.

"Shut up, Hades! That's not it."

"Why didn't he come?" I ask. When neither opens their mouth to reply, I press. "Hades?"

"Don't ask me. Hecate was the one who texted him."

Ah, now things are starting to make sense.

"He was a jerk, if you must know. He said, 'Thanks, but no thanks.'"

Wow. I'm shocked he'd say something that rude considering how desperate he was to score a date with her.

"I'm sorry. I thought he was nicer than that," I say.

"He's the son of Zeus. I'm not surprised."

"I don't buy it," Hades pipes up. "Something is going on. It isn't Hermes's MO to act like that."

Hecate snorts. "If you say so."

My pocket vibrates, reminding me that Helen was supposed to text me when she arrived. After we returned to Hades's place, I called her back. I decided it was high time to tell her about him, but I want to do it in person. I won't tell her the sordid details of how he came into my life—that secret I'm still determined to take to the grave. But now that I know more or less where I stand with him—we're clearly a couple—I have to tell her.

I check her message and then say, "Helen is here. I'm gonna meet her by the food truck area."

"I'll come with you." Hades places a possessive hand on my lower back.

"Oh great. Leave me alone here with this rowdy crowd," Hecate complains.

"You need to save our—" I start, but then see a familiar face coming down the steps toward us. "Uh, you won't be alone."

She follows my gaze and then gasps. "He came."

"Awesome. Now you can stop whining," Hades pipes up.

Her expression is still frozen into a scowl, but there's a spark in her eyes that most definitely isn't anger. Hades and I exit the row just as Hermes reaches us.

"Hey, you guys leaving already?" he asks.

"I'm meeting a friend by the food trucks," I explain. "I'm glad you came, though."

His eyes darken for a second, but then he smiles. "Yeah, me too."

"Everything okay?" Hades asks, watching Hermes closely.

His expression turns somber again. "No, but my issues are my own. You don't need to worry about me. You have enough on your plate." He looks past our shoulders. "On a scale of one to ten, how mad is she at me?"

"Eleven," Hades replies.

"Great. My chances were already low, and I brought a shovel."

"Don't beat yourself down. You're more ahead of the game than you think," I tell him.

His eyes widen. "Really? Did she say anything about me?"

"I thought your friends were waiting for you," Hades cuts in like a grump.

Hermes shakes his head, grinning. "Don't worry. I'll find out one way or another. Getting intel is my specialty."

Hades steers me up the stairs, keeping his hand on my lower back the entire time. I can't deny that I'm loving how he is with me. I never felt protected growing up. My father died when I was too young, and my mother, well… no comment.

I glance over my shoulder to see how Hermes is faring with Hecate. When she doesn't punch him in the throat, I take that as a good sign.

The noise is less deafening when we're out of the bleachers. I stop and turn to Hades, determined to find out the source of his foul mood. It can't just be because I insisted on coming here.

"Tell me what's wrong." He frowns, and I can guess exactly what his answer is going to be, so I add, "Besides the obvious."

"There are way too many people here. I don't like crowds."

"But you fought at the underground tournament. The crowd there was probably the same size as this one."

His eyes soften, and the corners of his lips twitch upward. "Do you remember how my last fight ended?"

Heat creeps up my cheeks. "You were doing well until you lost focus."

He reaches over and tucks a loose strand of my hair behind my ear. "My entire world shifted when I saw you in the crowd. I should have known what it meant right then and there."

I step closer, tilting my head up. "I couldn't keep my eyes off you either. It felt like there was a magnetic pull drawing me to you."

He chuckles. "Must have been the Fates, then."

"Must have been," I whisper as my eyes drop to his lips.

He leans closer, but right before he kisses me, someone calls my name. Startled, I jump back and turn.

"I knew it!" Helen says with accusation in her eyes.

"Hi, Helen," I reply sheepishly.

She puts her hands on her hips and glowers. "You have some explaining to do, young lady."

Next to her, Paris has his focus fixed on Hades. He looks a little awestruck.

Hades takes a step forward and offers his hand to Helen. "Hi, I'm Hades. Nice to meet you."

His approach knocks her outrage down a peg. In a daze, she shakes his hand. "I'm Helen, and this is my boyfriend, Paris."

Hades shakes his hand too. "Nice to meet you, Paris."

"Yeah, sa-same."

I can't believe he stuttered. He's Mr. Confidence personified.

Helen seems recovered from the Hades effect, though. She points at us and asks, "When did this happen?"

Hades wraps his arm around my waist, pulling me closer. "If you're asking when Persephone finally decided to give me a chance, then it's fairly new. Less than twenty-four new."

Relief washes over me. He's lying to cover for me, and I never told him I've been lying to my best friend this whole time.

Helen's eyebrows arch. "Oh, really? I thought you guys had been going out longer than that."

"There was an attempt that backfired royally," he replies, "but it was my fault."

I bet he's referring to the incident at Pantheon, and I don't want to go there, so I interject, "He redeemed himself by saving me from Prof. Cashore, though."

Her eyes widen, swimming with remorse. "Oh, Seph. I'm so sorry I couldn't be there for you. When I arrived at the café, you were already gone."

"What did that asshole do?" Paris asks.

Hades tenses next to me, and I decide that's another subject we should steer away from. "Best if we don't talk about it."

"All that matters is that motherfucker will be lucky if he can find a job scrubbing floors," Hades seethes. "He won't teach anymore... *anywhere*."

I glance at him with a question in my gaze. We didn't speak about Prof. Perv after the incident, but I should have known Hades wouldn't simply do nothing about the man.

"Good riddance," Helen replies.

"I need a drink," Hades announces suddenly. "Do they sell beer in this place?"

"I think the burger truck does," Paris replies. "I need one too."

Hades looks at me and seems to hesitate. I'm sure he wants me to stay glued to his side the whole time, but I'd like a chance to speak with Helen alone for a couple minutes.

"Go on. Helen and I will wait here." I can already hear the argument on the tip of his tongue, so I add, "It's fine. We won't go anywhere."

He leans down and kisses me softly on the lips. "You'd better not."

I watch him walk away, almost daydreaming. Women and teenage girls alike turn to stare at him. I can't believe that beautiful man is mine.

"Damn, girl. You have it bad." Helen steps next to me. "I don't blame you, though. He's a fine specimen."

"Yes, he is."

"So when did you two flip?"

"What?" I blink a couple times, too lost in my lustful feelings for Hades to process her question properly.

"You said he was a dick, and if I remember correctly, he also didn't like you very much because of the accident."

"Oh yeah. I don't know. It's like a dream. You don't know when it starts before you realize you're in the thick of it."

"Aww, is my best friend finally in love?"

My face feels like it's made of lava. I drop my gaze to the ground. "I think so. Is it crazy?"

"Not at all. I've always known that when you fell in love, it would be hard and sudden. I hope he's worth it."

"I think he is."

"So, have you guys done it yet?" she asks in a cheerful tone that's a little too loud.

"Shh." I look around us, making sure no one's eavesdropping on our conversation.

"You did, didn't you?" she squeaks.

Blushing furiously now, I look into her eyes. "Yes."

She grabs my arms. "How was it? Oh, please tell me he's good in the sack. It'd be a shame if he wasn't."

"He's... very good. More than good, actually."

She pulls me into a hug and spins me around. "I'm so happy

for you. Now we can finally dirty talk without it being awkward."

"It's always going to be awkward to me."

I lean back, breaking free from her hold. I want to say more, but from the corner of my eye, I see a familiar face.

"Mom?" I blurt out.

"What?" Helen turns. "Where?"

She ducks around the corner of the gymnasium, but I know it was her. I can't let her disappear again. I need to know about my father.

"I'll be right back." I sprint toward the building, hoping I can catch up with her before she vanishes again.

I don't know what she's doing here. She never cared about Perseus's games before.

When I turn a corner, I see her leaning against the wall, smoking a cigarette.

"Mom, what are you doing here?"

She stands straighter and looks at me as if she was caught doing something wrong. Her flight mode is engaged. I have to be careful now.

"I came to see my son. Is that a crime?"

"No. How have you been?"

She narrows her eyes, and her mouth turns into a slash on her face. "How do you think? You kicked me out of my own house. Don't you dare stand there and pretend you care about my fate."

A sliver of guilt pierces my chest despite the fact that I had every right to kick her out. I can't let the sentiment take root. That's how she got away with all the crap she pulled over the years. Because I let her.

"I do care. Where are you staying?"

She takes a drag of the cigarette before she answers, "With friends."

"Are you clean?"

She whips her face to mine so fast it almost gives me whiplash. "I don't live with you anymore. I don't owe you any explanation."

That means she isn't. I'm not surprised.

"As long as you don't use me as a form of payment, I don't care."

Remorse takes over her features, and she looks away. "At least now you won't be called a frigid bitch anymore. Virginity is just a thing that gets in the way."

I curl my hands into fists as the anger simmering low in my gut begins to bubble to the surface. Of course she had to twist things around and find a way to criticize my choices. But I bite my tongue because I still need something from her.

"I want to ask you about Dad." I step closer, ready to tackle her if she decides to bail.

She snorts. "Oh, I can't wait to hear what you want to know about Walter."

"Did he know a man named Salas Ciriano?"

Mom won't look me in the eye, but her body visibly tenses at the mention of Salas.

"I don't know. He was on the road all the time. He met many people."

"Please don't lie to me, Mom. This is important."

She turns and spends a couple beats scrutinizing me. "Are you sure you're ready for this, Seph? Once I tell you what I know, there goes the image of the perfect father you have of your dad."

I swallow the huge lump in my throat. I'm not ready, not in the least. My stomach is already coiled tight, and my chest is heavy. But sticking my head in the sand won't help me.

"Yes, I'm ready. Whatever it is, tell me."

She flicks her cigarette stump away. "Your father wasn't a simple truck driver. He was a mule before we moved to Olympus Bay. He transported drugs in his cargo."

"No," I whisper as the ground vanishes from underneath my feet. "That can't be."

"How do you think we met, child?"

I shake my head, still in denial. "He wasn't a junkie."

She laughs without humor. "No, that he wasn't. I guess he was smarter than me. He never touched the stuff. It's why he lasted so long in the business."

"So, did he work for Salas?"

A shadow crosses my mother's eyes. "No. Meeting Salas was a chance encounter, one that killed your father in the end."

"I don't follow. Dad died of a heart attack."

"Yes, because of the deal he struck with that man."

The small hairs on the back of my neck stand on end. "What deal? You're not making any sense."

She runs her hand through her greasy hair. "Your father took you with him on a trip across the border once. You were seven. Do you remember that?"

"Yeah. To meet my grandparents. You didn't let Perseus come."

"No. And you know why? Because that was a fucking delivery trip, and I was sober enough to forbid him to be so reckless."

I flinch. "But you let me go?"

"No, I didn't! You snuck out, brat that you were, and hid in his truck. He should have turned around when he realized what you'd done, but he was a stubborn man."

"I don't remember that part."

"Anyway, you were there when he delivered the goods to that Salas fella. The perv took one look at you and decided he wanted you."

My blood runs cold. "I was seven."

"He didn't care. He's a demented motherfucker."

I'm going to be sick. I hug my middle tighter, trying to keep my food in my belly. "What did Dad do?"

"He made a deal with the devil. He knew if he said no on the spot, he'd be killed, and you'd be taken. So he bargained with the man. Told him he could come for you when you were older."

My vision is blurry, and I'm so choked up, I'm afraid I can't get the next question out, but I manage somehow.

"How much older?"

"Twelve."

I shake my head as I step back. "He wouldn't have."

"He did. But then he died the next year. He told me that sordid story just before he passed, and he begged me to protect you. I did the best I could. We moved to Olympus Bay, and I tried to stay out of trouble and not draw the wrong kind of attention to ourselves."

And it did work. Salas never came for me when I turned twelve. I can't believe my mother tried to protect me. I thought she didn't care.

"You must be hella confused right now." She laughs in derision. "The woman who you thought was the worst mother in the world was the one who kept you from being raped by a pedophile."

"But then he did find me in the end, and you handed me over to him on a silver platter."

Her eyes grow larger. "What are you talking about, child?"

"The auction. Salas was there. He bid for me."

I wait for remorse to shine in her gaze, but she simply stares at me with her dispassionate eyes. "Well, you're a grown woman now."

I want to say rape is rape no matter the age, but it would be wasted on her. I am thankful that she kept Salas away from me when I was a child, but that doesn't erase all the harm she's done to me and Perseus along the way.

"Yes, I am. Take care, Mother."

I turn around and walk away. I don't realize I'm crying my

eyes out until my nose gets stuffy. I wipe my cheeks with the back of my hand, but it's pointless. The tears keep coming.

"Persephone!" Hades calls a second before his strong arms wrap around my body.

I press my face against his chest, and then I lose it completely.

30

HADES

Persephone is shaking in my arms, crying, and there's not a damn thing I can do besides hold her tight until she calms down. When I returned to the spot where I'd left her with Helen and found out she'd gone somewhere alone, I lost my mind and almost ripped the girl's head off. I managed to rein in my emotions long enough to get from her that Persephone had gone after her mother.

"Is she okay?" Helen asks.

"Does she look okay?" I snap.

"Hey, you don't need to talk to her like that," Paris retorts.

"It's okay, babe," Helen assures him. "He's just distraught. That's all."

Persephone pulls back and looks at her friend. "I'll be fine, but I need to go home."

"Hercules will make sure Perseus is safe," I tell her.

"Who's Hercules, and why does he need to keep Perseus safe?" Helen asks.

"It's a long story. I'll tell you another time, okay?" Persephone replies in a voice so small it makes my chest ache.

I see her friend is gathering herself to insist but seems to change her mind in the last second. Good. I really don't want to yell at her again. I did plenty of that when I discovered she'd let Persephone run off alone. It probably wasn't the smartest thing to antagonize her best friend, but I wasn't thinking clearly.

"Will you please call me later?" she asks.

"Yeah, I will. Promise."

I have my phone to my ear and Hercules on the line as I steer Persephone to the exit. I only need to exchange a few words with him. He knows the drill.

Persephone is still shaking when I stop next to my car. I help her inside and then get behind the steering wheel as fast as I can. I want to know what happened that left her in this state, but I can wait until she's ready to talk.

I turn the engine on and start backing up.

"Aren't you going to let Hecate know we're leaving?"

I grumble. Shit, I forgot about her. I hand my phone to Persephone. "Would you mind texting her? I want to get us out of this zoo ASAP."

She stares at my phone, then back at my face. "You're letting me use your phone?"

Frowning, I say, "Yeah. Why are you looking at me like that?"

"It's so private."

"Sweetheart, I have nothing to hide from you. It's already unlocked. Hecate's contact is saved in Favorites."

"Okay."

It takes a few seconds for her to type a message and then set the phone in the storage compartment between the seats.

"How are you feeling?" I ask.

She lets out a sigh and looks out the window. "Awful. Can we wait until we get to the house? I need a moment to process everything."

I reach for her hand and squeeze. "I can wait for as long as you need, my love."

"My love?" she squeaks.

Ah hell. I can't believe I said that. Not that it isn't true, but now she's staring at me like I've sprouted a second head. *Can't backtrack now.*

"Yes, my love." I smile. "Do you have a problem with that?"

Her lips quiver, and then her face crumples. She covers it with her hand and turns away, but I can still hear her sob.

Fuck. What did I do?

I find a place to park because I can't drive with her in this state, especially knowing I caused it.

"Skulls, look at me, please."

"Don't mind me. I'm just overreacting."

I unbuckle my seat belt and lean across the divide between our seats. "Come here, babe."

She turns, and her tear-streaked face makes my heart shrivel inside my chest. I've never felt this raw ache over anyone before. "Tell me what to do to fix this."

Her eyebrows arch. "Fix this? Do you think I'm upset because you called me 'my love'?"

"Aren't you? I made you cry again."

"Oh, Hades. I'm crying because I can't believe someone like you would call me that."

I flinch. "Someone like me?"

Her cheeks turn a delicious pink color. "You're powerful, and beautiful, and I'm a nobody."

I capture her face between my hands. "Don't say that. You're not a nobody. You're everything to me, darling. Can't you see what you do to me?"

"I'm afraid this is all in my head."

I kiss her hard, trying to convey how much she means to me. I pull back fast and say, "It's not in your head, my silly girl," I whisper against her lips. "I love you, damn it."

She lets out a shuddering breath. "I love you too."

No woman has ever said that to me and meant it, so I'm caught by surprise by her confession. She's the one who captures my lips this time, setting my entire body on fire. I need to be much closer to her, so I pull her across the gap and onto my lap. I'm glad I didn't drive the Bugatti tonight and took the Escalade instead. I push a button and the seat slides back, leaving plenty of room for Persephone to straddle me.

I grab a fistful of her hair, curling it around my hand as I thank God she's wearing a skirt tonight. Her sweet pussy presses against my cock, and the friction alone is already driving me wild with need. She gyrates her hips, making everything ten times worse—or better—and I groan.

"Don't do this to me, Skulls. I'm reaching the point of no return," I whisper.

"I don't want to stop. Don't make me."

I pull her head back so I can look into her eyes. "If we don't stop, I'll have to fuck you in this car."

"Do it, then. I want you to." She runs her tongue across my jaw and then down my neck.

Fuck me.

I let go of her hair so I can unzip my pants. My hands are shaking as if I were a teenage boy about to have sex for the first time. I'm too horny and impatient to figure out how to get Persephone out of her panties, so I slide the fabric aside and guide her pussy to my cock. She's already dripping wet and slides down with ease. I hiss. She's still tight as hell. This is going to be over fast.

A whimper escapes her lips. She closes her eyes and stops moving. It didn't occur to me that she might still be sore from earlier.

"Are you okay, babe?"

"Yes, I just need a second."

"If it hurts, we can—"

She shuts me up with her tongue, and then with her hips when she starts moving again. I dig my fingers into them so I can help her ride me. This feels too amazing, and I'm about to have an embarrassing moment and come too fast.

"Hades, I'm so close," she moans, spurring me on.

I work her faster, bringing her hips up and down until she blurts out all the yeses and ohs against my lips. That's my undoing. I explode inside her tight heat, groaning like a caveman. If we were in my bed, I'd flip her around and keep fucking her until we both climaxed again. But that's not the case, and I don't want to hurt her. When she's no longer shaking, I let her rest.

She hides her face in the crook of my neck, breathing hard against my skin. This close to her, I can feel the drumming of her heartbeat, thumping away at the same speed of mine. I kiss her head and then stroke her hair.

"Will this ever change?" she asks me softly.

"What?"

She leans back and searches my eyes. "This feeling of wanting to be with you all the time, anytime?"

I caress her cheek. "God, I hope not."

"Have you ever had this craving for someone else before?"

I chuckle, making her frown. "No, babe. You're the first woman who's ever made me feel this way, and you'll be the only one."

Her eyes become brighter. "I don't want anyone else either. Are we crazy?"

"No. We're lucky."

31

PERSEPHONE

I can't believe I went from virgin to sexcapades in a car within a day. The windows are tinted, but I felt naughty just the same, and that brings a grin to my lips.

We're on the road again now, but Hades keeps his hand on my thigh, under my skirt, and dangerously close to my sex. Caught in the heat of the moment, we didn't use a condom. I don't mind the mess, but I don't want him to think that I'm trying to trap him with a baby. I won't ruin the moment by talking about practical things, though. It can wait until we're home.

"Penny for your thoughts," he says.

"Huh?"

"You were smiling. I want to know what caused that."

"I'm pretty sure you know who's responsible."

"Uh-uh. You have to tell me." His lips curl into a boyish grin, and my heart goes crazy, jumping up and down like a kid in a bouncy castle.

"I was replaying our performance in the car."

"Is that so?" His hand inches farther up my leg.

My pussy throbs, and he hasn't done anything yet. "Hades…."

"What?"

"Your attention should be on the road," I say under my breath.

God, has he turned me into a nympho? I've never gotten turned on this fast before.

"I can multitask." His fingers brush against my panties, and I arch my back involuntarily, gasping out loud. "Besides, I only need one hand to steer."

He pushes the fabric aside and strokes my clit. I reach for the door handle, gripping it tight so I can tether myself and not fly sky-high.

"I love that you have my seed all over you," he says in a voice that's rough and tight.

I clench my jaw, trying to keep my moans inside. But Hades's fingers are magical—something I already knew. Now, he's more adventurous, shoving three fingers inside me while applying pressure on my clit with the heel of his hand.

"Holy fuck!" I blurt out.

"Do you like that, Skulls?"

"Uh-huh." I close my eyes because I'm already getting dizzy with pleasure.

He fucks me with his fingers, plunging them in and out at a steady pace as if he's not in a hurry to finish. I press my legs together, squeezing his hand between them in the process. I can't help it, though. My body has a will of its own.

"You have no idea how much I want to taste you right now," he says.

Just the visual of his mouth on me, licking and sucking my pussy, is enough to send me over the edge. I cry out, almost jerking off my seat as the orgasm crashes over me, sending me careening into a pool of bliss.

"Ah hell," Hades says in a strangled voice. "Fuuuck."

Worried, I look at him. His expression is pinched as if he's in pain. He keeps moving his fingers, though.

"What's wrong?" I ask.

"I…. It's nothing. I'm fine. I'm fine."

I cover his hand with mine, stopping his action between my legs. "You don't look fine."

He pulls his fingers from inside me and licks them as if they were covered in chocolate. "I can't get over how good you taste."

I watch him closely. He's trying to hide something. But then the familiar tall walls to his property come into view, so I decide to wait until we're inside to get to the bottom of it.

Hades pulls into the garage and gets out of the car first—which doesn't happen often—but he waits for me. I give him an overall glance and then see what he was trying to hide. There's a wet stain on his crotch.

"You came while you were fingering me, didn't you?"

His face turns beet red, and it's a shame I don't have my phone out to take a picture. I don't think many people have seen Hades blush before.

He rubs the back of his neck. "I…. That hasn't happened in a long time. Since I was a teenager, to be exact."

I laugh. "Are you embarrassed?"

"Of course I am. I don't jizz in my pants, Skulls."

I step into his space, wrapping my arms around his waist and tilting my head up. "You do now because of me."

"Yes, you're a minx who makes me lose control of my body. Don't let that go to your head."

"Too late." I rise on my tiptoes and kiss the corner of his mouth.

He grabs the back of my head and slants his mouth over mine roughly. My toes curl in my shoes, and here I go again, getting hot and bothered in the span of seconds. Maybe I'm trying to make up for all the years of sex I've missed.

Hades pulls back and almost growls, "I'm not going to fuck you in this garage, at least not tonight."

"Let's get to the house, then. We have an hour or so until Perseus gets home from the game."

"Shit. I'd already forgotten he was coming." He lifts me in his arms and rushes up the stairs.

"Oh my God, Hades. Put me down."

He only does when we reach his back patio with the pool. It's the first time I've set foot here, and it takes my breath away. The view, especially at night, is breathtaking. The pool is lit, and when I dip my fingers in the water, I'm pleasantly satisfied that it's also warm.

A shirt hits my face. Hades's shirt. When I turn, he's already naked—and totally ready for round three. "Come on, Skulls. Swim with me."

He dives into the pool like an expert swimmer and doesn't emerge until he reaches the other side. He's watching me now, which means I have to undress while his hungry gaze devours me. I don't know why I'm shy. He's seen me naked and put his mouth on every inch of my body already. I do it quickly though and then jump in—probably less gracefully than him.

He meets me in the middle and seals his mouth to mine underwater before we emerge. I cling to him, curling my legs around his hips. He glides in the pool, kissing me like he's afraid this is the last time. When my back hits the wall, I guide his shaft to my entrance, desperately needing him inside me again.

His thrusts are hard and precise. He breaks the kiss and holds my face in his hand, playing with my lips with his thumb.

"Feel how hard you make me, beautiful."

I'd reply if I could, but he once again robs me of the ability to utter words. I hold his stare, getting lost in the deep blue of his gaze. It should be unnerving to stare into someone's eyes for so long, but with Hades, it's the most natural thing in the world.

He captures my lips again, only this time his tongue moves with mine slowly, seductively, a contradiction to how hard he's fucking me. I surrender to his kiss, to everything he's doing to me, and it doesn't take long for me to fall apart again in his arms.

I've always prided myself for never using any kind of drugs, but Hades is more addictive than anything I could have experimented with. He's a high I never want to come down from.

HADES

I shouldn't have let my libido take over my actions like they did. I took advantage of Persephone and her feelings for me when the meeting with her mother clearly upset her. We're now in my bed, interlocked in a lovers' embrace. Her head is resting against my chest, and my fingers lazily glide up and down her arm.

I'm dying to know what her mother told her, but at the same time, I don't want to cause her any more pain, so I wait for her to broach the subject. Hercules should be back soon with Perseus, and that's going to burst our little bubble of privacy.

"Hades?"

"Hmm?"

She lifts her face. "I want you to know that I'm on the pill."

My eyes narrow, but then I see the worry in hers, and I can't let another issue weigh on her.

I smooth the line of worry that formed on her forehead. "And did you think I was concerned about that?"

"We didn't use protection twice."

"I'm the one who should be putting your mind at ease. I'm clean, so you know."

"You weren't concerned I could possibly be trying to trap you?"

"A baby trap?" I chuckle, but then begin to imagine what it would be like to have a kid with her, and that makes me deliriously happy. "It didn't even cross my mind."

But now I'll be thinking about it. More like obsessing, really. I shouldn't let Persephone suspect how crazy my thoughts are. I don't want *her* to think I'm trying to trap her with a baby.

She turns, folding her arms over my chest so she can rest her chin on them. Now she's covering me with her body, and my dirty mind immediately takes the next exit to "a million orgasms in your lifetime."

"You're probably wondering what my mother told me that sent me into hysterics."

And just like that, she rescues me from my filthy ideas. Apprehension takes hold of me as I search her face.

"I was waiting for you to tell me when you were ready."

She releases a shuddering breath, and a tear drips from the corner of her eye. I wrap my arms around her body, hugging her tight. "Babe, if it's too hard, you don't need to tell me."

"No, I have to, or this ugly truth will keep smothering me." She takes a deep breath. "There's a connection between my father and Salas."

Hell, I was hoping Aphrodite's source wasn't correct.

"It seems everything I believed my father to be was false. He wasn't a good man. He was a criminal, transporting drugs across the border."

My heart takes off, drumming away in my chest. I'm sure Persephone can feel it.

"Into Olympus Bay?" I have to ask, because if that's the case, then he was working for Zeus.

"No. We lived in a small town close to the border before moving here. One time, he took me on one of his work trips. He wanted me to meet my grandparents, and he thought he'd kill two birds with one stone. It was on that trip that he met Salas."

Chills of dread lick the back of my neck. "How old were you?"

"Seven."

I begin to see red, and she hasn't even told me the whole

story yet.

"It seems Salas's obsession with me started then. He wanted me, and my father…." She closes her eyes, and her entire body trembles.

"It's okay, babe. I'm here."

"My father made a deal with him. He said he could come back for me when I was a few years older. He knew if he gave a flat no on the spot, he'd be killed, and I'd be taken."

I hug her tighter, not only for her benefit but for mine too. I'm seething with rage, shaking now from head to toe. If I'd known this beforehand, Salas wouldn't have walked away the day he tried to kidnap Persephone.

Things are crystal clear to me now. There's only one possible outcome for this story. That motherfucker must die.

"My father told Mom that story on his deathbed. He begged her to protect me. That's when we moved to Olympus Bay. Despite all the horrible things she's done over the years, she did keep me safe from Salas. He never came for me when I turned twelve."

"Twelve?"

She nods and then turns her face away, hiding her eyes from me. "Dad was my hero. I thought he could do no wrong. I had no idea he was involved in any illegal activities."

I have zero respect or empathy for the man, but saying anything horrible about him now won't make a difference. It'll only make Persephone sadder.

"I'm sure he was a good father to you and Perseus. He made a mistake—a terrible one, I won't sugarcoat that—but he clearly loved you very much."

"Thank you for saying that." She looks at me again, sporting a pitiful smile.

I pull her toward me so I can kiss her until her heart isn't as shattered, until she knows she's my world and that I'll die before I let anyone hurt her again.

32

HADES

I slept for maybe a couple hours, that's it. I'm wide awake before dawn and already making a list of things that I need to take care of today. Screw biding my time. I can't let Salas loose, not now that I know the truth about his depraved mind. Also, sitting on my ass only makes Zeus believe I'm weak. This needs to end now.

Persephone is sound asleep in my arms, and I don't want to wake her. She's been through hell and deserves to rest. It's almost impossible to slide off the bed without kissing her on the cheek, but if I fall into temptation, she might wake up.

I get up and walk to my desk to jot down a quick note for her. I don't want her thinking I abandoned her again.

She stirs when I return to her side of the bed. I freeze, not daring to breathe.

"Hades," she murmurs in her sleep, and it's a throaty sound that turns me on immediately.

I want to answer the call so badly, to get back in bed with her and eat her pussy until she comes on my tongue, but I can't do that now. I've been selfish enough as it is.

I leave the note on the nightstand, put on the pair of sweatpants that I left draped over the chair, and stride out of the room as fast as I can. I'm still displaying a nice tent when I reach the kitchen; thank fuck there's no one around.

I let Cerberus out of his crate and then take him outside. Spending time with him usually helps lift my spirits, but today, there's too much darkness swirling in my chest. I can't get Persephone's story out of my head. I'm gutted that her memories of her father are tainted now. I'm fucking livid that he'd risk her life by taking her with him on a drug delivery trip. If he'd been alive, I'd give him the beating of his life.

I'm still playing with Cerberus outside when Hercules finds me.

"Please don't tell me you have more bad news," I grumble without meeting his stare.

"No, boss. I'm just reporting for duty."

An exhale of relief whooshes out of me. I wouldn't have been able to handle more crap. The truth about the connection between Salas and Persephone's father is too horrifying. It needs a swift action from me. No more playing the nice guy. I'm sure Zeus knew from the start about Salas's obsession. Everything he did was by design, and Persephone was targeted. He might have kept from Salas that Persephone was the girl being auctioned, fearing he would simply kidnap her, but I doubt Salas made the connection yet. He's an evil man but not the sharpest one.

Fuck Zeus, and fuck everyone who supports him. Even if I have to blow this town to smithereens, I'll stop him.

"How was Perseus? Did he settle in all right?"

We didn't see him when they got back. Persephone fell asleep in my arms before they came home, and I wouldn't leave her side then even if I could.

A twinkle of happiness shines in Hercules's eyes. "Oh yeah. He was like a kid on Christmas morning. He even jumped on his new bed a few times."

A sliver of happiness pierces my chest, and I chuckle.

"Explain to me how you managed to get close to him. Your job was to watch him from afar, if I remember correctly." I smirk.

His expression twists into one of consternation. "I'm sorry, boss. Like I said, he caught me, and then he invited me to hang out. He's a good kid, and I don't want to sound presumptuous by saying this, but I think he's starving for a father figure in his life."

I nod. "It makes sense. He lost his dad when he was young."

And good riddance. I'm sure the man tried to be a good father, but I can't forget that he made a deal with Salas. He would have given Persephone to that monster when she was still a kid if he hadn't died.

"I don't have any problem with you being that person for him, Hercules."

His eyes widen. "I don't know what to say."

"As long as it doesn't interfere with your work for me," I add.

"It won't, boss."

I nod. "I'm sure Persephone wants to spend time with her brother today. Being the weekend and all, you won't have to play chauffeur and bodyguard, which works out perfectly. I have a job for you."

"Whatever you need."

"I want all your men ready to engage. No more scare tactics. Zeus wants to hurt the woman I love, and that's a declaration of war in my book."

Hercules's demeanor changes in an instant. He worked for my brother for a long time before switching sides. He knows about him and what he's capable of more than I do.

"My men are loyal, but that's not enough. Salas brought his henchmen, and that combined with the scumbags Zeus has at his disposal puts us at a serious disadvantage."

That's not news to me, hence why I've been busy gaining allies.

"I know, and I'm working on it. I want extra security around my property and my business."

He nods. "It's already been taken care of, boss."

I nod. "Good."

"Do you want any security detail on you?"

"No. It's best if I don't have shadows with me today."

He narrows his eyes. "I don't like that. You could be ambushed."

"I'll be careful."

"Where are you going?"

"To pay a few visits. It's high time Zeus's offspring pick sides."

Hercules's eyebrows rise. "You mean Hermes and Ares?"

"They're the only ones who can help. Athena is too close to Zeus, and Apollo and Artemis are too young."

Frowning, he rubs his chin. "Besides Athena, all of Zeus's children hate him. But he's a master at manipulation. Do you think they'll turn against him?"

"Hermes will. Ares… it's to be seen."

"What about Poseidon? Is he staying out of this one? I haven't heard about any moves from his end."

"He's always been on Zeus's side, but surprisingly, he hasn't shown his hand on this matter yet. We need to keep an eye on him, and his son."

Hercules snorts. "I wouldn't worry about Triton."

"Why do you say that?" Even though Triton and I are close in age, I don't know much about him. He lives with his mother, and Poseidon's ex-wife hates my brother with a passion.

"He's more interested in catching the perfect wave than getting involved with a family feud."

In my experience, that means nothing. My brothers have the gift of reeling their children into their affairs despite their personal interests. My old man did the same to us. No matter how hard we try, we can't ever escape being a Godaire.

I DON'T SEE Persephone before I leave the house, but I do call Hecate despite the early hour. It rings and rings, and I fear she's not going to answer. Hell, I should have stopped by the guesthouse before I left, but I took too long to leave, and now I'm running late.

When I fear the call will go to voice mail, her annoyed voice comes through. "What the hell do you want now, Hades? Someone better be dying."

"I need a favor."

"Of course you do. I'm beginning to think you only let me stay in your guesthouse rent-free so I can be your lackey."

"You know that's not true. And what I'm asking is hardly a burden."

"I'll be the judge of that. Spill it already."

"I need you to hang out with Persephone and Perseus today and not let them go anywhere."

"Are you for real? You want me to babysit your grown-ass girlfriend and her brother?"

I pinch the bridge of my nose. "This is important, Hecate. New information has come to light, and I have to handle things. It's not safe for them in the streets."

"I don't like the sound of that. Please tell me you're not planning to do something stupid."

"When do I ever do anything stupid?"

She sighs loudly. "Hades, you'd better not get yourself killed trying to be a hero."

The last thing I need is a sermon from her. "Will you stay with Persephone in the house, please?"

"Fine. But don't think you're not in the doghouse with me. You left me alone with Hermes last night. Not cool."

"Yeah, whatever. Stop denying the obvious."

"What the hell are you talking about now?"

I sigh. "Never mind. I don't have time for this conversation. I'm counting on you."

I end the call before she can say another word, then look at the time and curse under my breath. If I don't press the pedal to the metal, I'll arrive late for the meeting I set up. Ares doesn't know I'm ambushing him at his gym. At this hour, it's only open for his personal use. But I convinced another player to meet me there, and if she arrives before I do, I can forget any help from her. Aphrodite doesn't tolerate people who waste her time.

I should have driven the Bugatti, but it's too flashy and recognizable. I'm trying my best not to draw attention to myself, because a trap isn't a far-fetched possibility. The Escalade is generic enough, though.

When I arrive at my destination, I see Aphrodite has just pulled in. Unlike me, she's unconcerned about being inconspicuous. Her red Ferrari could very well be a neon sign flashing on the highway.

It's not even seven in the morning yet, but she's dressed to the nines in a pinstripe skirt suit and stiletto heels that could work as weapons if she were in a pinch. Her long blonde hair cascades in luscious curls down her back, and it's no wonder she has a legion of men fawning at her feet. The woman is gorgeous, but her looks never did a thing for me.

She pushes her sunglasses up her head and watches me walk over. "This better be worth it, Hades."

"We won't know until we talk to him."

Her red lips become a thin, flat line. "I still don't know what my presence here can do for you. I gave you my support. Isn't that enough?"

"No. Ares needs to know I'm not alone in this, and unfortunately, he has severe trust issues. He needs to hear it from you."

She rolls her eyes. "Your nephew sounds hella fun."

I narrow my eyes. "He's never come to Playground?"

"No. And don't look so surprised. Not everyone in Olympus Bay is into what I offer."

"So you've never met him?"

She tilts her head. "What are you getting at, Hades? What's wrong with Ares?"

I shake my head. "Nothing. Well, not exactly nothing. But I'll let you judge for yourself."

The door is locked, which isn't an issue since I memorized the code. Ares has trust issues, but he's surprisingly unconcerned about security. He gave me the code a while back, and I know he hasn't changed it since. But again, who in Olympus Bay would be crazy enough to mess with his property?

As soon as I step inside, I can hear Ares's grunts. He must be in the ring. Aphrodite's high heels make a sharp sound against the concrete floor, and it echoes loudly in the open space. The noise doesn't break Ares's concentration, though. He's in the zone, giving hell to his trainer, who, even with all the padding, must be feeling the power of his punches. I rub my chin, reliving the moment when Ares knocked me out.

Aphrodite and I stop near the ring, and I begin to wonder how long she'll wait before she storms out of here. I flick my gaze to her, expecting to find an annoyed or bored expression. But she's neither. In fact, she seems captivated by Ares. Maybe her presence here will have more than one benefit.

"He's not bad," she says, "but his form could use some work."

Her comment is loud enough that Ares hears it. He glances in her direction, clearly annoyed, and then punches his trainer so hard that it sends the guy to the floor.

"Jesus!" I blurt out.

"You were saying?" Ares asks her.

She shrugs. "I stand by what I said."

Ares narrows his eyes for a second, and I wonder what's going to come out of his mouth. But surprisingly, he doesn't say anything to her. Instead, he goes to check on his trainer.

"I think we're done for the day," the man grunts as Ares helps him up.

"Oh, come on. I didn't hit you that hard."

"Excuse me? If I hadn't been wearing protection, I'd probably be unconscious."

He shakes his head and smiles in my direction. "You're worse than my uncle."

I fight the urge to flip him off. I have to remember why I'm here. Ares takes his time getting out of the ring and walking over to us. I notice he doesn't make eye contact with Aphrodite.

"To what do I owe the pleasure of your surprise visit, Hades?"

"The time has come to end Zeus's control of Olympus Bay. Are you in or out?"

His eyes go round, and for the first time since he learned to talk, he's not ready with a quick answer.

"I think your news short-circuited his brain," Aphrodite pipes up.

He quickly blinks a couple times and turns to her. "You're the owner of Playground. How do you fit in this?"

Her lips curl into a sardonic grin. "You know I'm more than a club owner, darling. Let's not pretend otherwise."

He squints, clenching his jaw, then turns to me. "When is this happening?"

"As soon as possible."

"You and my father have been waging a cold war for years. Why the urgency to dethrone him now?"

"Things have changed. He's brought another player on the field and made it personal."

Ares's eyes widen. "This is about the girl you bought at the auction, isn't it? Persephone."

"I didn't buy her," I growl.

He throws his head back and laughs. "Oh my. Now everything makes sense. My dear uncle has fallen in love."

"Okay. Are we done here? I have a busy day," Aphrodite complains.

At the sound of her voice, Ares's amusement vanishes. "Why did you come? Are you an offering to sway me to Hades's side?"

The punch comes swiftly, too fast for Ares to block it. His head snaps back, and then he's holding his bloody nose and cursing.

Fuck. This is not what I planned when I asked Aphrodite to tag along.

"I'm not a plaything, asshole," she grits out.

He wipes the blood off with the back of his hand, smearing the protective band around it. "Clearly not." He looks at me. "I'll join your effort to get rid of Daddy Dearest under one condition."

Crossing my arms, I watch him through slitted eyes. "Let's hear it, then."

"I want her to train with me."

"What?" Aphrodite blurts out, and then flicks her gaze to mine.

"No one has ever caught me by surprise like that," Ares explains. "I want to train with you."

"I'm not a trainer," she replies through clenched teeth. "Hire someone else."

"No. I want you. That's my price," he replies casually as he begins to unwrap his hand.

Shit. Now I'm screwed. There's no chance Aphrodite will agree to Ares's insane demand.

"I'm not going to train you."

Disappointment flashes in his eyes.

"But I'll commit to sparring with you once in a while," she adds.

He studies her for a moment, then looks at me with a crooked grin and a deranged glint in his eyes. "Let's end Zeus's reign."

33

PERSEPHONE

I find Hades's side of the bed empty and cold. He's been gone a while. My heart constricts in my chest, but I fight the emotion. I won't let my low self-esteem get in the way of my happiness. There could be a myriad of reasons why he's not here, one of them being that it's super late already. My phone says it's past ten in the morning. But it's Saturday, so…

"Shit!"

I sit up fast, remembering that I'm supposed to be at the flower shop at eleven. I almost trip over the tangled sheets as I get out of bed, and it's only a miracle that keeps me from falling face-first on the floor. I brace my hand on the nightstand and then see the note Hades left for me.

I'm frantic, but I can't help the smile that tugs the corners of my mouth. Quickly, I read his note. It's short and to the point, but it ends sweetly.

Good morning, beautiful. I'm sorry I couldn't say this in person. I have a million errands to run, and you looked too peaceful sleeping. I'll be back as soon as I can.
Love, Hades.

I press the note against my chest and sigh like a silly, enamored girl. If this was a cartoon, my eyes would be the shape of hearts.

I set the note on the nightstand again and hurry to get dressed. Ten minutes later, I'm showered and ready to go, but as I make my way to the kitchen, Perseus finds me in the hallway, his eyes round and worried.

Oh hell. What now?

"Thank God you're up," he says a little out of breath.

"What's wrong?"

"I dropped some of my chocolate-covered cereal on the floor, and I think Cerberus ate some."

My stomach bottoms out. "You think, or are you sure? This is serious, Persi."

He pulls his hair back, yanking at the strands. "I don't know. I had my back to the mess for a second. I was looking for something to scoop it up, and when I turned, he had his nose right in the middle of it."

Hell, I can't believe Cerberus is in trouble because of me again. Technically, I didn't do anything this time, but since Perseus is my brother, I still feel responsible.

"Are you able to carry him?"

Perseus looks at his cast, then nods. "I'll manage. What are we doing?"

"We need to take him to the vet."

His eyes bug out. "O-Okay."

I have no idea what car Hades took this morning, but when I spot the fob for his Bugatti on the console in the hallway, I don't think twice, just grab it and rush to the garage with Perseus right on my heels. I don't know how he was able to scoop up Cerberus while one of his arms is in a cast, but I sure as hell wouldn't be able to in my current state. That dog weighs a ton.

"Are you driving that?" he asks when he sees where I'm headed.

"Yes. It's the fastest car Hades owns."

"Do you even know how to drive that thing?"

"It's a stick shift, just like Petunia was."

"Only you would compare that piece of junk to this beauty."

"Shut up, Persi. You're not helping. Just put Cerberus in the car."

Cerberus barks and wags his tail, probably believing we're going to take him someplace nice. I hope that's a sign he didn't ingest any of the chocolate.

I turn on the ignition, trying not to freak out when the powerful engine comes to life. Perseus was right. This is nothing like Petunia.

"Put your seat belt on," I tell him.

"You don't need to ask me twice."

The slightest pressure on the gas pedal makes the car lurch forward. I grab the steering wheel tighter and grind my teeth.

Come on, Persephone. You can do this.

"Oh my God. We're going to die," Perseus whines.

"If you're not going to say something useful, just shut your cakehole."

Mercifully, I get the hang of the car when we hit the road. We pass a black SUV that immediately darts behind us.

"Shit, I think we're being followed, Seph," Perseus says.

I didn't even think about the possibility of the enemy waiting for us outside the gates. *Let's see them keep up with us.* I press the pedal to the metal, reaching a hundred miles an hour in less than five seconds.

"Holy shit," Perseus blurts out.

"Hang on, Persi. I want to lose our tail."

"Just please don't kill us in the process."

I've never driven a car at the speed I'm going now. It's scary as hell but also exhilarating. I check the rearview mirror, and when I don't see any sign of the black SUV, I slow down. I can't claim I'm an excellent driver, and it wouldn't do us any good if I crashed.

"Can you look up the nearest vet on your phone?" I ask Perseus.

"Uh, I don't have my phone on me."

I curse under my breath. I didn't bring mine either. Or my purse. I guess I'll go to the vet near Styx. My heart is beating at the speed of light, and dots of sweat have formed at my hairline. I want to know if Cerberus is still doing okay in the back, but I don't dare take my eyes off the road.

"Seph," Perseus whimpers.

"What is it?"

"Please slow down. I think I'm going to be sick."

When it rains, it pours. "Did you get food poisoning too?"

"No, you're going way too fast, and it's making me queasy."

I definitely don't want him throwing up in the car, so I slow the car to below a hundred. A moment later, a couple of black SUVs rush past us, scaring the crap out of me. I try not to lose my mind. They just raced by us, so maybe they aren't after us. But when another SUV runs parallel to the Bugatti, I fear the worst.

"What's that asshole doing?" Like a dumbass, I slow down instead of accelerating.

I'm jolted forward when another car bumps us from behind.

"What the hell?" Perseus turns in his seat.

I look at the rearview mirror in time to watch the SUV crash into us again. The impact makes me lose control of the steering wheel, and I collide with the car next to us.

"Seph! Watch out!" Perseus shouts.

Ahead of us, the first two SUVs are now blocking the road. *Shit!* I slam on the brakes, hoping I can stop the car before the crash. The tires screech, and the seat belt digs against my chest painfully. Cerberus whines, and I remember he's loose in the back seat. But Perseus has the presence of mine to stretch out his arm and prevent him from flying out the window.

The car finally stops a few inches away from the two vehicles in front of us. My pulse has skyrocketed, leaving me gasping for air. I barely have time to check on Perseus before a bunch of mean-looking guys get out of their cars carrying semi-automatic weapons. My blood runs cold when I recognize one of them.

Salas.

HADES

I'm on my way back from meeting with Hercules's team when Hecate calls. It's not even eleven yet, but I can guess she's calling to complain I'm taking too long.

"I'm almost home," I say before she can get a word out.

"I can't find Persephone and Perseus."

The beep of another incoming call comes through, but I ignore it.

"What do you mean you can't find them?" I grit out.

"When I came by the house, they were gone, and so was Cerberus. They took the Bugatti."

I pass a hand over my face, willing myself to calm the fuck down.

"I asked for one thing and one thing only."

"I'm sorry. Hermes came by, and I didn't go up to the main house until they were gone."

The second caller tries to reach me again. I see it's Hercules. *Hell.* "Hold on a second. Hercules is calling me."

I switch over and ask, "What's going on now?"

"I just received a call from the security team assigned to your house. They told me Persephone left the house in the Bugatti, but they lost her."

"How could they fucking lose her?"

"She's driving one of the fastest cars in the world."

"That's no excuse," I bark. "I want them all fucking fired."

I end the call with Hercules, not even trying to rein in my temper. Then I get back to Hecate.

"What did Hercules say?" she asks.

"The security team couldn't keep up with the Bugatti."

"Did you tell her about them?"

"What do you mean?"

"Maybe she thought they were the bad guys, hence why she left them eating dust."

I pinch the bridge of my nose. "Fuck! Have you tried calling her?"

"She left her phone, purse, everything behind. There was a mess in the kitchen, chocolate-covered cereal everywhere."

My heart shrivels into nothing as my worry doubles. "Were there any signs of a struggle?"

I can't discard the possibility of a home invasion. The team assigned to protect the perimeter is clearly composed of a bunch of idiots.

"No, the cereal mess was the only thing out of the ordinary. I'm so sorry, Hades. Hermes and I are already on the road looking for them."

A light bulb turns on in my head. "The Bugatti has GPS." I pull off the road so I can use the app to pinpoint Persephone's location. "She's not far from the house. She took the highway toward downtown."

"Okay, we're close."

I end the call and stare at the phone screen. She isn't moving. Sheer terror takes hold of me. I put the car in gear and peel off the side of the road, merging with traffic without bothering to look first. A loud horn sounds, and then the car I cut in front of swerves to the side.

I pray to every god I know that my worst nightmare hasn't become a reality. But when I arrive, I realize they were wasted prayers. I see the Bugatti, mangled from behind, and black tire marks on the road. Hecate and Hermes are already at the scene. I press on the brakes and jump out of the car, leaving the engine on. Hermes has his phone glued to his ear, and Hecate has a pitiful expression on her face.

I ignore them both and walk to the driver's side, looking for clues. My stomach twists with a vengeance when I see drops of blood on the asphalt.

I'm going to kill every motherfucker involved in this.

Without uttering a single word, I turn around and stalk back to my car.

"Hades, where are you going?" Hecate calls.

"To commit fratricide."

34

HADES

I burst into Zeus's lavish home like a man possessed. My vision is tinged in red, and that's exactly what I want to see splattered all over the pristine walls—Zeus's fucking blood. I always knew this confrontation with him was inevitable, but for the sake of his kids, I tried to be civilized. I'm done being the nice guy. He should have never messed with my loved ones. He brought a monster back into Persephone's life, handed her over to him, and now he's going to feel my wrath.

He has a full house today, people who came for Apollo's and Artemis's eighteenth birthday bash—a party I was invited to attend but not expected to. I know without looking that not even one of these sycophants is friends with the twins.

I seek the bastard out in the crowd, but all I see are startled strangers staring at me.

Ares breaks away from a circle of well-dressed women and makes a beeline in my direction. "I didn't expect to see you again today."

"Where's Zeus?"

His eyes widen. "Is it happening now?"

"What is?" Athena joins us. "Hades, you look positively deranged. I think you should leave."

"Fuck off. And stay out of my way if you know what's good for you."

I walk around them. Time is running out, and I can't waste it by throwing barbs at Zeus's favorite spawn.

"I'm not—" she starts.

"Stay out of it, sis. Trust me," Hermes interjects.

I don't know how he got here so fast. I had a head start, and I was driving like a maniac.

My quick search of the room yields nothing. There's no sign of Zeus. It seems my asshole brother isn't at the party yet, so I veer for his private office. The door is closed, but I'm too furious to open it like a normal person. I kick the solid wood, busting the lock and breaking the door off its frame.

Zeus is behind his desk, smiling as he speaks on his cell phone. When his gaze connects with mine, I see the victorious glint shining there.

"I'll have to call you later," he tells whoever is on the other end of the line.

He barely has time to set the device down before I'm on him, pulling the asshole up from his chair by the lapels of his jacket.

"Where are they, motherfucker?"

"You'd better let go now before you get hurt real bad, baby br—"

I flip him around, locking his arms behind him, and then I smash his face against the desk, getting the satisfaction of hearing his nose crack. He realizes then that I'm not here to be civilized and struggles. But I've been preparing for this moment my whole life, and I'm fueled by rage.

I pull him back, keeping a firm hold on him. "Where are they?"

Ares, Hermes, Apollo, and Athena storm in, but I keep my eyes glued to Zeus's bloodied face.

"You'll never find them," he grits out. "By now, your precious Persephone has been fucked six ways to Sunday by Salas, and your precious dog is shark food."

I let go of his jacket to pull the gun from behind my back. Pointing it at his temple, I say, "Do you think I'm joking? Tell me where they are, or your brain will be all over your office furniture."

He laughs hysterically. "Go ahead. Kill me. Then I'll take the information you so desperately want to the grave."

"You're right. Blowing your head off would be too easy a death for you."

I change my aim and shoot his leg instead. He howls, and someone else screams too. From the corner of my eye, I see Athena being restrained by Ares and Apollo.

"You motherfucker! You're gonna wish you'd never been born," Zeus shouts.

"Oh, I already do wish that, big brother. How long do you think it will take for you to bleed to death? I gather I can aim for your kneecap next, or maybe your hand?"

"You can torture me for as long as you like. I'll never tell you anything."

"Maybe I should shoot your nose off." I press the barrel of the gun against his nostril.

"No!" Athena yells. "Stop hurting him."

I turn to her. "If you want me to stop, I suggest you convince your father to tell me where Salas took Persephone."

She's crying as she glances at Zeus. It's obvious she truly loves the monster, but looking at her brothers, it's clear only she harbors those feelings. Zeus was a devoted father to her—and only her, for reasons unbeknownst to me.

"I know where. Just stop shooting him," she begs.

"Athena, don't you dare say a word," he growls.

Her eyes shine with remorse as she holds his stare. I've known her my entire life. She's never been duplicitous. She has honor, which is mind-boggling considering who her idol is.

"I'm sorry, Dad."

"If you say a thing, you're dead to me."

"Trust us, sis, you won't be missing much," Ares replies.

"You and your brothers are all scum, unworthy of my name," Zeus spits back.

I press the gun harder against his face and stare at Athena. "Just tell me now, or say adios to daddy."

"Salas has a yacht anchored at the Triton Cove Marina," she blurts out. "They plan to leave around noon."

My stomach bottoms out. That's not enough time.

"Fuck. That's forty-five minutes from here," Hermes pipes up.

"You stupid bitch," Zeus screeches. "I warned you to keep your mouth shut. You're just as worthless as the rest of them."

Athena's face contorts into a look of pure agony, doubling my fury against Zeus. Since I don't need him now, I hit his temple with the end of my gun hard enough to render him unconscious.

Athena gasps, but at least she doesn't accuse me of being a heartless asshole. Her brothers finally release her, and she runs toward us. I step away, but my body is still riddled with tension. Even hurting Zeus wasn't enough to release my aggression. I have it in spades within me, all ready to be unleashed on Salas.

"You'll never make it to Triton Cove before the yacht sails," Apollo points out.

"He will if he flies," Ares replies. "Come on. My helicopter is on the helipad in the back."

Hermes eyebrows shoot up. "You flew here?"

"Why are you surprised? Ares doesn't miss the opportunity to upstage me," Apollo grumbles.

I stalk past them and then sprint down the stairs.

"Hades, wait up," Ares calls.

I have blood all over me, but that doesn't seem to faze most of the guests. They hang out with Zeus; they know he isn't an innocent flower. I lock gazes with Artemis, and I feel the need to say something as I walk past her.

"Happy birthday, honey. Sorry about the drama."

"Is that his blood?"

"It ain't mine."

She smiles. "Best birthday gift ever."

I'm outside when Ares catches up with me. "For fuck's sake, Hades. I asked you to wait for me."

"In case you didn't hear Athena back there, I have less than half an hour to make it to Triton Cove."

"I heard her, but since when do you know how to fly a damn helicopter?"

I glance at him and can't find a retort. In the heat of the moment, I forgot about that pesky detail.

"Fine. You'd better get me there as fast as you can."

He gives me a deranged look. "Don't worry. We'll get there in time and then it's showtime."

"You're out of your mind if you think you're going without us," Hermes pipes up as he joins us with Apollo in tow.

I nod at him, but when I look at Apollo, I ask, "Are you sure you want to do this on your birthday?"

"Between kicking some ass and entertaining the geriatric fest inside that house, you think I'll choose the latter?"

I wish I weren't worried sick about the love of my life and could appreciate the magnitude of this moment. Zeus's offspring ganging up against him to help me is monumental. That's gotta hurt more than all the blows and the bullet wound I gave him.

"Let's do this, then," I say. "But remember Salas is mine."

35

PERSEPHONE

I'm still bound and gagged when I'm pushed onto the luxurious yacht anchored at the Triton Cove Marina. Salas didn't bother covering my eyes when he shoved me in the trunk of his SUV, and I could read the signs along the way. The long drive worked to calm me down from the panic attack, and now I can think logically. I know what he wants, and even though the mere thought of him touching me brings bile to my mouth, I can go through with it if it'll keep Perseus and Cerberus alive.

My brother is ahead of me in the same situation. They tied his good arm alongside the cast, and he has a gag in his mouth too. One of Salas's men has Cerberus tossed over his wide shoulder. A cord is keeping his muzzle shut. I should say a prayer that they didn't kill them on the spot, but the little I know about Salas doesn't give me comfort. If he spared my brother and Cerberus, it's because he has something vile planned for them. I'm terrified about their fate, but strangely, I'm not afraid of mine. Maybe because I know what awaits me. I take solace in the fact that he won't be my first, that I have the memory of Hades's love to protect me from his corruption.

He leads me inside the yacht and shoves me to a leather couch in the main area. From the corner of my eye, I see Perseus is getting tied to a chair, and Cerberus is dumped at his feet. The poor thing lets out a whimper that I can feel deep in my soul. It makes my blood boil, and I struggle with my restraints.

Salas steps in front of me, smiling from ear to ear. "Finally, after all these years, you're mine."

The gag in my mouth prevents me from telling him to get fucked, but I hope he can see it in my eyes.

"It's a pity I didn't have you when you were young and pure, but now that you're all grown up, I can fuck you as hard as I want without fear of breaking you too soon."

"What do you want to do with the dog and her brother, Salas?" one of his men asks.

He spends a moment scrutinizing them. "That's a beautiful dog. The pearl of Hades's eye, so I hear. We'll use it for gun practice later. He'd make a nice target."

My eyes go wider, and I scream against the gag in my mouth.

"As for her brother...." He glances at me, and a vile smile spreads across his odious face. "I have no use for him. You and the rest of the crew can have your fun. I'm sure you'll appreciate a tight virgin hole."

The guard smiles maliciously in Perseus's direction, making me see red. My brother shakes his head and flinches as the tall man approaches him.

Adrenaline makes me reckless. I jump from the couch and try to make my way to him, but Salas grabs me by the hair and yanks me back.

"Where do you think you're going, bitch?" He removes the gag from my mouth. "Go on. I want to hear you scream."

I spit on his face instead. His nostrils flare, and the evil in his eyes shines brighter. He releases my hair to slap me hard across my cheek. The hit is so violent that it sends me to the floor and makes my ears ring. Before I can get up, he's on top of me, spreading my legs with his knees.

"I wanted our first time to be special. I was going to take you to my private quarters and show you what a real man feels like, but I think I'll fuck you right here in front of your brother."

"Go ahead. Do your best, but know that you'll never measure up to Hades."

Pure hatred flares in his gaze. He curls his hands around my neck and squeezes in a vicious hold; I don't have room to gasp. In the background, I hear Salas's man laughing while Perseus struggles. I'm resigned to being raped by a monster; I can't handle the knowledge that it's going to be my brother's fate too. Tears of frustration gather in my eyes. I wish I was stronger, but I can't pry Salas's fingers away from my throat no matter how hard I try.

There's a loud crash in the room that draws Salas's attention. His hold on my neck slackens, and then his hands are gone and he's on his feet. I take a deep, ragged breath, getting as much air in my lungs as possible. Then I turn on my side and watch Perseus grapple with the asshole who was trying to take him. But Perseus is winning despite his arm being in a cast. He managed to break from his restraints, and he's now straddling the man, pressing his cast against his face. I wish he'd pull a *Game of Thrones* move and pop the guy's eyes like a grape.

Salas just stands there, watching the whole scene with a perverse grin on his lips. He's enjoying the show even though one of his men is losing the fight. I notice more of his guys standing far back, sporting the same expression of amusement. They're all sick bastards.

I spy the handle of Salas's gun sticking out from under his waistband and make a hasty decision. I jump to my feet and go for it. I only manage to slip the gun free before Salas turns and grabs my wrist, bending it at a sharp angle until I'm forced to drop it. He keeps twisting it, and the bone snaps. White-hot pain shoots up my arm, and I cry out.

"Stupid bitch." He shoves me back so hard that I lose my balance and fall on my ass near Perseus, who's now restrained by three of Salas's men.

One is pressing his knee to Persi's back and holding his face flat against the floor. Another is holding his legs, and a third is pulling his arm back at an angle that must be excruciating for him.

I guess my ill attempt to get the gun from Salas prompted the other fuckers into action. My vision is blurry thanks to all the tears of rage that are falling.

"I'm going to make you pay for your little act of rebellion." Salas points the gun at my brother, then changes the target at the last second, aiming at Cerberus.

All it takes is a split second before the gunshot. I don't have the knowledge of consciously moving my body toward Cerberus, but I cover him just the same, and then my thigh burns as if pierced by a flaming rod. The pain is agonizing. A strangled scream rips from my throat.

Perseus shouts my name, but my eyes are closed, and I have no idea what's happening to him now. My head is getting lighter, and the pain seems to be subsiding. No, that's not it. I'm slowly fading into nothing.

HADES

I hear a gunshot, and Persephone's name gets lodged in my throat. My gun is out as I rush down the dock to where Salas's yacht is still anchored. Ares, Apollo, and Hermes flank me, plus the local backup sent by Aphrodite. In total, we're twenty, all packing enough ammo to start a small war.

Aphrodite's men are all wearing bulletproof vests, but I'm not. Taking the lead is a huge risk, but my need to reach Persephone before Salas hurts her trumps all common sense. The guards stationed at the back of the yacht see us too late. I fire, my aim certain, getting both before they can pull their guns from their holsters. The loudest noise is of them falling off the boat since our guns have silencers.

I rush up the ramp, and then I'm inside the yacht. A punch comes at my face, which I block and then toss the man to the side. Salas comes into view, holding a gun in his right hand. Persephone is on the floor, unconscious, her body draped over Cerberus, and bleeding from a wound in her leg. My rage erupts from the pit of my stomach, and I'd have blown his brain to pieces if he wasn't aiming his gun at Persephone.

"Lower your weapon if you want her to live."

He'll fire before I have the chance to shoot him first. I lost track of where the others are. I can't follow the noise of battle around me. I know Salas will shoot me as soon as I lower my gun, but I can't risk Persephone's life. My arm begins to drop when a bullet pierces his shoulder. He staggers back with a cry, and his barrel is now pointing at the floor.

I don't waste any time. I pull my trigger, putting a bullet through his head before he fires his own gun. He drops like a sack of excrement, but my attention is no longer on him. I run to where Persephone is and tug her into my arms.

"Skulls, my love, please talk to me." I press my fingers against her neck, trying to find a pulse. It's there, but it's weak.

Someone stops next to me. "Is she okay?"

I look up and find Hermes. "She's losing blood fast. I have to take her to a hospital."

"The area is secure," Ares tells us as he walks over.

Across the room, Apollo is helping Perseus to his feet. The kid has blood on his face from a busted lip and a cut on his forehead, but other than that, I don't see any obvious wounds that need immediate attention.

Cerberus makes a pitiful noise, but Hermes reacts before I can, cutting the cord those sons of bitches put around his muzzle. He inches closer to me and rubs his nose against Persephone's prone form. I'm relieved beyond measure that they didn't hurt him too.

I stand up with Persephone in my arms and head for the exit.

Perseus rushes to my side, his face ashen. "The bullet got her leg, but she'll be okay, right?" He looks into my eyes, his expression pleading and also full of hope. He's putting his faith in me that I'll take care of his sister.

"She will, but I need to get her to a hospital."

He nods. "You take care of her, and I promise I won't let anything happen to Cerberus."

"What?" I whip my face to where Cerberus is. "Did they hurt him too?"

How could I have missed that?

"He looks fine, Hades," Hermes tells me.

"He might have eaten chocolate-covered cereal. That's why we took your car. We were taking him to the vet."

Son of a bitch. This cannot be happening. It's a nightmare. It has to be a nightmare.

"You take care of Persephone, and I'll take Cerberus to a vet," Hermes says, already carrying him toward the dock.

"Thank you." I glance at Perseus. "I'm glad for your offer to stay with Cerberus, but I'm sure Persephone will want to see you when she wakes up. You're coming with me."

He wipes tears from the corners of his eyes. "Okay."

The lump in my throat almost threatens to choke me. It kills me that I have to choose between the love of my life and my best friend. Chocolate is toxic as hell to dogs but not usually fatal. I can't say the same about Persephone's wound. I hold her tighter against my chest and pray to a god I don't believe in that she'll make it through.

36

PERSEPHONE

My eyes fly open, but my vision is blurry, and I can't tell where I am. Discomfort comes first. The side of my face is tender, my left thigh hurts, and my wrist is in a cast. Memories of my torment at the hands of Salas come to the forefront of my mind. The last thing I remember is jumping to protect Cerberus from a fatal shot.

Movement in my periphery makes me turn my head. Hades's face comes into focus, and my heart overflows with a myriad of emotions: love, relief, gratitude.

"You're awake. Thank God." He squeezes my hand and cups my cheek.

"How long have I been out?" I croak. My voice is still hoarse from all the screaming, so hopefully not long.

"Nearly twenty-four hours. They had to operate to remove the bullet. And your wrist is broken."

His eyes grow darker.

"Is he dead?"

"Yes. My only regret is that I can't kill him more than once."

An ache presses against my chest. I hate that Hades was forced to soil his soul to protect me.

He runs his fingertips across my forehead. "What's this? I don't want to see you frown, sweetheart."

"I can't help it. I wish you didn't have to kill anyone because of me, even if the asshole deserved it."

He presses his lips softly against mine. "If you're worried about my soul, don't be, Skulls. It was already damned before you ever came into my life. And even if it wasn't, I'd gladly spend an eternity in hell if that meant you were safe."

I thought I couldn't love this man more, but my heart expands to contain the overflow of emotions.

"I love you so damn much." I wipe the tears from the corners of my eyes.

"Not as much as I love you." He kisses me again, but this time he lingers, prying my lips open with his tongue.

All the aches in my body fade into nothing as I get lost in him.

A throat clearing interrupts our moment, and sadly, Hades pulls away.

"I see Sleeping Beauty is awake," Hermes pipes up, smiling from ear to ear.

A moment later, Perseus comes into view and rushes to my side. "Seph! I was so worried."

"I'm okay, Persi." I watch him closely, trying to not flinch as I count all the bruises and cuts on his face. "How are you?"

"I'm fine. I look rougher than I feel."

"He's truly fine," Hecate says. "Damn, girl. You're a trouble magnet, aren't you?"

"Seriously, Hecate?" Hades complains.

She shrugs. "Just stating a fact."

"Who else knows about what happened?" I ask.

"Just my inner circle," Hades replies. "We're still in Triton Cove."

I exhale in relief. Helen doesn't know. She worries too much, and I'm glad she didn't have to suffer alongside everyone else.

"What happens now?" I ask.

"Now we wait until the doctor says I can take you home."

"That's not what I meant."

He glances at his friends, avoiding my gaze. Something is troubling him, and I don't like it.

"I don't think we have to worry about Zeus anytime soon. Dad is still licking his wounds," Hermes replies. "And now that Ares and I have fully supported Hades, it's unlikely he'll try anything. He's arrogant, but he's not stupid."

Hecate crosses her arms. "I'm not worried about Zeus. But what about Salas's brother?"

"We won't worry about Dimas now," Hades retorts. "The most important thing right now is for Persephone to recover."

He kisses my temple, making me melt a little, but it isn't enough to diminish the anguish in my chest. I *am* worried about Zeus and this Dimas person. Hades killed his brother; that means he'll most likely seek retribution.

"I hear you loud and clear. Come on now." Hermes waves Perseus over. "We should let Persephone rest."

"All right." He kisses me on the cheek. "Get well soon, sis."

It's not until my brother leaves with Hermes and Hecate that it occurs to me to ask about Cerberus. My mentioning him brings a smile to Hades's lips.

"He's fine. It turns out he didn't eat any chocolate."

"Oh thank God."

He runs his fingers through my hair. "You should get some rest, darling."

"I've been sleeping for a whole day," I complain.

"True, but your body needs the rest. The quicker you recover, the quicker I can take you home."

Home.

Hearing Hades say that gets me all choked up again.

"What's this now? Why are you crying?" he asks.

"I don't know. I'm a fucking mess. Don't judge me."

"I'm not judging you. I want to know what I said that made you sad."

"Sad? These aren't tears of sadness, you big goof. They're happy tears."

Relief washes over his face, and then his lips unfurl into a radiant smile. "If you keep this up, I'm going to cry my eyes out too."

"Please do." I laugh.

His eyebrows scrunch together. "What are you trying to prove here, Skulls?"

"That you may look as tough as nails, but you are in fact a big softy."

"I am. A big softy for you, but let's keep that between us. I have to maintain my reputation." His eyes twinkle with mischief.

"Oh yeah, your bad boy reputation?"

"That's right." He nods.

I grin. "I don't mind if you play that role in the bedroom either."

Pure heat sparks in his eyes. "As soon as you get better, babe, I'll show you all my bad boy moves."

His stance changes in the blink of an eye when a man wearing a pristine suit enters my room. Hades straightens up and pulls a gun I didn't know he had on him. My heart jumps up to my throat, getting stuck there when I notice the resemblance between our visitor and Salas. He must be Dimas.

"I hope I'm not interrupting," he says in a smooth voice.

Hades points the gun at him. "What the hell are you doing here? How did you get past the guards?"

Guards? I had no idea there was a security detail outside.

The man smiles slowly. "I assured them I meant no harm." He opens his jacket and shows us his empty gun holster. "See? I came unarmed."

"That means nothing," Hades grits out. "You also didn't answer my question. What are you doing here?"

He buttons his jacket again, unfazed by Hades's aggressive stance or the gun pointed at him. "I came to thank you."

"Thank me? For what?"

"For getting rid of my irresponsible brother. Salas has been a thorn in my side for the longest time, but thanks to a promise I made to our father on his deathbed, I couldn't kill him myself."

My jaw drops as I listen to him talk casually about fratricide. But then, I shouldn't be surprised considering how Salas was. I'm sure Dimas isn't any better. He's smiling, but his eyes are dead, soulless.

"What about Zeus? Do you intend to form an alliance with him after all this?"

His eyes narrow. "My dealings with your brother are my concern. You have my thanks for helping me out with an inconvenience, and in return, I'll let you live your life in peace. But if you get in my way, you'll discover I'm not a tolerant man."

My stomach coils tightly, recognizing the threat. I flick my eyes to Hades, but he doesn't show any sign that he's afraid of Dimas.

He curls his lips into a grin. "That we have in common. I'm not a tolerant man either. Just stay the fuck out of my town, and we won't have any problems."

Dimas raises an eyebrow. "*Your* town?"

"Haven't you heard? Olympus Bay has a new king."

The man doesn't say a word for a couple seconds as he stares at Hades. I flick my gaze between them as they engage in a staring contest.

Finally, Dimas chuckles. "You can have Olympus Bay... for now." He looks at me. "I wish you a speedy recovery, honey. *Antio sas.*"

He walks out, and Hades immediately follows him. My heart

is hammering in my chest, and it doesn't return to a normal pace until he comes back sporting a grim expression.

"Is he gone?" I ask.

"Yes. I made sure of it. I also had a talk with the guards. They shouldn't have let Dimas in."

"Are they cops?"

Hades chuckles. "No. They're Aphrodite's men."

"I didn't expect that answer."

He's smiling as he walks over. "She's an ally now, but I'll explain everything to you later. Now, I want you to rest."

"I'm too wired to fall asleep."

He frowns. "Anything I can do to help?"

It's my turn to curl my lips into a mischievous grin. "Hmm, I remember your fingers had the ability to make me sooo relaxed."

He smiles once more. "Is that so?"

I nod.

"In that case, they're all yours."

37

PERSEPHONE

A MONTH LATER

I've tried my best to hide the stupid scar on my leg when Hades is around. Not because I think it's hideous—it ain't pretty, but I'm not self-conscious about it. His eyes dim whenever he sees even a hint of it, and I suspect he feels guilty that I got it. At least the cast around my wrist is off.

Tonight, I've decided on a different approach. I'm going to flaunt my battle scar and make him appreciate it instead of feeling sad about it. The dress I'm wearing is Greek-inspired. It has a plunging neckline and big openings on the sides. There's no hiding the scar in this. I smile. It's also sexy as hell. I can't wait to see the look on his face.

A little bird—Hermes—told me it's Hades's birthday today, a detail he failed to mention. He must have told Hecate to keep her mouth shut too, because she felt hella guilty when I approached her earlier to ask for her help with a surprise for him.

Perseus is spending the night at a friend's house, something I highly encouraged so I could have the house to myself. What I have planned requires total freedom and zero chance of people walking in on Hades and me. I don't intend to keep our activities confined to the bedroom.

Hercules is also in on the surprise. He's keeping Hades busy at Styx longer than necessary. I wonder if Hades suspects what we're up to.

My phone pings on my desk, announcing an incoming text message. It's Hercules saying they're five minutes away.

I hurry downstairs to make sure I have everything set. I ordered food from Hades's favorite restaurant because I'm not a great cook. It was delivered ten minutes ago, so it's already cold, but I doubt we'll be eating first anyway. I grab the bottle of champagne from the fridge and stick it in the ice bucket.

Then I turn to Cerberus and crouch in front of him. "You know what to do, right, buddy?"

He barks once and wags his tail. His cast is off; he doesn't need to be confined to the crate anymore. His job is to lead Hades to the pool area where the surprise will take place.

The little monitor in the kitchen shows the feed from the security camera and lets me know the moment he pulls in the garage. I hurry down the hallway with the ice bucket in hand, careful not to fall. I don't plan this evening ending with a trip to the ER. I walk past the swimming pool and veer for the pergola that I decorated with twinkling lights and a few sheets of see-through fabric for the extra romantic feel. Underneath the pergola, I threw comfy cushions and blankets. It's a lovely evening, and all the stars are out. This couldn't have been more perfect.

The champagne glasses are already on the small table, and I also got a bowl with grapes that, for whatever reason, I thought worked with the setting. I set the ice bucket next to them and then bite my lower lip. Maybe I should have brought more snacks. I bet Hades didn't eat anything all day.

I'm still lost in thought when his arms circle around my waist, and I let out a little squeak.

"What's all this?" he asks near my ear.

I turn around in his arms. "You scared me."

He chuckles, kissing me softly. "I'm sorry."

"Why must you always sneak up on me? *I* was supposed to surprise *you* tonight." I pout.

He takes my hands and steps back. His eyes drink me in first, and when his gaze meets mine again, I lose the ability to breathe. I'll never get used to how beautiful he is, or how he looks at me as if I were a goddess.

"You're breathtaking," he says.

My blush spreads through my cheeks. I'm still not used to receiving compliments from him. "Thank you."

"What are we celebrating tonight?" His eyes dance with mirth, and his lips curl in the crooked grin I love.

"Don't play innocent with me. It's your birthday, and you didn't tell me."

"I... I don't celebrate my birthday."

"Wait, like never?"

He shakes his head.

"Oh, Hades. That's the saddest thing I've ever heard."

"It's by choice." He shrugs nonchalantly, but I know him better now. I can see through the walls he erects to protect himself from a deep ache.

"*Was* by choice," I correct him, then release his hands to grab the small gift I got for him. "Here. Happy birthday."

He raises an eyebrow. "What is it?"

"It's called a gift. The only acceptable reply is 'Thank you.'"

The corners of his lips curl upward as he unwraps the box. But when he sees what's inside, he rewards me with a broad smile that lights up the entire place. He lifts his gaze to mine, holding the pair of cute skull-print boxer briefs I got for him. "This. Is. Awesome. Thank you, babe."

I push the fabric of my skirt to the side—thank you, slits—revealing my underwear. "They match mine."

It just so happens I'm showing my scar in the process, and Hades's gaze immediately drops to it. His smile wilts a fraction.

Oh no. We're not having that.

I step into his space and cup his cheek. "Hey, I don't want to see that look on your face every time you catch sight of my scar."

"I can't help it."

Frowning, I say, "Don't you dare feel guilty about what happened to me. Instead, you should be proud of what you've accomplished."

A myriad of emotions swirls in his eyes as he holds my gaze. "It's hard for me... being proud of myself. Confidence is something I fake well."

"We'll work on that. *Together*. You're the best man I've ever met, Hades. I love how fiercely you protect everyone close to you. I love how you treat your friends with kindness and patience, even the pain-in-the-ass ones. I love how you adore your dog. And I love how you love me."

He captures my face between his hands. "I don't know what I did to deserve you, Skulls. I'm glad you barreled into my life."

I squint. "Hmm, maybe not as glad that I ran over Cerberus."

"God, I can't begrudge you that either. Not anymore, anyway. You brought so much joy into my life. I didn't know how lost I was until you found me."

Tears roll down my cheeks, and they're probably smearing my makeup.

"You have to stop making me cry all the time, damn it," I say.

He wipes the moisture from my face with his thumbs. "If you're prone to crying when you're happy, I'm sorry, babe, but I can't promise you that."

"Fine." I step away from his embrace. "Are you ready for your next gift, then?"

He arches his eyebrows. "There's more?"

I reach behind my back and pull the zipper down. The straps slide off my shoulders, and the dress falls in a heap at my feet. "Yes, babe. There's more. Much, much more."

THE END

Thank you for reading Savage Impulses. I hope you enjoyed my modern take on Hades & Persephone's story.
I have plans for the other gods.

If you would like to receive news about the Kings of Olympus U series, sign up for here:

https://mhsoars.activehosted.com/f/18

FREE NOVELLA

CATCH YOU

Want to read another enemies-to-lovers sports romance? Then **scan the QR code** to get your free copy of *Catch You*.

Pride and Prejudice meets Veronica Mars in this enemy-to-lovers romance.

Kimberly

I had always thought Owen Whitfield fit the mold of the

brainless jock perfectly. Group of idiot friends? Check. Vapid girlfriend? Check. Ego bigger than the moon? Check. As long as he stayed out of my way, coexisting with his kind was doable. Until one day our worlds collided, changing everything. He pissed me off so badly that I had no choice but to give him a taste of his own medicine. Little did I know that my act of revenge would come back to bite me in the ass. How was I supposed to know Owen would turn out to be the best partner in crime I could hope for?

Owen

I never paid much attention to Kimberly Dawson, but I knew who she was. Ice Queen was what we called her. She was gorgeous, no one could deny that. But she was also a condescending bitch, which was enough reason for me to stay the hell away from her. She thought I was a dumb jock, and that was okay until she came crashing into my life. Against my better judgment, I let her embroil me in her shenanigans, forcing us to spend too much time together. It was my doom. She got under my skin. She was all I could think about. I never thought I would be the knight in shining armor to anyone, not until she came along.

Scan the QR code to get your FREE copy!

ABOUT THE AUTHOR

USA Today Bestselling Author Michelle Hercules always knew creative arts were her calling but not in a million years did she think she would become an author. With a background in fashion design she thought she would follow that path. But one day, out of the blue, she had an idea for a book. One page turned into ten pages, ten pages turned into a hundred, and before she knew it, her first novel, The Prophecy of Arcadia, was born.

Michelle Hercules resides in Florida with her husband and daughter. She is currently working on the *Blueblood Vampires* series and the *Rebels of Rushmore* series.

Sign-up for Michelle Hercules' Newsletter:

Join Michelle Hercules' Readers Group:
https://www.facebook.com/groups/mhsoars

Connect with Michelle Hercules:
www.michellehercules.com
books@mhsoars.com

facebook.com/michelleherculesauthor
instagram.com/michelleherculesauthor
amazon.com/Michelle-Hercules/e/B075652M8M
bookbub.com/authors/michelle-hercules
tiktok.com/@michelleherculesauthor?
patreon.com/michellehercules

Printed in Great Britain
by Amazon